Good
As
Any

Good
As
Any

Stories

Timothy A.
Westmoreland

Harcourt, Inc.
New York   San Diego   London

Requests for permission to make copies of any part of the work should be mailed to the following address: Permissions Department, Harcourt, Inc., 6277 Sea Harbor Drive, Orlando, Florida 32887-6777.

www.HarcourtBooks.com

Library of Congress Cataloging-in-Publication Data

Westmoreland, Timothy A.
        Good as any: stories / Timothy A. Westmoreland.—1st ed.
            p.   cm.
        Contents: Near to gone—They have numbered all my bones—
Good as any—Strong at the broken places—Buried boy—Darkening
of the world—Blood knot—Winter Island.
        ISBN 0-15-100852-3
        1. United States—Social life and customs—20th century—Fiction.
I. Title.

PS3623.E87 G6   2002
813'.6—dc21   2001024955

Text set in Granjon
Designed by Jeff Puda
First edition
KJIHGFEDCBA

Printed in the United States of America

"Near to Gone" appeared in *Scribner's Best of the Fiction Workshops 1998* and *Quarterly West*. It was a finalist for the Heekin Fellowship and The Texas Institute of Letters' Brazos Short Fiction Award. "Darkening of the World" was published both in *The Indiana Review* and in *The Best New American Voices 2001*.

For Debbie,

always Debbie,

Mary and, now,

Annabel . . .

Because I am never alone.

Contents

Good
As
Any

Near
to
Gone

I walked up the road to talk with the lineman who had been busy for several days watching a downed power line. Since my wife, Anita, had left for Buckland I'd observed him for long hours to see what it was a man with a job like this does. Not much, I thought. He drank coffee and read the newspaper, smoked cigarettes in the afternoon, and at night I could smell cannabis drifting in the air. His truck sat around a curve a couple hundred feet up the road from my house, but I could keep an eye on him from my bedroom window.

Heavy, wet snow barely fell from the sky. Ruts left behind by Anita's car were still visible in the driveway and on the road heading south, away from the house. It was an hour before dark, and I wanted to see what this watchman could tell me.

"How long before we get power?" I asked.

"I'm just paid to make sure nobody touches it," he said. "I don't fix them." The man wore a thick wool vest over his coveralls. He sipped coffee from the cap of his Thermos. Brown stains seeped down the back of his deerskin shooting gloves. "Snow's near to gone."

"Foot and half to two on the ground," I said, running the palms of my gloves together. "Tonight?" I asked.

He looked straight ahead, down the road. "Another day or two." He cranked the engine and turned a vent toward his face, sipped coffee.

I looked toward the sky and could see breaks opening in the clouds. "It's about over." I pointed upward.

He leaned his head out of the cab. His neck was thick and rusty with two-day beard. His forearms, bare below the turned-up shirt cuffs, were at the wrist the size of good kindling wood—delicately reaching into the glove's gauntlets.

"I can see my breath inside the house," I said.

He watched the line. "Bundle up. It's going to be cold."

"What's your name?" I asked.

He looked me in the eye. "I'm doing my job," he said. "They'll tell you that if you call."

"I don't mean that," I said. "Just wanted to know."

He was quiet. "Norm," he said, finally.

"Norm?" I repeated.

"Yeah."

I lied. I said, "Buzz," and I reached my hand out to him. The palm of his glove was warm from the coffee. "Live down at seventy-nine."

"Seventy-nine."

"How much runs through a line like that?"

"A lot," he said.

"How much?"

"Don't know. I just make sure no one touches them."

"So if I got hold of it, I'd really fry?"

"Sure," he said.

"How long would it take?"

"Seconds."

"Would I feel it?"

"Maybe."

"Just for a second?"

"At least."

"Longer?"

"Maybe. Maybe a little longer."

"Son of a bitch would hurt?"

"Probably. But not for long."

"What would it feel like though?"

"Don't know."

I put my hand on the lip of the truck bed and leaned inward. A shiver ran up my back, as the cold worked through my glove and up into my arm. A blue haze ranged on the snow around us. The torsos and limbs of pines fell in black shadows across the road. I could hear the way everything was beginning to seize up from the cold.

I felt warm air from a heater vent meet my face. "Toaster-oven warm in there," I said.

"Not so bad." He raised the cup to his mouth.

I shifted my weight, leaned back from the truck, felt an aching in my leg. I glanced up the road toward the power line. Across the pavement, down a long ravine, I could hear that the Saw Mill River was still running hard. Brenda Clark's bluetick, Chalk, ran the wetland. You could hear his bellow, echoing through the beech and hemlock.

"Cigarette?" he said. He tapped the pack on the steering wheel and offered one my way.

"Not anymore," I said. "Is this what you do for a living?"

"Not particularly," he said. He cupped his hand over a cigarette and lit it. "I do a variety of things."

"The electric company just calls?"

"When they need bodies." He paused, then asked, "What do you do, Buzz?"

"Not much," I said. I pulled my stocking cap down over my skull and balanced on my other leg.

"Want a seat?" He gathered newspaper up from next to him and tossed it onto the floorboard.

"I could take one."

"Come around."

I walked around the front of the truck and slipped into the cab next to him, the air stale with coffee and damp pulp. "Where you from, stranger?" I jested.

"You've got a limp."

"I know."

"New Hampshire," he finally answered. Smoke streamed from the edge of his lips and from his nose. "You?"

"Around," I said.

"You don't work?"

"Not anymore."

"You have?"

"Not very well."

"At what?"

"Mostly being lazy," I said. "I subcontracted roofing jobs and boiler work."

"I hate shingles."

"I never touched them."

"You're lucky."

"Not so much."

"Coffee?" he asked. He tilted the lip of his cup in my direction and then took a sip.

"Thanks," I said. "That'd be great."

"All I got is Tupperware," he said as he shifted in his seat and reached back behind me. "It should work."

"You've done this before?" I asked.

"What?" He spilled coffee into the bowl.

"Watched power lines?"

"It's hot," he said, offering me the coffee. He leaned forward and turned off the ignition. "Yeah."

"Ever seen anyone fried?"

"Not yet," he said. "But I expect to someday."

"You expect to?"

"People will drive right past you. Road signs and all."

"They're grounded."

"Not when they get out." He turned toward me and winked.

I laughed and held the bowl tightly, afraid the weakness in my fingers would somehow let me down. I had numbness too, and wondered if the coffee might not burn through my gloves and scald my hands. I reached down and rested the Tupperware between my feet.

"If you don't mind my asking, what's with the limp?"

"Surgery," I said. I slipped my cap off and he looked at my head, then at my face, and then, without blinking, right into my eyes. "I go for Taxol twice weekly."

"That's tough."

"Sometimes," I said. I leaned down and brought the bowl to my face. "Good coffee."

"Got a Coleman in back."

"I was wondering—"

"Set it out late when the chance of traffic is slim," he said. "I cook up coffee, pork chops, and eggs. I like to eat well."

"Listen," I said. "At night I can smell something."

"How's that?"

"I mean, sometimes it's good for the nausea."

"Pork and eggs?"

"No. The smoke," I said. "I recognize the smell."

"You've got a nose."

"I do."

Between us there was nothing but darkness. The cloud cover was gone and moonlight burnished everything in black and white. The road in front of us, hunkered down beneath snow, was cut by the tangled power line. We could see each other's breath hanging in the air like dust. Norm cranked the engine and turned on the heat. He lit a cigarette and turned his window down a crack.

"I can spare some," he offered. He took a drag off his cigarette, then leaned over and turned on the dashboard lights. "You ever smoked?"

"A few times," I said. "Years back." I shifted in my seat, turned so that I might get an idea what was on his mind. He didn't carry an expression on his face that told me anything. He seemed to be without judgment.

"Well," Norm paused, staring in the direction of the power line. "Let's get the Coleman going." He reached beneath the seat and pulled his stuff out and tucked it into his vest pocket. I watched him hunch over for a moment and get the feel of the heat coming from the vents. He closed his eyes and didn't move, letting the warmth get deep into his body. "Ready?" he asked. He killed the engine and opened the door. "Let's move."

The neighborhood was dark and all I could hear was the sound of our feet in the snow and Chalk baying somewhere down by the Saw Mill. The air burned my lungs. Norm let down the tailgate and then stood and looked up at the stars. The stillness of everything had made us both go silent.

"Need some help with that?" I asked.

"You shovel," he said, pointing toward a spot near the edge of the road.

I grabbed a garden shovel out of the truck bed. "Listen," I said, "I don't mean to come down and panhandle."

"Don't think about it," he said. He lifted the Coleman from the truck. "You can watch the line while I cook." He moved gingerly, putting the stove to rest in the place I'd cleared. "You a bacon-and-eggs man?"

"Sure."

"Got pork chops too."

"Bacon is fine."

"Maybe some of both?"

"Sure."

"How about some fresh coffee?"

"That'd be nice," I said.

Norm lit the stove and got a cooler from the back of the truck. "You should take some weight off that leg," he said. He brought me a camp stool from behind the front seat, opened it up, and offered it to me. Patting the vinyl, he said, "Warm that puppy up."

"You're a real Boy Scout," I said.

"Semper Fi," he said, giving a salute.

I paused. "Always be prepared," I corrected.

"Vietnam," he said without looking up.

I watched this man, Norm, while he removed a skillet, coffeepot, coffee, eggs, bacon, pork chops, a package of paper plates, and plastic utensils from the cooler. Norm was a man of practical leisure. He made a table, as they say, and it wasn't so bad. He was careful, orderly, keeping things clean, and in the heat from the stove I felt almost at home.

"Let's get a smoke before we eat," he said as if it were an order of business. He stood up from in front of the stove.

"Sure," I said. I leaned over and put my elbows on my knees.

"Keep your seat," he said. Norm reached into his vest pocket and pulled out a joint. "I plan ahead," he said. "They're tough to roll in this kind of weather. By the time dinner is done your hands won't feel like yours at all."

Norm put the stub between his lips and lit it and then squatted down in front of me. "OK," he said. "OK. Like this," he said. He took a drag and then held it in. He seemed to swallow something that was bitter. "Like that," he said, offering the stub my direction. "Hold it in," he said.

I started with a small breath and let it out. Norm nodded to me, and I took in some more and held it as long as I could. I felt a stinging in my throat and tried to hold back a cough.

"You'll get it," he said.

I took another pull, and this time I could feel my throat and lungs open up and take the smoke all inside. I closed my eyes and tried to locate any change, even the vaguest hint of one that might be happening to my body. I held the stub out for Norm.

"It's all you," he said, motioning for me to finish the whole thing.

Norm stood up again and took a walk out toward the power line. Then, turning, he looked back over me and our setup, toward my house. "You live there alone?" he asked, taking steps back toward the stove.

"Not always," I said.

He kneeled beside the Coleman. "Better than always," he said, smiling. He cracked the eggs with one hand, directly into a cast-iron skillet, tossing the shells out into the snow. He whisked the yolks around a moment and then shuffled the coffeepot a bit closer to the flame. Thoughts looked to be strolling around in his head. "So why not always?" he asked finally.

"Wife's gone for a while," I said. But the truth was Anita had left me. Gone to stay with friends; people who had a gas generator—lights, hot water, heat.

"With you lame?" he asked.

"Yeah."

"That's tough." He paused a moment to shift the eggs onto one half the pan. You could tell he was attempting to conjure up my story. He laid strips of bacon out on the skillet. "How do you get around?"

"Walk."

"I mean, to the doctor and stuff," he hesitated. "For chemo? To the store for food?"

"Don't know," I said.

He divided the eggs onto plates and draped more bacon on the skillet. "I'll get the chops last," he said.

"She's just gone," I added, in an effort to make sense of it for him. I turned sideways on the stool and tried not to let the roach burn my fingers. I was worried about this, about how not to look like I didn't know how to handle the situation. I took a drag and tried to pass it on. He refused and so I touched the burning end lightly into the snow.

Norm drained the bacon grease and forked several strips onto each plate. "Fuel," he said, handing the eggs and bacon my way.

"Thanks."

"For good?" he asked.

"That might not be long," I suggested.

Anita had left a few days back, the first morning we were without power. Winter had hardly come at all. Then I felt something in my leg, and overnight two feet of heavy snow settled in over the valley—early for these parts, the first week of November. The night before she left, Anita was driving me home from the hospital when the streetlights went dark and along the road the houses sat like coffins. We drove twenty miles in the dark, over forgotten routes, between open fields just cleared of corn, and then into Buckland where even the traffic signals were out. We live over some hills from town, at the base of a range that rises up and makes the northern rim of a valley. I'd always felt like this was a good place to be.

Norm had a Ziploc bag with flour in it that he dropped a couple of pork chops into. He shook them around a bit and then fingered the meat into the skillet with a bit of bacon grease. The smell of fried pork swelled around us.

"It hurt?" Norm asked, pointing to my leg. He turned the chops.

"There's a rod in it," I said. "I can feel it get cold."

"I knew a girl once. Had lots of metal in her."

"Yeah?"

"Years ago, in high school." He put his hand out for my plate. "Biology teacher had her bring X rays to class."

"What happened?"

"We started saying things like 'Fat Amy's insides'." Norm put a pork chop on my plate and handed it to me. "She'd walk by and we'd say that under our breath."

I shook my head, thinking how things like that happen when you're young.

"Those X rays though," he paused. "She had bones."

"I guess."

"There were all angles. Dozens of them." Norm swallowed. "Close in. Far out. Just the knee, where the bolts and screws and all kinds of contraptions were, and then the whole leg up to where there's the crease. They put some kind of something on her to protect her parts."

"A real *Gray's Anatomy.*"

"Yeah. Really."

"So what happened?"

"We looked at those snapshots for days," he shook his head. "I studied the close-ups. It was like all those shadows and curves—the bones—were people. Tight. Together. Doing things, you know."

I didn't know, but I shook my head like I understood.

"I got to where I wanted her," he said.

"From X rays?"

"Seeing her insides all the way up. That leg just really got me."

"What happened?"

"She got herself killed somehow. A few years back. Left two kids. A car accident."

"Fat Amy's insides?"

"Yeah."

"How fat?"

"Not too," he paused. "Just enough, you know."

"That got to you?"

"Those bones," Norm said. "Some nights I'd just run my hands down her hip, along her thigh. I'd just try to feel them."

I watched Norm close his eyes and figured he was back trying to locate what it was that made him want to look inside a person. He sat for a moment, hunched over his plate, and then he reached over for the coffeepot. "Warm up?" he asked.

"Sure."

He was delicate, pouring carefully into the bowl. "I saw enough in Vietnam to cure me," he offered. He managed the bowl with both hands, delivering it to me like a child.

"I was wondering."

"Enough bone to make a thousand bodies."

"You ever marry?"

"Sure."

"What happened?"

"I don't know," he said. "What about you?"

"She said I didn't know how to be scared."

"That—I could teach you."

"She was terrified."

"Kids?"

"No."

"Well—"

"It's not like I've got a choice," I said. I lifted the bowl of coffee to my face and held it there for a moment. The steam brought moisture to my skin. I took a sip and held it in my mouth.

"You should be scared," Norm said, almost as if he were asking me to do this for him.

"She began to be angry with me," I explained. "About the pain and the treatments. It was a lot for her. Driving me around and taking care of stuff at the house."

"I've seen a lot of bad things happening," he said. "It takes a lot to watch. I saw Amy's daughter for instance. I see her around up in New Hampshire. She looks like her mother did and she sees that herself every day."

"I don't see much."

"In 'Nam I watched people waste away. From the inside out."

"Who doesn't?"

"It's frustrating," he said. "It's like they won't admit anything's wrong. Their silence . . . it's like being blamed."

"What's to say?"

"I don't know."

"There's nothing."

"Just saying you're scared is something."

"For the sake of others?"

"Why not?" He paused and took a drink of coffee. "That's what we want to hear."

Norm stood up and looked off in the direction of the power line. We hadn't seen or heard any cars coming up the road all evening. "Let's warm up in the truck," he said, offering to take my plate from me. I walked around the side and got in while Norm went across the road and dumped the scraps along the tree line.

"That dog'll get them," he said when he got in and cranked the engine.

"Chalk," I said.

"Odd sounding."

"Bluetick," I said. "They all sound different."

A cold blast came from the vents. Norm raced the engine trying to get the heater to produce something decent. I thought of Anita down in Buckland, keeping warm. She might be trying to figure things out, come to an understanding, wanting to run her hands over my leg, along my spine, across my chest.

In the moonlight I could see the power line in a tangled mess. "Suppose you touch that," I said. "What would you feel for just that second?"

"Surprise."

"Yeah. But that's like a thought."

"A last thought."

Norm turned to face me. The heat was beginning to kick in, and I could feel my body loosening up—the muscles letting go. My hands ached.

"I imagine carbonation," he paused. "The tiniest bubbles. You feel the tingle in your blood."

"No thoughts."

"No. Just knowing."

"Not the life-flashing-before-your-eyes thing?"

"More immediate."

"Tiny bubbles," I said, in a half song.

"Wires."

"Really. Yeah," I said. "I think so. All your cells—for that less than a moment—one."

"There's that moment when you're both there and not there. In between."

"I guess that's what it means to want to get inside?" I said. "That point when you're not alive, not dead. We want to know that."

"Sure."

For a moment I thought I knew what we were saying, but just as quickly I realized I hadn't a clue. I was just talking, just saying things, words, that might belong to someone else. Norm was there, across the seat from me, staring like he was waiting for me to tell him something. We both went quiet. Norm turned the ignition and we sat and listened to the engine cool down.

In front of us I could see the silhouette of Chalk shuffle around the food Norm had left out—dancing, doing a jig, tail wagging, in a nervous kind of way.

"Brenda would not like this if she knew," I said in a childish, instructive way. Chalk carried pork a little at a time, a few yards away, and then chewed like he was snapping at air.

"Brenda?"

"His owner."

"Well, Brenda doesn't know."

"She keeps him fit," I said. "On a diet."

Norm reached between the seats and pulled out a package of dried beef. "I hate this shit," he said. He rolled down his window and tossed a handful out in front of the truck. Chalk appeared luminous, blue, darting in the moonlight to pick up the stalks of jerky. His speckled ticking hovered about the snow. He stopped as if on point, then went for a second handful Norm had pitched out of the truck. Norm began to laugh and check behind the seat, then in the glove compartment, looking for something else to throw. He came up empty-handed and seemed lost for a moment.

Then it was as if our senses struck flint—a flicker of light, a crack, a brief yelp, maybe not one at all—and we both called, "Ohh." A shadow drifted across the road in front of us and came to a stop along a snowbank.

"What the fuck—"

"Chalk," I said, letting my hand search for the door handle. We both sat motionless for a time and just stared at what we had not quite seen. I felt my insides turn cold.

You could smell burned hair in the soft breeze, and down the hill I heard the river. I stood over the dog, looking up the way toward the line.

"Let it alone," Norm called. "Don't touch it."

"Son of a bitch."

"May be hot," Norm said, coming to my side with a rubber-handled gaff.

"Could he be alive?"

"No chance."

"Sure?"

"Very."

We both stood over the body, confused, amazed. Norm nudged the dog. "All this time and then this," Norm said. "I'm in deep now."

"What could you do?" I bent down and ran my hand along Chalk's face. He could have been sleeping. My own heart was beating strong, pumping in my ears.

"What *can* I do?" Norm asked. He wasn't interested in suggestions. His mind was made up. "I'll have to call this in," he said. "Where's this Brenda live?"

"Up the hill," I said. And then I suggested, "It was an accident."

"No such thing."

I got to my feet and I could feel my leg was really beginning to hurt. The rod running through the inside of my thigh was cooling off, or that was the impression it gave. I hadn't left the house to come down here for all of this—some dope, a watchman, and a dead dog. I'd come to find a few things out. Now we had a situation. I glanced at the power line and then turned and looked back over the truck toward my house, at the dark windows from where I could be watching. I considered the options.

"Don't report this," I said, finally. "Don't say anything."

"If I don't," Norm said, "she will."

"Don't tell Brenda, either," I said.

"She's going to notice the dog's missing."

"She lets it run loose. Something could happen."

"Something did."

"I noticed," I said, trying to smile. My thoughts were going flat, and for the first time I realized the dope had put its fingers on me, but was now losing hold. I turned and headed back for the truck. I hated what had happened to Brenda's dog. Shameful. It pierced me somehow, got to me while I sat there in the truck with Norm, us not talking, just waiting for the warmth to emerge.

"Take him down to the river," I said.

"She needs to know."

"No. She can think he's run off. Or been picked up. The truth is she doesn't need to know."

"It's better knowing."

"Is it?" I asked. "Does it help you—*knowing?*"

Norm considered the question.

"He'll drift far enough before things freeze up."

"And if they look for him?"

"Who looks for a dead dog?"

Norm didn't try to answer. I watched him keeping an eye on Chalk. Norm lit a cigarette and took a sip of coffee. A trace of blood ran in the snow, coming from the dog's body. In the light I realized I could see steam rising from the dog. I knew Brenda would call down the next day, or in a few days, and ask if I'd seen

Chalk. She might even take the car through the neighborhood streets, looking. She wouldn't stop though, only slow down, study the landscape, keep driving. She could keep her hope up that way.

"Lend me a smoke?" I asked.

"Cigarette?" Norm said, surprised.

"I've never seen anything like that," I said, holding out my hand.

Norm hesitated then handed me the pack. "You scared?"

"Maybe of being alone."

"You are alone."

"You go through it like that dog," I said. "Not knowing much."

"There's no other way to do it. That's fear—no one in your shoes."

"I guess." I tapped a cigarette out of the pack and lit it.

"I was beyond scared," he said. "I'm talking 'Nam. Waiting."

"Hmm."

Norm frowned. He opened his door and emptied his coffee. "I knew a guy," he said, then halted. Reaching behind my seat he found the Thermos and poured a fresh cup. "Lukewarm," he said after taking a drink. He handed me the cup to share. I took a swallow and handed it back.

"Spider," Norm said, "was a buddy in 'Nam." He paused, took another sip, and let himself fall backward through his thoughts; he slipped down into his seat, slackened. "A real gunner, I mean."

"A walker?" I asked.

"You couldn't hear him two-step across gravel. A genuine Jungle Jim."

"GI Joe."

"With balls."

"OK."

"You've heard this story a thousand times, I'm sure. But listen."

"I'm listening."

"Incoming hit and I heard all kinds of wails. Inhuman kinds of sounds. I ran to see. Spider had bones poking out of him, some not

GOOD AS ANY

even his. A dirt hole with just a mess of flesh. Couldn't tell how many men there were. The mortar just made a deep grave."

Norm was quiet for a moment, and I could see his breath in the air. He was beginning to breathe slower, deliberately. I looked away from him, out onto the snow that was losing definition in the rush of moonlight. I stubbed my cigarette into the ashtray.

"I came up on Spider in that hole and I stayed over him. My mouth started watering. I just kept drooling. His bowels stank, the stench spilling out of him as he rocked side to side."

"Jesus."

"Spider said it was like seeing pussy for the first time, seeing it in the flesh, balls tightening up—" Norm halted. "Watching him, it was like everyone was the same person. Seeing his senses firing all at once like that made me go empty inside, except for the fear."

"Did he tell you things? What it was like?"

"It wasn't like the movies. He didn't just close his eyes. Spider turned on himself, tugged at his own insides, wanted to be used up."

"What'd he say?"

"He looked to me like he wanted me to be afraid. But *his* eyes, they were calm. I got so pissed at him." Norm closed his eyes. He seemed to forget his job, the power line, and the dog lying in the street, and me waiting to hear what he had to say. "I wanted him to die," Norm said, pausing. "I left him behind and went on."

I sat quietly, stared out at the trees along the shoulder of the road. I began to feel the mechanisms inside me at work—my anatomy going all cockeyed. My muscles pulled tight, my bones ached. "It's getting colder than hell," I said, finally. Norm didn't respond. I imagined Chalk floating downstream, his body calm, forgiving. "This has got me by the short hairs," I admitted.

Norm let out a brief laugh. His cigarette had burned down to the filter; he lowered the window and tossed it out. A dampness settled at the corners of my eyes. "It's cold," he said. He cranked the engine and sat up in his seat.

"You take Chalk down to the Saw Mill," I said. "Make sure he doesn't snag. No one will know."

"We're going to take care of this one," he said. Norm reached into his vest pocket and pulled out the Ziploc bag and rested it in his lap. He put his hands up to the vents, warming his fingers, and then rubbed his palms together.

"Get the snow out there too," I said, pointing to where the blood had stained the ground.

After his hands were warm, Norm turned the vents away from himself. He undid the bag, culled a paper, and began to roll a joint. I watched his fingers work, nimble and quick, practiced. In a few minutes he'd made up several. "Take these," he said when he had finished. He tucked them into my shirt pocket. "This'll get you through a few times." He tugged the zipper up on my coat.

With the engine running, Norm got out of the truck and walked to where Chalk was lying in the snow. He shook his head and bent down to examine the dog. For the longest time Norm just kneeled there, waiting for something to happen it seemed. I let the heat pour across my face and hands. I thought about joining Norm, offering to help. But he gathered the dog into his arms, gently holding him to his body. It was as if he had hold of a child, or a lover. I could see he was steady on his feet, looking down occasionally, cradling Chalk, shifting his weight for support, until I lost sight of him between the trees.

I stepped out of the truck and I tried to listen for the sound of Norm thrashing down toward the water, but all I could hear was the engine running, and as I turned and headed for home that noise faded and the echo of the river made it up the bluff. Wood burned in a fireplace down the road. I saw the smoke, silvery in the light, coming from a chimney. Even after all Norm and I had consumed, I was bare. I had a hunger and my stomach turned. I needed something to eat.

The house was dark, but not as cold as I'd imagined it would be. I stood in the kitchen taking in the smell of vacant rooms and listened to water dripping from the faucet onto a stack of unwashed dishes. This and the boards that creaked under the kitchen linoleum were the only sounds I could hear as I shifted my balance, wanting to feel something in my leg beyond the cold. I opened the refrigerator and used a flashlight to look around inside. I touched the tops of jars and casseroles, packages of meat and a carton of milk; everything was damp, almost tepid. The freezer meat was half thawed. Everything inside was on the verge of going bad. I decided to save what I could and took the flashlight down in the basement and returned with boxes.

I began to empty the refrigerator. First, the milk and half-and-half that Anita used in her coffee, then deli mustard, tomato ketchup, jars of kosher dill halves, and Hellmann's mayonnaise. A smell, dead air, escaped the refrigerator. My thoughts were mechanical, measured by the dripping faucet. I focused on packing the box—half jars of pasta sauce; a container of Cool Whip and Imperial margarine; a few cans of beer; and on top of this I spread packages of Parmesan cheese; Danish Emmentaler; smoked turkey and ham slices; and a carton of eggs. I felt solid, a part of the thick mess this early winter had brought on. I worked with an even motion, emptying the beef round, shell sirloin steak, boneless chicken breast, and pork ribs. I put the pie crusts into a separate box. In with those I put a half-full bottle of Lindemans merlot and an unopened bottle of Mumm cordon rouge. I wrapped the boxes in plastic trash bags and took them outside.

Behind the house I knelt beneath the limbs of a chestnut tree and began to remove the thick covering of snow with my bare hands. I worked my fingers into the packed layers, lifting clots out into a mound until I could see a dark slip of earth, a space large enough for the boxes. I set each box flush against the frozen ground and then I paused to get my breath. Sweat ran down my back. In the moonlight, the hole in the snow appeared bottomless.

I wanted to laugh. It was all but done. I dug in with my feet, shouldered a bank of snow over the boxes, smoothed the surface until there was no sign of what was underneath. I worked until I couldn't feel my hands. Air scorched my lungs and my head felt on fire, burning from the inside, and my mouth was dry.

I lay back in the snow and watched my breath drift upward. Snow-covered branches creased the sky. Around me, everything was bowing under the weight. In the distance I heard Norm's truck engine stop, and I imagined him sitting in the front seat looking out at the power line, drinking coffee, considering whether he should walk up to Brenda's place to tell her the truth. I listened to the quiet, to the occasional snap of branches, and for a while I thought of Anita. A hollowness opened up in my stomach. I had the sense of falling, a fear of being trapped in a small place, of moving so quickly that I could barely keep my eyes open.

They
Have
Numbered
All My Bones

A long straight road through colors, leaves twisting on the air. Pavement between dust fields. Corn, farther out. A graveyard and aloft, a skein of geese winging south. What are the chances? Buckley thought, his window down, the chill showing on his forearm. He watched the geese. They passed overhead, then out over the fields.

A glimpse, a deer, in the pale of evening. Is there anything more frightening? Buckley swerved. There wasn't a thump, just tilting, tires, darkness.

———

Darkness, nothing, was what Buckley Miller believed in. It's what gave him comfort. Constant failing was the human condition, and there was no judge, no retribution, no afterlife in which to pay for one's habits. Habits, after all, are almost always sins. Buckley liked to drink, for instance. He would drink in the afternoons after a long day of putting shingles down on other people's houses. His own home was a wreck, and he was sure in some church doctrine that was a sin. He showered and then dropped into the Taproom. He was on a first-name basis with the bartender, because at three in the afternoon who else was there to talk with? He had two beers and one whiskey. In the spring, the barroom door was propped wide and the breeze would get all up in his hair and make him feel lonely. Sometimes he'd get ideas. Get a porn magazine from the Dairy Mart and sit in the parking lot in his Explorer. That's why people own SUVs, so that no one can see in on the business at hand. Buckley would drive around town at rush hour and look in on women at stoplights. With their windows down, sometimes the flurry of air would lift their short skirts. Buckley would palm himself. Certainly, if he had believed in anything, this would be a sin. But Buckley knew the only thing he was guilty of was being lonely. There was no one to hold his shingle-worn hand.

As a habit, Buckley drove. It calmed him. He imagined one day a lady might catch his attention at a gas station or convenience store and ask him about the lettering on his truck—"Buckley Miller Roofing Services. Free estimates. We're not just roofers." In fact, that's all they were. But Buckley had that stenciled as an invitation to the world, to anyone, to ask questions. He imagined someday an attractive businesswoman would ask if he could come take a look at her roof. She might say, "I have the map of Idaho stained on my living room ceiling where the rain has leaked." Buckley imagined he would say, "I'm an expert on Idaho. It's where I'm from." He thought this could happen. He let conversations play in his head while he drove. He drove long distances without remembering how and when he made turns, lights, intersections.

———

"Mr. Miller," a voice called. "Mr. Miller, can you hear me? We're giving you something for the pain. You may feel it."

Buckley couldn't speak.

GOOD AS ANY

"We've intubated," she said. "Don't try to talk. Can you open your eyes, Mr. Miller?"

Buckley felt the tube down his throat; he could hear equipment. He wanted to rest, to remain in the comfort of dreamless obscurity.

"You've been in an accident," she said. "I'm Doctor Faris. Can you open your eyes?" She held his hand. "Mr. Miller?"

Buckley felt her touch. The questions came to him from far away, as though from across a busy train station. There was noise and conversation and the sound of feet, hurried. He rose from the crowded station, up steps into the brilliant glare of the emergency room. He was strapped to a gurney.

"Good, Mr. Miller," the doctor said. "We're getting ready to send you up to the O.R. You've sustained internal injuries. We're waiting on the head CT. Mr. Miller?"

Buckley wished she'd call him by his first name. He wished she'd let him go, to descend the steps into the train station, to take the train down the dark tunnel into oblivion. She reached for his IV, used a syringe to inject something into the tube. A strange taste matured, something that recalled him to a time he longed to forget. He hadn't always lived in a small town.

Miles was an art student at Columbia. He always called her by her last name, though he didn't know why. He thought of becoming a journalist. They took chemistry together. Their names followed on the roll. "Miles," the professor called, "Miller." He announced grades. "Miles. Ninety-two. Miller. Thirty-six. An all-time low for you, Miller. Perhaps you should seek help." Buckley tucked his paper into his book. He hadn't studied. The city, the place, had overwhelmed him.

"I can help you," he heard a voice say from behind him.

He turned. "Miles," he said. Her smile was mischievous. "You think you can?"

"I know I can," she said. She stood on the landing above him, dangling one foot off the steps. She dipped her head. Her hair was shaggy, curly and long on top; short on the sides. He remembered the glint in her dark eyes. "I work at a diner on 112th. I get off at midnight."

"Miles," he said.

She walked with him down the steps, out onto the sidewalk. She put her number on the corner of a page in her literature book, tore it out for him. Buckley still had it.

"Mr. Miller," the doctor called. "Stay with us. We need you to try and stay awake. We sent for the chaplain."

How odd, Buckley thought. What a useless thing to do. He drifted off and then back. Opening his eyes, he saw the doctor leaning over him. Her face was lily, smooth, high-cheeked. She had long, dark hair that was braided. When she leaned close, over him, he could detect the scent of soap and he felt, strangely, embarrassed. Shy. This was the closest he'd been to a woman in years. What an awful intimacy the emergency room offered. What a vulnerable feeling. Yet it was as though everyone rebuffed you. They wore gloves and were careful to treat you as an aimless body.

"Are there relatives we can call for you?"

Buckley shook his head. There was no one. He was an only child and his parents were both dead. The world had a cruel way of reminding him of this. If there were a God, would he go to all this trouble to punish a person? A car, a thought, a deer, a ditch, and then an ambulance and an emergency room doctor? All to say that by way of habit you are a failure. To recall the express train downtown, where there were bars and music. Places he and Miles frequented. The corner music house where he lost ground, flunked out of school. Miles slept on the uptown train, her head on his shoulder. He could taste that scent now, the scent of her shampoo, remember the exact curve of her neck. No matter how late they came home, they made love, and then she would read for several hours before settling into the arch of his back.

"... found a copy of the Douay Bible in your truck," the doctor said. "The chaplain's not Catholic. Mr. Miller, stay with us."

Buckley opened his eyes. They were wheeling him down a corridor. Lights passed quickly overhead.

"He's not Catholic," Doctor Faris continued. "But we have a priest on the way."

Catholic? he thought. How ridiculous. The Bible had come from a used bookstore. It had been on his backseat for several days now. A curiosity. A roofer doesn't have to be an uninformed man. It takes something to run a business, to make it work. As he had settled, in his thirties, he'd become a steady reader. Not just trash. Buckley liked Kafka, Joyce, Saramago. He liked a world he could fall into. It was a method of forgetting.

———

Buckley kept a small, stainless-steel Thermos of coffee in his Explorer. The long winters chilled him so that he couldn't do without it. Even early mornings, in summer, ran chill bumps up his arms. Seasonal days, in late March, with the snow melting and work beginning to pick up, he sat in his Explorer, drank coffee, watched his workmen, and read. He walked into novels as if they were rooms in his own home. He searched for clues of his own existence, for guidance on how to better know his past. Time, it seemed to Buckley, was the enormous uncertainty, puzzle, we all touch in our waking moments. It was true. Buckley not only drank, but sometimes he slept on the job. He slept because his truck was warm, his wool vest rode up on him, rubbed his chin, lay on him like a blanket. In his waking everything was possible, was real, because those moments were abundant with complete forgetting. There was no realization yet, no sense of time, or rather there was a closeness, a snug and cozy crowding, a euphoria, of the best moments of his life. His dreams were often full of his dreams, and in that instant of opening his eyes it was as though they'd breached the boundary of slumber and entered the living world. For a brief second, he was happy. He might wake as a married man with children, a journalist who traveled the world, the owner of an art gallery. Then, awareness would come, and he would uncap his Thermos and drink the bourbon-laden coffee. The bourbon was an addition of late. It'd come this autumn.

Autumn was the season of book sales. Buckley drove Route 9 from Deerfield to Whately, to the Antiquarian Bookseller and to the Raven. Discounts. Everyone thinning their stock for the long season of snow. New Englanders were Milquetoast. Allegedly hearty, they stayed in for the winter. It was dark by five and they were in for the night. Booksellers, like roofers, had an extended, dry season in winter. While his workers pounded nails, Buckley walked among aisles of used books. Weren't they the lost choices of others' lives? He fingered the spines of novels he thought of trying. He took his time among the smell of dust and burnt coffee.

The owner was loud, talkative. He rambled on with a customer who was also a dealer. There always seemed to be a dealer in the store. Buckley hated the gargle of the owner's voice. He wove his way to the back of the store. Religion. There were scholarly books on heretics and saints and scriptural analysis. And, to his surprise, a shelf of Bibles. Who would sell a Bible? he thought. Then it occurred to him, Who would buy a used Bible? It made Buckley dislike the owner even more.

Buckley pulled a copy from the shelf and inside he found the dates of births and deaths and confirmations. It was a family Bible. There were names and social security numbers. Godparents' names. It was a Catholic Bible, an old Douay translation. It reminded him of a girl he'd known years before. Miles. She had been Catholic. He'd thought of her now and then over the years, the way people do when they wonder what life would be like if other choices had been made. To Buckley's mind, everyone must think of past lovers. They come into your life on occasion, stay in your house with you for a week or two, and then go away. It was the closest thing Buckley ever had to visitors.

He and Miles had been friends, lovers, for the year he attended

Columbia. He wished he'd married her. It was the closest he'd ever come to marriage. She was, he knew, the love of his life. Does a person ever have more than one? No, he didn't think so.

For Columbus Day weekend they had rented a car and driven to Maine. They stayed in a room at a monastery. It was cheap and clean. She tutored him in chemistry, and they made love and walked the grounds, which were expansive and peaceful. There was a monument, he remembered, that had one of the Psalms engraved on it. He could not remember which one, but he recalled something, a phrase, "They have numbered all my bones." It had struck him as odd and beautiful. Miles had told him it was from the Douay, that it came from the Latin Vulgate, that most churches didn't use it any longer.

But here in the bookstore this memory was as fresh as if it had only happened a week ago. He flipped the pages but couldn't find the passage. Miles had had such a way about her, a sense of constant flirtation. Even in the chapel where she kneeled, prayed. He sat dumbly next to her thinking how she looked in nothing but a T-shirt, showing him how to balance equations. The bookstore owner droned on, and Buckley decided to buy the Bible. It seemed wrong, too terrible, to leave it behind for others to delve into someone else's past. Besides, he felt less lonely, even if he was only in the company of a ghost.

———

Buckley felt claustrophobic. He wanted to free his arms. He was surrounded by nurses. They wheeled him into a waiting elevator. Dr. Faris held the door, then stepped in. The doors closed.

"Mr. Miller," she said. "We're going to hand you off to Dr. Umana. He's a top-notch surgeon. OK?"

Buckley nodded.

"You may be under for several hours," she continued. "We're going to call in a specialist. We're concerned about possible swelling in your brain."

The elevator doors slid open and they maneuvered the gurney out into the hallway. The nurses moved quickly, precisely, without talking. As they breezed along, Buckley felt a chill in the air. He wanted a blanket, something to cover up with, to warm himself. They bumped through several doorways and then into the operating room.

The lights overhead were bright, so much so that he had to close his eyes. He listened as the nurses busied themselves, moving trays around and rolling equipment. Each seemed to have a specific job and none of them talked. For the first time Buckley heard the heart monitor, the rhythmic beeping. He wondered if the time came, would he hear the last beep? Would he hear the beginning of the long, steady tone that meant death? These thoughts worried him. He tried to shift his weight, to loosen his body from the gurney. He wasn't able to move. Buckley began to hear his heartbeat in his ears. This wasn't unfamiliar to him.

Earlier in the week he'd felt something weighty grow within him. After a gloomy afternoon of dusting through used bookstores, he elbowed his Explorer home—a Bible on the backseat. A cold rain was coming down when he pulled into the driveway. For a few minutes he waited for it to slacken. It didn't. He left the book in the backseat, ran for the porch. In the dark house, Buckley turned up the furnace and climbed the stairs to retrieve a recollection. On a shelf in the spare bedroom there was a copy of Emily Dickinson's poems. He could hardly touch it. It was a book Miles carried with her everywhere she went, from the time she was in junior high. She had given it to him, inscribed something that at the time had sounded strangely distant. The thought of leaving him must have already been in her mind, buried, secret. "If you forget my thoughts," she had written, "they are here. Read a little each day and try not to rebel against it too much." Buckley had rebeled, and then when she left him it hurt too much to open the book and too much to throw it away.

Buckley splayed the pages and there was Miles's handwriting. It was as if she were in the next room. Folded into the book was the page from Miles's literature anthology with her number on it. She had always been so deliberate. For the first time he noticed the number shared space with Dickinson's poem, "Wild Nights— Wild Nights!" He sat on the edge of the bed, his heart beating in his ears, and cried.

Together, on their trip back from Maine to New York they had passed through Amherst and visited the Dickinson homestead. The docent had been generous, had spent time before and after with Miles. Buckley remembered how easily they had gotten along. Miles was that way with everyone.

In all of these years he'd not admitted it to himself, but Buckley had settled here, near Amherst, in hopes of finding Miles one day. Perhaps her passion would draw her back to this place, and per- haps he would see her on the street. Maybe she would apply for a job. Emily's brother's home, The Evergreens, was next door and was being refurbished. It would be opened to the public soon, and there would be jobs, he was certain, for specialists. Buckley remem- bered, now, that Miles had written down the docent's name in the collection of poems. Perhaps he could find the docent, inquire about Miles.

"I'd like to see the view from the copula," Miles had said.

"You could work here summers," Buckley suggested.

"Maybe," she said. "Maybe someday."

He dried his eyes on the sleeve of his shirt. He flipped through the pages and found the name—Kohler. He thought he'd call the homestead and inquire.

———

Buckley awoke, squirmed, had an itch on his nose he couldn't touch. He couldn't even ask someone else to do it for him. They had moved him to the operating table, secured him so that now he couldn't move his head.

"OK," a man said, pushing into the room. He walked over and

looked into Buckley's eyes. "I'm Doctor Umana. No need to stand," he said, jokingly.

Buckley blinked.

"You won't feel a thing," the doctor said. "This is Reeder." Umana nodded to the head of the table. "He's our anesthesiologist. He'll make sure you're comfortable. Doctor Bromley will join us shortly. He's our brain-trauma specialist. He'll be looking for swelling." The heart monitor beeped in the background. "Are you ready?" the doctor asked.

Buckley blinked again. Reeder gradually dropped him into unconsciousness. How easily, Buckley thought, as the sounds of the operating room dissipated and darkness took him.

———

Miles had pulled the blinds and the late morning sunlight fell across the bed brilliantly. Buckley awoke, turned away. He kept his eyes closed.

"Wake up, Miller," she said. "It's the last good day of fall." She tugged the window open and the noise of the quiet street lifted. Cool air spilled in. "I've got a plan," she said. "Now wake up!" She took a pillow, boxed him with it.

Buckley rolled over, shaded his eyes. "What?"

"Shower," she said. "And hurry up. Before the sun goes home."

Buckley lay motionless. She struck him with the pillow again. "Now!"

"OK," he said. He rolled up and off the bed, a mattress and box springs that sat flush on the wooden floor. He barefooted to the bathroom, turned on the water to let it warm. Buckley stared at himself in the mirror. It was the weekend and he liked to sleep late. He tested the water and stepped in under the nozzle. It didn't matter, the plumbing was fickle, the temperature would fluctuate from warm to cold to scalding. He scrubbed. Los Lobos Tex-Mexed from the stereo. Miles loved mornings. He knew she was probably dancing, swirling about the apartment.

Buckley shut off the shower, toweled. He took a dry towel and draped it around his waist. He stepped around the corner. Miles was leaning against the doorjamb of the kitchen, dressed in a short black dress, white ankle socks, white sneakers, and a straw hat. She had a bota roped over her shoulder and a wicker basket at her feet. She pretended to look at a watch on her bare wrist.

"OK," Buckley said. "OK." He slipped into jeans and deck shoes. Pulled on a light sweater. "Who lit a fire under your skirt?" Buckley asked, sliding his wallet into his pocket.

"You," Miles said. "Always you." She smiled.

Buckley laughed. "Ready," he said.

They took the train down, crossed over to Central Park. Miles took Buckley by the hand, led him out across the sun-washed lawn. She was deliberate, slow. She seemed to know just what she was looking for, and then she found it just out of the shade of a large, reaching tree. Above, the leaves hung in full color. Buckley helped spread the blanket and Miles settled gently to her knees. She unpacked the basket.

Buckley had never been as happy. To his mind he'd had a sad and sorry life. There had been nothing to do but read and study. There was an inadequacy to him, he thought, which couldn't be defeated. Self-conscious was Miles's word. He needed coaxing. A surprise now and then to remind him that life isn't always what you expect. Habits, she said, were the enemy of joy. They are a sign of resignation. So Miles was always complete with the absence of ritual. Catholicism, she'd say, forces one to invent life. The constant guilt can wear you down to nothing. Buckley had never seen any sign of that. Though faith bothered him. Its company made him feel certain something would go wrong. The faithful are always punished.

Miles laid out a plate of fresh fruit, slices of apple, peach, pineapple. There were grapes and cheese and crackers. She'd brought fresh turkey and croissants.

"Close your eyes and open your mouth," she demanded.

"Why?"

"Just do it."

"I don't trust you."

"That's good," she said. "Now. Close your eyes and open your mouth."

Buckley did.

Miles squeezed the bota and a stream of wine shot into his mouth. It startled him and he turned away. Wine streamed down his chin. He swallowed, laughed. "You trying to drown me?"

"Claret," she said. She fed him a cracker with cheese. "What do you think?"

"Very nice," he said. "My turn."

"Oh, no," Miles said. "I'll do it." She pinched some wine into her mouth. "It's good." She took a cracker and cheese.

Buckley leaned and kissed her. He peeked into the basket and she quickly closed the lid. "What else did you bring?" he asked.

She looked at him, tilted her hat back. "Myself," she said. "That's it then," he said. "I'm leaving." He acted as if he was getting up.

"Sit down," she said. She pushed him back on the blanket. "I've got to practice my French."

Buckley smiled. "I'm not going to argue."

"The French language," Miles said. "I'm going to read an important book to you. *Le Petit Prince.*"

"Oh, no."

"Shut up."

"I don't know French."

"That's why you have me," Miles said, "to translate."

"You brought me all the way here to torture me?" Buckley asked. "You could have done this at home."

"It's a very good book."

"It's silly."

"Only if you're not listening," Miles said. "I'm here to show you."

"If you have to," Buckley said, resigned.

Miles brought out two glasses and filled them with wine. Buckley took off his sweater, rolled it up, and used it as a pillow. Miles began to read, translating every few passages, skipping some altogether. She knew the book well, read with an exaggerated accent. She was playful with her translations. She made up some things to enhance the story. Occasionally she'd ask Buckley to guess what a sentence meant. He'd taken Spanish in high school. His guesses were sometimes very close. He leaned up on his elbow, closed his eyes, and fell into the rhythm of Miles's voice. He thought he could spend a lifetime doing this.

The park began to fill here and there with people. Dogs running. Couples walking by. Far out, in the middle of the opening, two men tossed a Frisbee. Buckley sipped his wine, listened. The shadow of the tree reached over them and so they paused, pulled the pallet out into the sun.

"Are you listening?" Miles asked.

Buckley nodded.

"This is important," she said. "We are getting to an important part."

"OK," he said. "But I'm getting hungry."

"Make yourself a sandwich," she said. "I'm not your wife."

Buckley made a sandwich, sat up and ate, listened.

"Now here we go," Miles said. "This fox is smart. He's about to tell you something. Perk up."

Buckley smiled.

" *'Voici mon secret. Il est très simple: on ne voit bien qu'avec le cœur. L'essentiel est invisible pour les yeux.'* " Miles looked at him, smiled. *"Comprends-tu?"* 'And now here is my secret, a very simple secret: It is only with the heart that one can see rightly; what is essential is invisible to the eye.' " Miles smiled again. "This is important."

"I waited for that?" Buckley said.

"Yes," Miles said. "It's important."

"It's pretty simple-minded," Buckley said.

"Then you're not listening," Miles said, flatly. "*L'essentiel est invisible pour les yeux.* What is essential is invisible to the eye."

"I get it," Buckley said.

"Do you?"

"It's simple."

"Is it?" Miles asked. "It can mean a lot of things."

"Simple."

"And you understand it?" Miles sat up on her knees. She frowned.

"Yes."

"I'll show you something you've not thought of." She lifted the front of her skirt, pausing only briefly before dropping it. She was naked beneath the dress.

Buckley smiled, felt his breath leave him.

"You think you know so much, Miller." She looked angry. "You need to read this book."

"Come here," Buckley said, reaching for her hand.

She pulled hers away. "The things you can't see, Buckley, can drive you crazy. They've got power. More power than anything else. You need lessons on how to see rightly."

"Come here," Buckley pleaded. "I want to kiss you."

"Finish your sandwich," Miles said. "We're going to the Met. I'm going to show you how to see."

They ate their sandwiches, drank the wine. Miles folded the blanket and tucked it into the basket, the wind ruffling her dress. Buckley wanted to kiss Miles but she would not let him. They took a long walk through the park and then over to the Met. Miles told him about *Le Petit Prince*. At the museum she checked the basket and let Buckley hold her hand. They passed through the galleries. Miles wanted to show him the Impressionists. She told him about how they invented a new way of seeing. She let Buckley hold her hand, but when he leaned to kiss her she pulled her cheek away. The afternoon passed slowly, in front of Monet, Pissarro, Van

Gogh, and others. Many others. All masters. And all Buckley could think of, all he could see, was what Miles wasn't wearing under her dress. She learned how to break his heart with invisible things.

––––––

Buckley had phoned from the roof of a house, was told that Ms. Kohler no longer worked at the homestead, but that she now was a professional consultant and an administrator in the school district. He pocketed the phone, looked out over the rising hills. The colors of fall were on the trees. He knew the area well. He had lived here for almost sixteen years. There were no surprises. The school-district offices were at the middle school, off Chestnut Street. Close enough to swing by once he got things squared away. Buckley liked to start each day, to put down the first few shingles himself. It was the sense, the notion that he was a teacher, that gave him pleasure. The workmen drank their coffee and watched as Buckley pounded. Two taps, then one swift punch and the nail was flush. Someone could write a song to the rhythm, it was so precise. Two taps, then a blow. Two taps, then a blow. Never a bent nail. Going on sixteen years of this. He stood straight, spun his hammer like a revolver and belted it.

"Get to it!" he shouted.

The men slowly rose to their feet, went to work.

Buckley stood over them for a while and then shimmied down the ladder. They would slow down their work when he left. Who cares? he thought. It was the last job of the season and there wouldn't be snow for a couple of months. The longer they took, the colder the mornings would get. They were only punishing themselves. Buckley paid per job, not by the hour. He was generous with his money; figuring how long it would take him alone to do the job, doubling the time, and putting that to a reasonable rate. Buckley sat in his truck, the windows down. He closed his eyes and listened to the sound of the men hammering. Over the years he'd learned to love this noise. It was a comfort to him somehow, hammers and wood. He remembered the Bible on his backseat, reached for it and then flipped to the Psalms. He skimmed the words, tried to recall the passage from long ago. He was tired. He'd not slept well.

The night before, Buckley sieved through pages of books he'd tried to forget he owned. There was Updike, Cheever, Dillard, Sontag, Paley. Some writer named Carver. Carver she liked. Greene she loved. Miles had adored later Greene. All of these books were hers, they were gifts to Buckley. He knew there were notes in her familiar hand in each of them, sections highlighted, with questions scribbled next to them. But Greene, she had loved Greene. And besides the poems of Dickinson, she had given him her copy of *The End of the Affair*. He flipped through to read the highlighted sections. Buckley sat down on the edge of the bed and remembered laughing at the ridiculousness of the Catholicism. He remembered how angry Miles had gotten.

They had been in the diner where she used to work. She'd given that job up to clerk in an expensive bookstore in midtown. They carried mostly art and art history. Miles had sold books to many famous actors and New York authors. Often Buckley would meet her after work, and she would tell him excitedly, gesturing with her hands, her dark eyes wide and expressive, who had been in that day. Together they took the subway down to Union Square and crossed the park, walking a block down to the Strand. There, Miles could buy the same art books she sold, but at a quarter of the price. But the evening that they argued, only he'd come back with a book. *The Go-Between*. They sat drinking coffee.

"Where do you find these books?" she said, tracing her finger on the cover.

"It was just there on the table," he said. "It looked interesting."

"Did you ever start the Greene I gave you?"

"I finished it," Buckley said.

"You finished it?"

"It wasn't that long," he said.

"Didn't you have a math exam?"

"Yes."

"Did you study?"

"Some."

"Some?" she said. "Buckley, you're going to get kicked out."

"At least I was reading what you gave me."

Miles smiled briefly. "If you get kicked out, what are you going to do?"

"I won't get kicked out," Buckley said. But he knew he might. "I'll get a job."

"They won't let you stay in housing," Miles said. "You'd have to leave the city."

"We could find a place together."

"Buckley," she said. "I'm not ready for that. I need room to paint." A waitress stopped at the table, refilled their cups. "Thanks, Toni." Miles stirred some cream into her coffee. "Don't you want to be something?"

"Your husband," Buckley said.

Miles frowned. "What's going on with you? You had this drive to be a journalist when we met. Now you spend all your time lounging around reading novels. This is Columbia, Buckley. It's not bum-fuck Idaho."

This accusation soured in Buckley's head. "You're from Ohio, Miles. That's not the capital of the world."

"But I'm here now," Miles said. "And I'm going to make something of it."

"Maybe I'll change my major to literature," Buckley suggested.

"Now that's ambition," Miles said. "You want to be some old stiff who spends his time reading lecture notes written twenty years ago? Students nodding off? Who cares about dead writers?"

"You love Dickinson!"

"She's never been taught," Miles said. "No one's *really* taught her. She's immediate, like painting. You love her. Then you come to her again and again and she defies a dusty collection of notes. She means something new each time. It's as though she's still alive."

"You have an interest in the living," Buckley said. "I'm interested in the dead. It's the only way to say something substantial about an artist."

"I'm interested in the future," Miles said. "You're satisfied with the present. And the past."

"The present is the only thing we can trust," Buckley said. "The past is the only thing that is certain."

They both sat without talking. Buckley knew that something was changing, that Miles was growing impatient with him. They walked beside each other in the cold March air and didn't talk. Buckley walked her up the steps to her apartment and she didn't look at him. She turned the key in the lock, closed the door on him without a word, without even a kiss or a good-bye.

They fought on the phone later that night when Buckley had called Greene's Catholicism ridiculous. Silly. He said Greene would be a delightful writer if you took all the Catholic garbage out. Miles was so angry that she cried. She said that after what had happened that evening, maybe they should take a little time to reflect. Maybe, she had said, they could just date. She wanted their relationship to feel new again. She wanted passion. She wanted Buckley to find his motivation, to have his interests back.

Then, thinking of the book, Buckley asked her if she loved him when he was not there with her. She had said she wasn't sure anymore if she loved him at all.

Buckley sat on the edge of the bed and held the Greene novel in his hand. He remembered his habit when he lived in New York. He would frequent used bookstores and slip volumes off the shelf. He would hold them in his palm and let the signatures fall open of their own accord. This was like dipping into the life of the previous owner. He could discover what was most dear to that person. Now, this book was a way to travel backwards. He hoped he might get something new he could use. Were there things about Miles he'd forgotten or never known? Buckley let *The End of the*

Affair splay. There was a highlighted passage about geese flying over our future graves. How strange. How useless. He didn't remember these lines. They meant nothing to him. Buckley closed his eyes and lifted the book, smelled its pages. He'd swear there was the faintest hint of her. Miles. Her shampoo and her cologne. The way her long, slender finger used to trace the words of her favorite passages, for his eyes to follow as they rode the train. The train rocking, her shoulder next to his. The touch of her cheek when she had leaned to kiss him so many times. Buckley sat on the bed longing for the certainty of his past. Wishing he had been right. But he knew that people needed to anticipate the unknown that rushed toward them from the future. He had lain back on the bed, cried, fallen asleep. He tossed, woke up with the sickly overhead light casting about the room. He turned, slept again. The night had passed this way.

Buckley awoke, the Bible in his hand. He stirred in his seat, the sound of hammers knocking slowly. The day had warmed. The cab of his Explorer smelled musty, like the scent of the Bible. He uncapped his Thermos and took a sip of coffee. He thought he'd drive to Amherst to visit Ms. Kohler and inquire about Miles.

———

Buckley felt as though the veneer between his unconsciousness and his waking thinned. He couldn't feel the doctors cutting on him, but the presence of hands in his abdomen was there for him to know. Their voices seemed discernible, though there was no way of proving he was not dreaming. He could have even dropped into a coma, he surmised. The anesthesia elicited a mood, a feeling, of creamy warmth. It was as though he was happy, satisfied. Buckley had not known these feelings for a long time, and he wondered if it was possible to stay here, in this condition of elated carelessness, forever. He tried to immerse himself deeper into this sleep, but it was as though the voices called him, kept him aware with their chatter. There were random words—retractor, BP, suction, hemostat, clamp. They went on and on. Buckley's vitals were strong. He drew closer to the conversation.

"Doctor Bromley is here," he heard a woman say. "He's looking at the CT scans."

"Good," Doctor Umana said. "He scrubbed?"

"Yes."

A door opened. "What have we got?" a man said.

"Doctor Bromley," Umana said. "MVA. Midthirties. A blow to the back of the head. Must have been something loose in the vehicle. Metal, maybe? In an SUV."

"Figures," Bromley said. "They're moving coffins. I'm worried about intercranial pressure. Let's keep him deep."

"OK," Reeder said.

"There's a priest waiting," Bromley said. "Father Estes."

"OK," Umana said. "This guy's a mess."

"I'll want to relieve . . ."

What had struck him? Buckley thought. What kind of luck? Then, it was as if he had dunked his head underwater, the voices above muffled and unclear. It was difficult to breathe. Buckley felt himself fall deeper into unconsciousness. The euphoria left him.

He was driving. A long straight road through colors, leaves twisting on the air. Pavement between dust fields. Corn, farther out. A graveyard and aloft, a skein of geese winging south. What are the chances? Buckley thought, his window down, the chill showing on his forearm. He watched the geese. They passed overhead, then out over the fields. He recalled that geese never fly alone. If one of the flock is sick or injured, another will drop back with it, stay with it as a companion. Geese, he thought, take care of their own. He smiled, watched them disappear in the distance. A sudden loneliness came over him. How could his life have come to this? He closed his eyes for a moment.

A glimpse, a deer, in the pale of evening. Is there anything more frightening? Buckley swerved. There wasn't a thump, just tilting, tires, darkness.

———

Buckley sat in his truck, parked in the middle school lot. He was about to step on a train that would take him into his past. He recalled the excitement of his first train ride with Miles. How they rode hand in hand. He remembered the first time they kissed. How they had walked together across the Brooklyn Bridge and there, in the middle, the wind, the towers, the suspension wires, the kiss. For their six-month anniversary they spent student-loan money to stay for a night at the Roosevelt. They had kissed on the stairs of Grand Central. This played in his head like a stupid movie. It was foolish and he felt sorry for having come here, for having looked back. He felt he'd turned to a pillar of salt, that the weight in his stomach, that his hands, numb and motionless on the wheel, were punishments for not living in the moment. But Miles had come alive again and was here in the truck with him. She had, only the night before, traced her finger along the pages of books, showing Buckley what mattered to her. He'd read her inscription on the inside cover of the Dickinson poems. Her philosophy in a nutshell. Buckley thought how comical we all are for believing time travel was a scientific curiosity. We all do it every day. And that puzzle, if you go back to the past, perhaps encounter your grandfather, and interfere in some way with his meeting your grandmother, would the present be changed? Yes, of course, the present is always changed, each time we consider our burned and useless youth. Each time we remember what we've lost, we are altered. We walk through the world as a ghost, as a haunted, inadequate apparition.

Buckley thought of turning the key, driving away. But he'd come this far and maybe, somehow, knowing if Miles had ever returned to the homestead, to the streets in the town where he walked and lived, would ease his aching. He opened the door, crossed the lot, and entered the building. A receptionist led him down a corridor, past the superintendent's office, to the desk of an assistant.

"Debbie," the receptionist said. "This is Mr. Miller. He'd like to speak with Ms. Kohler."

"Hello, Mr. Miller." She reached and shook his hand.

"You can call me Buckley."

"Buckley," Debbie said. "Is Ms. Kohler expecting you?"

"No," Buckley said. "I called the Dickinson homestead and they said I could find her here."

"Let me see if she's available," Debbie said. She turned toward a side office. "May I tell her what this is about?"

"I'm curious about work at the homestead," Buckley said awkwardly. "We know people in common."

Debbie glanced at him. "Are you a Dickinson scholar?" she asked.

"In a way," Buckley said. "I know Dickinson. But I'm a businessman."

"You can have a seat at the table if you like." Debbie pointed to a long meeting table that filled an alcove.

"I'll stand," Buckley said.

Debbie studied him, then dipped into the side office, closing the door behind her. Buckley recognized her from around town. She was petite with pretty skin and long, soft hair. He'd seen her walking down Main Street with a tall, thin man who also had long hair. How *do* people get together? Buckley had always thought. She was too good for him. The man looked as if he'd never worked a day in his life. Sickly. A professor, maybe. Buckley tucked his hands into his pockets, then pulled them out. He tried not to look suspicious.

Debbie opened the door and both she and Ms. Kohler stood in the opening. "Hi, I'm Wendy Kohler," the woman said, holding her hand out.

"Buckley Miller," he said, taking her hand.

"What can I do for you?" she asked.

"Could we talk in private?" Buckley said sheepishly.

"We can talk here at the table," she said. "We can close the outer-office door."

Debbie went and pushed the door, shutting off the larger office. She went back to her work in front of a computer. Buckley pulled a chair back and sat down. Ms. Kohler sat across the table from him.

"We've actually met," Buckley said. "Years ago."

"I've seen your truck around," Ms. Kohler said. "You're a roofing contractor?"

"Yes."

"I've seen you parked up the street at the Dairy Mart," she said. "A man with a business might use more discretion."

Buckley was surprised at her impertinence. "We all have our habits," Buckley said. "You spend your time reading a poet whose poems can all be recited to the tune of 'The Yellow Rose of Texas.' "

Ms. Kohler looked surprised. "I hadn't thought of that," she said. She smiled. "What can I do for you?"

"As I was saying, we met years ago," Buckley said, "when I was a student at Columbia. My girlfriend and I came to the homestead. You were our docent."

"Really," Ms. Kohler said. "That long ago?"

"It doesn't seem so long," Buckley said. "But I guess it is." Buckley looked saddened. He felt hopeless. "Her name was Julie Miles."

"Julie Miles."

"You spent time with her, before and after the tour," Buckley said. "She asked you if you'd ever been in the copula."

"Yes," Ms. Kohler said flatly. She waited. "What's your point?"

"I was wondering if she ever came to work at the homestead?"

"Mr. Miller—"

"Buckley."

"Buckley. I'm not in the business of reuniting lost friends—"

"Ms. Kohler," Buckley interrupted. "I'm not asking you for much."

"What are you asking for?" Ms. Kohler stirred, as if she might get up and leave the office.

"Please," Buckley begged. His could hear his heart beating in his ears. He thought he might cry. "I need to know what happened to her. I need to know if she ever came back here."

Ms. Kohler stared at him blankly. "I don't think I can give you that information."

"Then she must have worked at the homestead," Buckley said. "You must remember her."

"I didn't know a Julie Miles," Ms. Kohler said.

"Did she marry?"

"Mr. Miller," she said, putting her hands flat on the table. "There are other ways of finding out about people. Many companies do that kind of thing. You could try the Internet."

"Ms. Kohler, please." Buckley had begun to plead. "Could we speak in private for a moment."

"Say whatever you have to say here."

Buckley stared at her, tears welling in his eyes. "I was in love with her," Buckley said. "So much so that I flunked out of Columbia. I gave up everything for her. And when I did, I gave up the parts of me she loved. I think that is the way it is with some people. They get lost in love. They lose themselves. And that's what screws everything up." Buckley paused. "I gave up everything. I just want to know if she every came back here?"

"What difference does it make?"

"I don't know," Buckley confessed. "I don't have a fucking clue."

Ms. Kohler stared at Buckley for a moment. "She worked as a docent for a while."

"How long ago?"

"Mr. Miller, I really shouldn't be saying anything."

"Please, Ms. Kohler."

"It's been several years."

"Only several years?"

"She was happily married, Mr. Miller."

"Was?" Buckley felt a sense of hope rise.

"She was married to a man named Hogue. Josh."

"Did she ever mention me?"

"No, Mr. Miller." Ms. Kohler settled back in her chair. "Julie was happily married." Ms. Kohler considered Buckley. "You have an overblown notion of love."

"Does she still live in the area?"

"I believe Josh does," Ms. Kohler offered. "Julie has paintings in the Michelson Gallery in Northampton."

"Where does Miles live?" Buckley asked. "Julie. Where is she?"

"Mr. Miller," Ms. Kohler hesitated. "She passed away."

"Passed away?" Buckley repeated. It had never occurred to him that such a thing could happen, that someone his age would have already died. When you're young, he thought, just leaving for college, you don't think of death. The thought doesn't come to you until you're older. Fifty, maybe. Fifty is still young. Maybe even older when you are balding or gray, and you look in the mirror and there is nothing there to remind you of yourself, when you were just coming into your own, your skin, your blood, your thoughts. Buckley sat stunned, wordless.

"Mr. Miller," Ms. Kohler said. "I'm sorry."

Buckley had nothing to say. He felt emptied out, despairing. There was no one he could tell, no one he could plead to. He couldn't even say he was sorry. Sorry for what? For being stupid? Miles had had faith and what good had it done her? She was dead. He tried to recall her face. How had she changed in her married life? Had her hair grown long? Had she gained weight? Had she lost her looks? He couldn't say. They had walked the same streets together for a few years and he'd not recognized her. With a new name and a new life, why not? Perhaps she had seen him, recognized him, and chosen to pass him by. If there were jobs less ambitious than a literature professor, surely roofing was one of them. Certainly, she'd seen his truck with his name on it.

"How long has it been?" Buckley asked.

"A couple of years, maybe," Ms. Kohler said. "She's buried at St. Brigid's. Off the highway."

Buckley knew the place. He slid his chair back, stood.

"I'm sorry, Mr. Miller."

"Thank you for telling me," Buckley said. "I know you didn't have to."

"This door leads out," Mrs. Kohler said, pointing.

"Did she spend time in the copula?" Buckley asked, though he couldn't say why. The question was meaningless.

"I think she did," Ms. Kohler said. "There's a beautiful view."

Buckley nodded. He thought he'd like to see it for himself sometime. He shook Ms. Kohler's hand, made his way to his truck, and sat inside. With the windows up, it was warm. Still, a coldness took him. It was as if his only friend had died. There was no one left to bear witness to his life, to his failing and his longing. It seemed impossible that Miles was gone. There had always been a comfort in knowing that she was out in the world living, going about her business, with the memory of him lying dormant, tucked deep beneath her consciousness. He had been there in her past. There had been that hope that one day, just like for him, something would spur the memory of their shared past. It might have caused her to look him up, call, even agree to meet him someplace. Buckley needed this possibility. It didn't matter if neither of them acted on it, tried to find the other. But Buckley needed the possibility. He wondered if only he was afflicted by the past; that distant memories were as ever present as the colors of the falling leaves, as people walking the streets, as words highlighted in books that had been closed for many, many years. What had Miles once read to him? *"L'essentiel est invisible pour les yeux."* It would have been better if he'd called Miles and she'd said she recalled him faintly. But now, his love for her, his memory, would be hardened. Miles's presence was complete, with a beginning and an end. The love for the dead goes on—it's the breathing in and out and in—always unreturned.

Buckley would never know Miles's thoughts. He wouldn't know if she had seen him from the copula and, perhaps, thought back happily on their days together. How had they lived together in the same town and not run into each other? A cruelty of time, he thought. Buckley looked out at kids on the playground. They have no idea, he thought, how much they will miss this, these days before memories begin to crowd them. How could he live in this world? To exist, he thought, there has to be someone there to see you, someone who knows every part of your life, both real and imagined. But there was no one now for Buckley. He would walk the town streets alone, with no memory.

Buckley reached for the Bible on the passenger's seat. He opened to the Psalms. He needed time to think before going back to work. The news had still not settled. It might take a lifetime for it to make sense. Buckley remembered worrying when he was a child that when he died he'd go to heaven, but that in heaven he wouldn't remember anyone's name. This frightened him. He'd said he'd put a list of everyone's names in his pocket, so that he wouldn't forget. But now, Buckley wished he could forget. Everything.

Buckley read. He wanted to find the passage. The afternoon eased. The school buses flooded the parking lot. Kids yelled. Some walked hand in hand. Other's carried musical instruments. Buses whined into motion. Buckley watched the commotion for a while then read some more.

Finally, he found it.

I am poured out like water; and all my bones are scattered. My heart is become like wax melting in the midst of my bowels. My strength is dried up like a potsherd, and my tongue hath cleaved to my jaws: and thou hast brought me down into the dust of death. For many dogs have encompassed me: the council of the malignant hath besieged me. They have dug my hands and feet. They have numbered all my bones.

———

Buckley could hear the heart monitor. They had moved him from recovery to the ICU. He had regained consciousness briefly, and both Umana and Bromley had told him he was critical. He wanted to move, but was strapped down. He felt trapped. They said there might be memory loss. A chance of coma. He had internal injuries. They had used language that floated through his thoughts without adhering. Something about his heart. An artery. He could not remember. He drifted off. Umana had said the drugs would cause him to sleep. He said Father Estes would be allowed in soon. Buckley could not talk. He wanted to tell them Father Estes could go to hell.

Buckley slept. He dreamed of Miles. He went to her grave. He had hoped there would still be a suggestion of its having been freshly dug. It would have, he felt, made a difference. But the grass, still green in the fall air, was thick and evenly settled. He wondered if anyone ever came to visit. There were no flowers, no letters. Buckley got down on his knees. He put his palms to the grass. He didn't know how to pray. He cried. There had been all these years and now he was so close to her. There was only the dirt and grass between them. There were only a few feet that separated them. He longed to talk to her. And he wanted to pray for her. How should he start? The cool evening was on him. He closed his eyes and it was as though someone whispered to him. *"Into thy hands, Lord, I commend my spirit. O Lord, Jesus Christ, receive my spirit. Holy Mary, pray for me. Mary Mother of grace, Mother of mercy, do thou protect me from the enemy and receive me at the hour of my death."* This prayer had come to him and he was glad.

Buckley left the copy of Dickinson's poems. He sat in his truck for a while and watched the wind carry leaves across the graveyard. He started the engine, but he couldn't imagine going on. He pulled the truck into gear. It was habit. We all do it, he thought, like manners. He drove along a straight road through colors, leaves twisting on the air. Pavement between dust fields. Corn, farther out. A graveyard and aloft, a skein of geese winging south. What are the chances? Buckley thought, his window down, the chill showing on his forearm. He watched the geese. They passed overhead, then out over the fields. He recalled that geese never fly alone. If one of the flock is sick or injured, another will drop back with it, stay with it as a companion. Geese, he thought, take care of their own. He smiled, watched them disappear in the distance. A sudden loneliness came over him. How could his life have come to this? He closed his eyes for a moment. How could he go on? This time of day, this time of season, there could be a deer. It's difficult to see in the pale of evening.

There could be a deer. Is there anything more frightening? Buckley closed his eyes, swerved. There wasn't a thump, just tilting, tires, darkness.

As though whispered to him, he had prayed. *"Into thy hands, Lord, I commend my spirit. O Lord, Jesus Christ, receive my spirit. Holy Mary, pray for me. Mary Mother of grace, Mother of mercy, do thou protect me from the enemy and receive me at the hour of my death."*

Buckley had kneeled over Miles's grave. All he could think of was her body, in a casket, beneath him. She had believed in the resurrection of the body. He wanted to believe too, there, crying. Buckley wanted to remain there for as long as it took, until he could find comfort and certainty. He closed his eyes, and it was as if he were asleep.

His sleep lightened. The heart monitor beeped. Buckley felt the heaviness of having cried for too long perch on his chest. The aching deep inside his chest spread into his head. His awareness seemed to rise and fall, as if surfacing from beneath waves of dreams. *"Into thy hands . . ."*

It was as though he could touch her. They were, again, on a

train. Her hand in his. Miles was reading. She read to him aloud *"L'essentiel est invisible pour les yeux."* He smiled and she kissed him. Her perfume. It was as if, after all these years, they had met again. He wanted to say something to her, but he couldn't find the words. For a moment, his memory faltered and her name escaped him. Miles. He closed his eyes, kissed her cheek. He felt a strange rush, a dizziness in his head. He rose, as if from a dream.

"*. . . hour of my death.*"

A rushing. He rose. There was the shrill of the train's brakes. It was constant, deafening. He was held down. He couldn't lean against the breaking, the momentum. He held Miles's hand. It was there for him. There were voices he couldn't make out. People jostling about the train. Rushing. Everyone rushing. He rose and then fell into darkness deeply, deeply.

Good
As
Any

Delilah left us when Rose Marie and I slicked a "Cats: The Other White Meat" sticker on the Bronco. That's the half of it. The epilepsy papers, too, were part of it. But they came later. And the truth was Rose Marie made Delilah feel like the other woman, the one less loved. Maybe she was, I guess. But Delilah was a twitch. Certifiable.

I said, "Don't let the door hit you in the ass on the way out."

She was no artist. Didn't understand the dexterity of leaving, of coming back for belongings or just forgetting them altogether. Delilah lugged a huge suitcase out of the bedroom, around the corner, dragging with both hands. I had to hold the door for her. "Fuck you," she said. I closed the door behind her. None of this seemed to bother Rose Marie. She sat on the divan, listening to her favorite compact disk. She's got the best brown eyes.

"It's just you and me, kid," I said, sitting down next to her. I put my arm around her, stroked her back. "We've got the whole bed to ourselves."

"Ave Maria" ended. She toed the remote and the song repeated again. I closed my eyes and listened. This was some strange fetish she had, one that I liked. It's part of what brought us together. I should've known better than to get involved with a woman who loved cats, I thought, with regard to Delilah. I should've known.

———

I had seen the ad in the personals. "Love to snuggle? I'm your girl. Constant. Loving. Headstrong, but obedient. The best you'll ever have. Favorite song, 'Ave Maria.' " Reading the ads was a weekend habit. I found them entertaining. Sunday mornings I'd get up early, make coffee, and finger through the paper. I wasn't looking for companionship. Delilah and I had been an item for a few years. She slept late. When she did scuff in around eleven, I had to put the paper away. She hated newspapers, demanded not to be stuck looking at the back page while I read. I folded the corner down, closed the paper.

"Coffee?" I asked.

"Yes," she said, plopping in the seat across from me.

I got up, poured. "You know the song 'Ave Maria'?" I asked, sitting the cup and saucer in front of her.

"Yeah," she said. "Why?"

"No reason," I said. I sat down across from her.

"Why?" she asked.

"Article," I said. "Just wondering." Obedient, I thought. Now there's a word. What kind of person calls herself "obedient?" I imagined leather.

"Don't know how you read that crap," she said. "Wash your hands."

Delilah'll tell you she's no good before noon. It's true. She won't let me touch her after I've read the paper. Says she can feel the ink. I got up and pumped soap out of the dispenser—antibacterial soft cleansing. I have to scrub like a surgeon. Afterwards, she'd want to smell them. I held my hands out, palms up, while she sniffed.

"OK," she said. "Kiss me."

I didn't mind this, lips that tasted of coffee. I bent and kissed her. "What's it sound like?" I asked, settling back across from her.

"Who cares?" she said. "What kind of article talks about 'Ave Maria'?"

"Forget it," I had said. "Let's not talk about it."

———

I left a message with the service while Delilah was taking a nap. "Be discreet," I said. "I've got an old Bronco." Afterward I took the truck out for a drive. I didn't know what I was asking for, why I'd made the call. I steered the winding roads, through the hills, up into the mountains. The engine groaned. It was late May and already it was hot. I watched the temperature gauge. Deciding to give it a rest, I parked at a summit, where there was a large community house with a view. Saturday nights a band played, people danced. Delilah and I had come here when we'd first started dating. Western swing was the theme of the night. She had the boots and the hat. I'd found some old calfskins in a secondhand shop. We danced and drank like it was some kind of gringo honeymoon. I knew for sure I was in love. But there I was, alone now. Delilah sleeping. I'd made that call. I took a walk on the large deck that surrounded the place. Below, a river snaked through farmland. I enjoyed the view and the breeze.

I took the Bronco by a wash, had it done up to the nines. Detailed even. It got dusky and I drove home.

"Where you been?" she asked when I came through the door.

"Got my truck done," I said.

"Some guy named Buddy called about the ad."

"Buddy?" I questioned.

"You finally selling that piece-of-crap Bronco?" she asked. "Good riddance. Number's by the phone."

I nodded. I hoped I'd not gotten myself into some kind of ring. Who the hell was Buddy? I lurked around the house with a beer.

Some sort of fudge packer had called. My lord, what had I been thinking? I figured I'd have to call, scare him off, before Delilah got wise. She was of a limited understanding.

I suggested ham, red beans and rice, fried okra. Delilah gave me the look. You know, like who the hell do you think I am? I fought back with my sorry-assed slump-shouldered forget it. She plugged in the Fry Daddy and I smiled inside. While the grease crackled, I made the call.

"Buddy?"

"Yeah," he said. "Who's this?"

"Mitch," I said. Before I could let him have it, he started with the questions.

"You got a dog?" he said.

"I'm—"

"Do you?" he interrupted.

"I'm—"

"What do you think this is, charity?" he interrupted again. "Do you or don't you?"

"No," I said.

"Good," he said. "Now we're getting somewhere."

What the hell was he talking about? I tried to wedge a sentence in, but he pressed on. "Fenced yard?"

"Listen," I said.

"Do you or don't you?"

"No," I said.

"That's no good," he said. "You got trees though?"

"Yeah."

"Big ones?"

I paused for a moment. Did he really mean trees? "Big enough," I answered, deciding that seemed safe enough and true.

"OK," he said. "You'll need a lead."

"Lead?" I said. "What for?"

"To tie her up," he said. "You can't just let her run free. Someone'll come along and take her."

"I see."

"What made you call?" he asked.

I thought for a moment. " 'Ave Maria,' " I said.

"You know the Willows?"

"The housing edition?"

"What other?" he said, sharply. "Thirty Teaberry Lane. Be here tomorrow at five."

"But—" I said, trying to object. I got a dial tone. I put down the receiver and went to the kitchen. Delilah was working over the stove, turning the ham. I leaned against the counter, sipped beer.

"Well?" she said.

"Well what?"

"He going to buy it?"

"I don't know."

"Did he sound interested?"

"I'll take it by his place tomorrow afternoon," I said.

"Is that a good idea?" she said. "He could be some kind of nut."

"You want him here?"

"No," she said. "You should meet him someplace public. Over at Lyle's body shop."

"I don't want to get Lyle involved in this," I said. "It's fine."

She let it rest. Delilah and I ate in the den. I puzzled about the call. She didn't ask questions. The TV played and she watched. We made it an early night, with work the next day. It took me a long time to get off to sleep. My nerves were working after the strange conversation with Buddy. He'd used the word *she,* so I guessed I better go and straighten things out. Keep him from calling and spilling the beans to Delilah. He might think she was game.

———

Rose Marie and I had a quiet evening. Just me and her sitting on the divan watching television. She liked to nap with the television on. She liked it when Delilah was out of the house. I figured she would be happiest now that Delilah had left for good. To be honest,

I didn't miss Delilah either. There was this terrific show on *The Learning Channel* about working dogs. You know, seeing-eye dogs, dogs that pick things up for the disabled. I knew all about that stuff. But then they had this segment on dogs that work with epileptic patients. They talked about how dogs could sense when a patient was about to have a seizure. The dog would give a signal and the person would know to take their medicine, prepare for an attack. I thought it was cool, something I didn't know. I fixed up chicken pot pies and Rose Marie and I ate. Then we went off to bed. She liked to sleep in the crook of my arm. Sometimes it kept me awake, but I let her do it anyway. My thinking was a trusting relationship was about give and take. I dreamed about the epilepsy dogs. I got this notion in my head.

———

I'd taken off work early to make it to Buddy's by five. I figured I'd make it quick and simple. Come home and tell Delilah Buddy's interest got me to regretting the ad. Just say I'd changed my mind. Delilah would be angry. But she'd get over it. What worried me was the talk Buddy and I might have. Some people don't hear so well. I knew about all those rings on the Internet. People hooked up from all over. All about a specific kind of fetish. Sick stuff. I knew there could be trouble. I tucked my .38 into the back of my jeans, pulled my jacket down so it wouldn't show.

Buddy's place was some kind of mansion. I parked on the street, sat looking for a while. Two stories, stone work, and fancy carpentry. That's the kind of money a perv can make. I left the keys in the ignition, in case I needed a quick departure.

The doorbell was one of those songs, you know. I backed up for some distance. He opened the door, cell phone in hand.

"Mitch?" he questioned.

"Yeah," I said. "Listen—"

"Come in," he said, backing away from the door and waving me in. "I'll be with you."

He ducked off into the house. I stood for a moment looking in. Leather couches, hardwood floors, real art on the walls. A haven of ill repute. All the kinky stuff downstairs in the basement. I felt for my gun. I stood on the entryway tile.

"Look," I heard him say. "I've got the bitch here if you want to come by." There was a silence. "When I'm here," he said, pausing. "Yeah. Locked up otherwise. OK. Good-bye."

Buddy hustled around the corner. "Sorry to keep you waiting," he said. "Business." He stepped up out of the sunken den, offered his hand. "Buddy Smith."

"Mitch," I said, shaking his hand. He had a grip.

"Let's have a seat," he said.

"I think—"

"Have a beer? Wine? Tea? Coffee? You look like a beer man to me," he said. He headed off, then turned. "Domestic or import?"

What the hell, I thought. "Import."

"Sure thing. In a jiffy."

Who uses the word *jiffy* nowadays? I adjusted my gun for the quick draw. I walked lightly, taking a look at his books along one wall. Some people think books are like furniture. I think of them as doorstops. He had a few that'd hold open some big doors. Lots of books on dogs. I kind of hoped for something juicy. Nothing.

"I forgot to ask light or dark," he said, moving quicklike. "I took the privilege of assuming light. Dark doesn't suit you," he added.

"Light's fine," I said, taking the Heineken. "I hate to run you through all this trouble, but I think there's been a misunder-standing."

"I'm sure there has," he said. "Please. Have a seat." He kind of swept his arm out like one of those girls on *The Price Is Right*. He fell back into the cushions of the love seat. "Coasters," he said. He tossed one across the table.

I sat down on the edge of the couch. This man was working it. I took a pull off the beer and held the bottle between two fingers.

"Let me ask you this," he said. "You called about the advertisement?"

"Yes," I said. "But—"

"Well, then you're the person," he said. "I'm looking for someone who wants a relationship. That ad had long-term relationship written all over it. Let me ask you this: You know how to love a woman?"

I tilted the bottle, took a drink. I kept my eye on him. "Yeah," I said, nodding. "I think I do pretty well."

"Well, this isn't any different," he said, touching the tabletop with one hand. "I've had all kinds of bitches and Rose Marie is the sweetest. Better than any woman you'll ever love."

"Hold on," I said. "This's gone on long enough."

"You have no idea," he said.

He stood up. I felt for my gun, putting the beer down on the table. For sure, I thought this was his move. This one's going to be hard to explain, I thought.

"Coaster," he said.

"What?"

"Coaster," he repeated. "That's expensive wood." He pointed to the table.

"I think I'd better go," I said. I moved the bottle onto the coaster. I stood up.

"Come take a look at what I've got," he said. "Out here in the backyard." He headed across the room to a sliding glass door. He motioned. "Bring your beer, if you like." He stood waiting, one hand on his hip.

"What's out there?" I asked.

"You're not a trusting man," Buddy said. "That's very good. You can't trust people these days." He paused, waiting. "Come on," he said. "We won't bite." He slid the door open, stepping outside.

———

I woke up and Rose Marie was snoring, snuggled up against me. I'd sorted out part of this problem in my sleep. The house was quiet. I guess I half expected Delilah to have come back during the night. No telling where she'd gone. I lay for a moment thinking the day through. Readjusting, I slipped out of bed without waking Rose Marie. I put coffee on for the both of us, called into work sick, and turned on the computer. Rose Marie hated the computer, would do anything to keep me away from it. But I had work to do, so I let her sleep. The thing was, she had cancer. We were running out of time. I surfed for information until she came around the corner, yawning, looking at me as if to say, "Why didn't you wake me? I missed you so." I took her into my arms.

———

Buddy's backyard was like a golf green. A damn country club. From the deck I could see the yard was divided. Halfway out there was a tall fence that was opaque with that green stuff. Like there was a tennis court out there or something. I knew better. It was some kind of perv factory. I remained on the deck, sipping my beer. I was nobody's fool.

Buddy was almost to the gate. He turned. "Come on," he called. "Just come take a look."

"No thanks," I said. "I'm fine here."

He held poised, one hand blocking out the afternoon sun. "She's a sweetie," he said. "You should take a look."

I had the gun. I figured there might be folks in trouble out there. I didn't want to make the news, but I didn't want to be one of those persons who stands by and does nothing. This turns bad, I thought, I'll plug him in the head. I felt for the safety. Released. I kept my eye on him, approached steadily. I was slow about it, but not hesitant. I'd never been yellow in my life.

"After you," I said at the gate.

"Certainly," he said, winging through. He stopped, turned. "Now these take some getting used to."

I kept my right hand near my back, my thumb hooked on a belt loop. All naturallike, casual, you know. Looking from the side it was clear there was a fenced enclosure, not a sound coming from it. Buddy walked out into the yard, turned to look toward the pen. I followed suit. There was a string of stalls, and when I got a good look I saw they were filled with dogs. The ugliest dogs I'd ever seen—white, brindle, combinations. I looked to make sure. They looked like goddamn pigs. But they were dogs. One barked at me.

"What the hell are those things?" I said. "A bunch of sows?" I was sure Buddy was some perv mixing dogs and pigs.

"Bull terriers," he said.

"Jesus," I said. "You're kidding me."

"Not pit bulls," he said. "There's no such thing as a pit bull. Those are Staffordshires. These are English bull terriers."

"I don't need a dog," I said. "Or a pig either."

"Rose Marie is something special," he said. "I promise."

"You advertise dogs in the personals?" I said. "What kind of twitch are you?" I let my hand fall from my belt loop. I thought I might hit him.

"I don't want people who are looking for dogs," he said. "I want people who are looking for relationships. People who are lonely and who have a lot to give. I prefer the company of dogs."

"Maybe it's the crowd you run with?"

"I think you'll come to see."

I put my hand up to block the sun, to get a good look. I swear, I just started laughing. We both walked over for a closer examination. Delilah would kill me, I thought. I go out to sell my truck, bring home a cartoon. She'd pitch a fit.

———

The Internet's a source for bucket loads of useless crap. Where before my exposure was limited, the day I brought home a computer my life opened itself to an invisible railroad of garbage. The equivalent of boxcars full of idiots babbling to me about how I should change my life. I didn't need this. I had Delilah. But Delilah was gone and I braved the Web, looking for information about working dogs, dogs that helped epileptics. I wasn't blind. I didn't have a wheelchair, nor did I want to pretend. I wanted to keep my freedom. But epilepsy? Who would know? Rose Marie was running out of time, and I wanted to be with her every moment.

I made some calls. No one was in the know. I was continually surprised at how stupid people were, on the average.

"We're not a veterinarian," a dull voice piped.

"I know that," I said. "I'm talking about epileptic people who *have* dogs. The dogs can sense an oncoming epileptic seizure. It was on *The Learning Channel.*"

"Never heard of such a thing," the person said. "Don't see how that's possible."

"Listen," I said. I was silent for about ten seconds. "Hear that?"

"What?" the person said. "Hear what?"

"My dog heard it," I said. "It was me calling you a fucking idiot in a high-pitched voice that only she could hear." I slammed the phone down. Sitting there, stunned, it occurred to me. If they don't know, who will?

Rose Marie was sitting at my feet, looking up. I fixed her coffee, cream and sugar. Put the mug down for her and stepped into the shower. I toweled off and we went out for our morning stroll. Rose Marie liked certain things. Particular plants and flowers. It'd been a mild winter. There were patches of snow. But there were daffodils already. She spent an hour going over them, smelling each one. I let her take her time.

———

Buddy let Rose Marie out of her stall, fawned over her. I was doubtful. I realized she was like the Spuds MacKenzie dog. Like the dog in the movie *Patton*. She was just like them except brindle. A stocky sausage with legs. I kneeled down beside her and ran my hand over her solid body. She had this pensive way about her.

"This girl is special," Buddy said. "You won't believe what she can do."

"I didn't come here for a dog," I said.

"You didn't come here to turn one down either," he said. "Let me show you what she likes." He turned for the house. "Come on, Marie," he said. "Up, up."

Rose Marie fell in pace behind him, smartly. She kept her tail low, her body stiff. She was a dog with a mission. I sipped my beer and watched her trot, stiff legged.

"It'll only take a minute of your time," Buddy called to me.

I figured I had to go through the house anyway. I reached back, put the safety on the gun. I followed them inside.

"Sit," Buddy said. The dog sat, watched him. "This here's how Rose Marie got her name." He held up a compact disk. "You have a player?"

"Yeah," I said. "Not a fancy one."

"Remote control?"

"Yeah," I said.

Buddy took the disk out of its case. He put it in the player and walked over to show me the remote. "See here," he said. "I put different-colored tape on each button. Play. Skip. Stop. Dogs don't see color. But Rose Marie can tell the different shades. That's why I picked these colors."

"Yeah," I said, looking.

"Marie," he said. "You want music?" Marie stood, wagged her tail. "Come get it," he said. He bent and held the controller down for her. She took it gently in her mouth and walked close to the stereo. "OK," Buddy said. " 'Ave Maria.' " She set the controller down. She pawed a button, skipping several songs. Finally a tune came on and she stopped. She sat and listened. I guessed it was "Ave Maria."

"Pretty good trick," I said, smiling.

"It's no trick," he said. "Gentleman brought her in this way, with the CD. Said he'd have the CD playing, leave the room, and when he returned this song was on. He had other CDs with 'Ave Maria.' She'd do the same with them."

GOOD AS ANY

"Yeah," I said. "What's the scam?"

"There is none," he said. "She likes music."

"Dog like this could make you money," I said. "You're going to put the screws to me."

"I'm a businessman," he said. "I breed and show bull terriers. Top of the line. This here's no show dog. She's what we call a rescue. A dog we put up for adoption to a good home. A person who'll take care of her. As breeders, we try to keep them out of the shelters. A lot of people don't know the difference. They think they're pit bulls. They want to put them down right away or try to fight them."

I sat studying him, wondering what the catch was, how I was going to pay. "You're saying you don't want this dog?" I asked.

"I'll keep her till I find a good home," he said. "She knows commands, is housebroken, and she likes music. I want her to be a house dog. She's not great with other animals. Some are that way. Definitely no cats."

Rose Marie lay down next to the remote. I thought about it. "How old is she?"

"Five," he said. "You read Jim Harrison?"

"Never heard of him," I said.

" 'It is easy to forget that in the main we die only seven times more slowly than our dogs.' From his book *The Road Home*. You should read it."

I nodded. I liked the sound of it. "How long's a dog like this live?"

"Difficult to say," he said. "Don't know all her history. As few as seven. As many as fifteen or sixteen years."

"So I can just take her?"

"No," he said. "There's an adoption fee. The money goes to keep the rescue organization running. There's some veterinary expenses. She's been spayed. You have to own a crate. She's crate trained."

"What's that mean?"

"Means she's used to staying in a crate while you're away from the house. I advise you keep to that. Dog like this can make a mess of the house. Rose Marie has a thing for leather."

I smiled, laughed.

"What's so funny?"

"Nothing," I said, remembering what I'd thought before I came. "What kind of money are we talking about?"

"Three-fifty adoption. Fifty for the vet. I'll give you a crate for thirty. That's a deal. I'll give you a lead and a book about the breed. You'd better read it. A Cressite ball," he paused. "Make it four-fifty even."

"Shit," I said. I knew I'd get screwed. I shook my head. "She's a beauty but—"

"Take your time," he said. "You can call around if you want. That's a deal. Adoption fee's the same all over. It's to keep the freaks away. People who want to fight them."

"How do you know I'm not one of them?"

"You wouldn't still be here," he said. "Besides I'm going to come by your house and check in on her every once in a while."

"That's a lot of money," I said.

"My pups are fifteen hundred," he said. "Call around if you like. She'll be here until I find her a good home."

He sat back on the love seat with his beer. He took a draw. "You know, I've got to make a few calls." He leaned forward, got to his feet. "Spend some time with her. I'll be with you in a few minutes."

He walked down the hallway and I heard him on the phone. My beer was warm. I drained it and got down on the floor next to Rose Marie. I ran my hands along her back. She looked up, had a gentle way about her. Rose Marie's eyes were deep and brown, as though there was a lot going on in her mind. I recalled Buddy's phone conversation when I arrived. I thought it might be about Rose Marie. I heard him hang up the phone. "Hey, Buddy," I called.

"Yeah," he said. He appeared in the doorway.

"You take checks?" I asked.

"Not usually," he said, pausing. "You give me your address and I'll take one."

"I'm good for it."

"You'd better be," he said. "I'll find you if you're not."

"Don't worry," I said.

"I won't," he said. "I'll throw in a couple of CDs she likes."

He helped load the Bronco. Rose Marie rode in her crate in the back. I put the classical station on the radio for her. I knew Delilah was going to pitch a walleyed fit. She'd been on me for a long time wanting a cat. I expected a real throw down. I'd never cared for cats.

———

There was a message on the machine when we came in from our walk. Rose Marie went back to her coffee, sniffed. My boss had called to check on my health. This was a busy time of the year for me. I worked as a river keeper. The early spring would create problems with ice flow, with rain. I'd missed a lot of days, staying home with Rose Marie. My boss said he'd need some kind of medical appointment verification. What a hump. I called and made a late afternoon appointment. I said I had the shits, that I was feeling faint. I'd heard something from Delilah's brother about this. He worked as an EMT. Brought home all kinds of stories. Old people, GOMERs he called them, dead on the toilet. Vagaled down. Heart slows, pressure drops. They die.

A river keeper's wages are low. The only reason I held on to the job was for the medical. If you're a sharp tack you can do a lot with medical, trust me. I got myself another share of coffee, spilled a little into Rose Marie's cup, and settled down in front of the computer. I popped an extra ten milligrams of Zestril.

Rose Marie lapped up her joe and sat beneath my desk looking up. I needed something official looking. I fished a certificate out of the filing cabinet—an environmental award that'd been given to me by the state a few years back. I got wise, stumbled upon the key words: "Seizure Alert Dog" and "Service Dogs." That gave me all I needed. I started up the office program, found a certificate template.

The State of Massachusetts, in accordance with the Americans with Disabilities Act and with the cooperation of the Civil Rights Division of the U.S. Department of Justice and the National Association of Attorneys General, hereby certifies Rosalind Marie Eve as active, in service and licensed, for aid and care to persons of disability. The above-named will have all rights and privileges, as stated under the ADA and as enforced by the Disability Rights Task Force, appertaining to the role of seizure alert care. Under State and Federal Law, no access shall be denied.

I ran the certificate out on the printer. Gave it the once-over and decided what the hell. I downloaded a letter off the Internet and traced the signatures of the Assistant Attorney General and the Attorney General with two different pens. Figured I'd go all the way. A clean photocopy, and nobody'd be the wiser. I also made an official-looking license, one that fit into a nice leather passport wallet. I scanned a color photograph. I'd go by the office-supply copy center on the way to the doctor and have the job laminated.

Rose Marie had had it with the computer work. She reared up, her front legs in my lap. She kept pushing my hand away from the mouse with her nose. I put in Don Henley for her, handed her the control. She found "The End of the Innocence." Over the years I'd discovered she loved piano music, all kinds. She hunched in front of a speaker.

I settled on the couch to look at an old section of personals I'd missed. Rose Marie brought her stuffed puppy, sat holding it. Years back, the doctor had botched her neuter, left part of the uterine stump. She was fourteen and still went into mock heat. She also experienced mock pregnancy and mock birth. Then she took to carrying around the stuffed animal, caring for it like it was her puppy. The vet's negligence was part of how she got cancer. Half the time she had an infection also, which I learned to smell easily. I tried my best to keep ahead of things, have mammary tumors removed and give her antibiotics wrapped in bread. She took her medicines like a champ. I tossed the paper aside, helped her onto the couch. We snuggled, took a nap.

———

I had stopped by the hardware store and bought colored tape. Dave's Soda and Pet Food City had Eukanuba in the fifty-pound bag. I hefted that into the backseat. I freed Rose Marie from the crate, let her ride up front with me. I turned on the radio. A classic rock station. Rose Marie lifted her right paw, worked the air. It was like she was pushing something away. Elton John's "Candle in the Wind" came on. Di's version. And Rose Marie settled, listened. She was picky, with questionable taste.

Delilah was out back, planting vegetables. I kneeled next to Rose Marie, pointed her the right direction, and let go of her lead. She sat. I lifted her back end, gave her a push. Rose Marie trotted off into the dirt, ducked her head, and butted Delilah over into the mud.

Delilah yelped—a quick, sharp note. Rose Marie's tail battered the air. She barked, forklifted her way on top of Delilah. Delilah screamed, did the stop, drop, and roll routine. She covered her head, tossed in the dirt.

"Help!" she screamed. "Attack!"

This sparked Rose Marie. This here was "Foghorn Leghorn." Rose Marie started jumping on Delilah, licking her all over, leaping here and there trying to get a lick on Delilah's face. Delilah writhed, covered her face. "Somebody help me!" Rose Marie grabbed Delilah's shirttail and tugged.

"Attack!" Delilah called. She continued to pitch about. "Somebody help!" Rose Marie, shirttail in mouth, swept her head wildly from side to side, pulling Delilah through the dirt. Delilah fought her off with one arm, Rose Marie snapping. I laughed so hard I couldn't call her off.

"Goddamn," Delilah screamed. "Help me!"

I laughed even harder. "Rose," I called, gasping for air. "Come here."

Rose Marie paused, wagging and panting. Delilah stood up, disheveled, mud caked to her where Rose Marie had licked her bare skin. She looked around, expecting blood I guess.

"What the fuck is that thing?" she screamed.

I laughed, buckled. I swear I almost pissed in my pants. Rose Marie sat, looking up at Delilah.

"It could've killed me!" Delilah screamed. "Where'd that god-damn thing come from? Whose is it?" She threw her hand shovel down and headed for the house.

Rose Marie stared at the shovel, then up at Delilah as she stomped off. Rose Marie ducked her head, took on her brooding expression. "Good girl," I said. I walked over and sat beside her. "She likes cats anyway," I said. Rose Marie stretched out, her legs jutting straight behind her. She rested her head in my hands. Maybe her tastes were better than mine.

———

I was feeling faint from the Zestril. I helped Rose Marie out of the Bronco. She had, over the years, come to a slow, majestic walk. Steady, head held high. She was regal, her fur tinged with gray. Everything about her said, "I'm better than you." As for me, I pretended there was nothing out of the ordinary in her presence at my side. Rose Marie and I strolled into the doctor's office and took the elevator up.

"I'm sorry," the receptionist said. "But there are no dogs allowed in the office."

"This is Rose Marie," I said, haughtily. "I am quite bad off. She is helping me. My service dog."

The woman stood, peered over the counter.

"Is there somewhere I could rest," I said, reaching to hold on to the counter. "I think I'm blacking out." I did my best weak-kneed tremble.

"Sir," she said, alarmed. "Sir, are you all right?"

"I don't know," I said. I bent, put my hands on my thighs.

"Hold on, sir," she said, hustling around the counter. "Pamela," she called, back toward the examining room. "Get us a chair. Let Dr. Anthony know we've got an emergency."

"I think I'm OK," I said, still bent. I winked at Rose Marie. She sat.

"Just hold on," the woman said. She put her hands on my shoulders. "If you need to sit down go ahead."

"I think I'll be fine," I said.

"My name's Beth Ann," she said. "Pamela's bringing a chair."

"I'm fine," I said. "I think I can walk."

"Just stand where you are," she said.

Pamela hurried a wheelchair out. They maneuvered it in behind me. "OK," Beth Ann said. "Can you just rest back into the chair?"

"I think so," I said. I fell into the seat.

"Exam one is open," Pamela said. "That dog can't come in."

"Service dog," Beth Ann said. "What's your dog's name?"

"Rose Marie," I said.

"What a pretty name," she said. "Come on, Rose Marie." Beth Ann began to push us through the doorway.

I held my hand up to my forehead, pretended to be faint. It wasn't all an act. My blood pressure was at bargain-basement numbers. Pamela wasn't biting. She had my card. She propped the door open, maintained an unsympathetic expression.

Beth Ann rolled me into the examining room. "Will you be OK if I leave you for a few moments?" she asked.

"I think so," I said.

"Have you had diarrhea long?"

"A few days," I said.

"Vomiting?"

"Yeah," I said. "Some."

"Dan will be in shortly," she said. "I'm sure he's going to want to push IV fluids. I want to go ahead and get that ready."

"Thank you," I said.

Beth Ann breezed out of the room. I told Rose Marie to sit and she did. Nurses whisked up and down the hallway, and I could hear someone in the background reciting my symptoms. Another nurse came in and checked my blood pressure. "Seventy-six over forty-two," she said. "You are low. Don't try to stand. The doctor will be in momentarily."

I heard the nurse calling out my vitals. In a few minutes the doctor came into the room, shutting the door. He stood for a second, looking down at Rose Marie. "That's no service dog," he said.

"I brought her for assistance," I replied. "I felt faint."

"You shouldn't have that dog in here," he said, without compassion.

"I'm sorry," I said. "I don't have anyone else."

"I'm Dr. Anthony," he said. "Let me check your blood pressure again." He put the cuff on, pumped. He released the air and took my pulse. "OK. Look toward the wall behind me." He shined a small light into each eye. He peered down my throat. "OK," he said. He took my arm, pinched the skin. "How long's this been going on?"

"A few days," I said.

"You don't seem dehydrated," he said. "But your pressure's low. We're going to push some IV fluids. With some dopamine. It's going to take an hour or so to get you up to speed."

"That's fine," I said.

"The nurse will set you up," he said. "I'll be back to check on you."

"Thanks."

"Leave your dog at home next time," he suggested. He closed the door.

I could hear him giving the nurses instructions out in the hall-way. Beth Ann and Pamela brought in some kind of recliner and helped me over into it. Pamela was all business. When I was seated, she washed her hands of me. Beth Ann hooked up the IV.

"What kind of dog is Rose Marie?" she asked.

"English bull terrier," I said.

"She's very unusual looking," she said. She raised the IV pole, adjusted the flow. She bent over. "Rose Marie, you're such a sweetie," she said. "Take care of your human." She headed for the door. "I'll be back to check on you two."

Rose Marie lay down next to the chair. We both rested. Every so often Beth Ann would come in and check the IV and take my blood pressure. When the bag was nearly empty she tested my blood pressure again. "It's come up some," she said. "I'll leave it in until Dan sees you," she said. "I'll let him know you're almost done."

"Thanks," I said.

The doctor stepped in about fifteen minutes later. He sat down at the small desk in the corner. "I'm going to give you a scrip for the nausea and one for the diarrhea," he said. He opened the drawer and pulled out a pad. "Are you able to keep down liquids?"

"Yes," I said. "Gatorade."

"Good," he said, writing. "If the symptoms persist you need to come back. Are you on blood pressure medication?"

"Yes," I said. "Zestril."

"You should lay off that for a few days," he said. He finished writing. "There any chance you took too much today?"

"I don't think so," I said. "I guess it's possible. I've been dis-tracted."

"By what?" he said, turning on his stool.

"Rose Marie has cancer," I said.

He looked down at her. "That's too bad," he said. He seemed to soften. "We lost our lab about a year ago."

"How?" I asked.

"Kidney problems," he said. "We had to put her down."

"That must have been hard."

"I stayed with her," he said. "Never do that. It wasn't like they tell you. It was horrible. She went while I was holding her. I never got that image out of my mind."

"I'm sorry," I said. "I don't know what I'm going to do. Rose Marie is all I have."

"What kind of cancer?" he asked. He bent, looked at her.

"It's in her mammaries," I said. I leaned over and rubbed her face. "Could you do me a favor?"

"What's that?"

"Could you listen to her lungs?" I asked. "She's been breathing kind of heavy."

He paused, deliberated. "I really shouldn't," he said. "I'm not a vet. We're going to have to sterilize this whole room."

"I know," I said. "I'm really sorry." I leaned forward in the recliner. "I lost my job," I said. "I can't afford a vet. Since we're here and all?"

"I really can't," he said.

"Can I borrow your stethoscope?" I asked. "You could tell me what to listen for."

"I'm not sure I know," he said.

"Breathing is breathing," I said. "Just let me use it?" I stared at him. "Those things are expensive."

"Hold on," he said. He went and locked the door. "I could get into serious trouble." He kneeled beside her.

"Rose Marie. Up, up!" She pushed herself up on her front legs. "I appreciate this so much."

He felt her chest, grimaced. "The tumors are pretty large," he said. He put the scope to her, moved it about listening. "I can still hear her heart. But there's a lot of crackling. She's got some fluid on her lungs," he said. "I think it's metastasized." He looked up at me. "I don't think there's much you can do."

"I know," I said, pausing. "I don't know what I should look for."

"I'm not a vet," he said, kneeling beside her and running his hand over her back. "Look for signs of labored breathing. It's going to get to where she has a hard time taking in air."

"I think she's got an infection, too," I said. "She gets them all the time. It's from a botched surgery. They left in part of the uterine stump. There's a discharge from her back end."

He bent. "I can smell it," he said.

"That's how I know," I said. "The vet used to give her antibiotics. Five hundred milligrams of Keflex."

"That'll do it," he said. "How's that on her stomach?"

"I give it to her with bread," I said. "She does OK. Towards the end it starts giving her trouble."

"You need to go ahead and get her on some," he said. "You don't want the infection to complicate matters. If you're wanting to buy time."

"How long's she got?" I felt my voice waver.

"Difficult to say," he said, looking down, holding her face in his hands. He seemed genuinely saddened. "With people, this can go on for a few days. I've seen it go on over the period of a year."

I wanted to say something, but my voice just froze.

"Not long," he said. "Maybe a few weeks."

We both sat giving her love. "What's the difference between human Keflex and Keflex for dogs?" I asked, finally.

"Pretty much the same," he said. "The human equivalent is just higher quality."

I gave her a rub on her ear. "Could you give me a scrip for that?" I asked.

"Out of the question," he said. He stood up and went to the sink.

"Just say it's for me," I pleaded. "Who'll know?"

"Can't do it," he said. "Fraud." He scrubbed his hands.

"What's fraud is that we can't get insurance for dogs," I said. "It costs me five dollars for Keflex. Forty or fifty for her. She's part of the family. She's my daughter."

"Sorry," he said. He sat down at his desk, tore open alcohol pads, and cleaned his stethoscope. "She shouldn't even be here." He stood. "I'll have Beth Ann come unhook you. Come back if things don't improve." He unlocked the door and left.

I stood, feeling a little unsteady. The prescription pad was still on the desktop. I reached and pulled off a few sheets, tucked them into my jeans pocket. In a few minutes Beth Ann came in and took care of me.

"I hope to see your Rose Marie again sometime," she said.

I smiled. "Thanks for your help," I said.

"You're welcome." She left the door open.

I took Rose Marie's lead and we headed out the way we'd come. I stood at the elevator, letting the doctor's news settle in on me. I had known this, had been to the vet's only a few weeks before. But then, her lungs were clear. I thought we'd have more time. Over the years, Rose Marie had been a fighter, and I'd used all my savings for surgery, to remove lumps as they grew. Each time it'd taken a little more out of her. Things just dwindled, converged, and the natural order took hold.

"Sir!" I heard Beth Ann call. "Wait. You forgot your prescriptions."

I turned and she was waddling down the hallway. "Don't want to get home without these," she said. She handed them over— three. "Hope that takes care of you. That's some nasty infection going around."

————

"Half a month's rent?" Delilah yelled, scrubbing herself behind the shower curtain. "You go out to sell the Bronco and come back with a goddamned pit bull. Half a month's rent!"

"Rose Marie," I said. "And she's not a pit bull. She's an English bull terrier." I leaned against the doorjamb. "And dogs like this usually cost thousands. She's got a champion bloodline in her."

"You don't want a cat in the house, you say," she turned off the water, pulled the towel down off the rod. "Don't want an animal in

GOOD AS ANY

the house, you say. You bring home a dog that looks more like a pig than a dog. You brought home a damn pig!"

"First off," I said. "Cats shit in the house. Rose Marie is housetrained. Second of all, not only do cats shit in the house, but then they play with their shit. Toy with it like it's some kind of mouse. They're fucking stupid. Don't know their names. They claw you. They lick their own fur off, swallow it, cough it back up on the furniture. They're stupid. And oh, by the way, did I mention they're stupid."

"Dogs slobber," she said.

"Some dogs slobber," I said. I lowered the lid on the toilet and sat down. I pulled a roll of tape out of the bag and cut a strip. I put it on the remote the way Buddy had told me. "You know dogs work for people. You ever seen a seeing-eye cat?"

"They're too smart for that," she said. "They are independent."

"OK. You tell me," I said. "What kind of person would you rather be friends with? A person who answers when you call them. One you can rely on. Or one who acts aloof when you need comfort? Who do you admire more? A person who helps the blind. Or a person who'd let them walk out in front of an oncoming car?"

"That's not the same," she said. She stepped out of the tub, wrapped the towel around herself. "What are you doing now?"

"I want to show you something," I said. "I want to show you how smart Rose Marie is."

"Oh, please," she said. She padded off into the bedroom. "What kind of name is Rose Marie? What is she, Catholic?"

"When you're done, come into the den," I said. I finished taping the CD changer. I walked in and Rose Marie had her head tucked into the potted plants. "Rose!" I shouted, thinking she was eating them.

"What's she done?" Delilah yelled from the bedroom. "See, that's what I'm talking about."

Rose Marie looked up, seemed to enjoy the feel of the leaves on her face. She had this calm, peaceful way in her eyes. "Nothing!" I yelled back. "She's done nothing. She's in here enjoying your plants."

"Don't let her eat them."

"She's not eating them." I went to the kitchen, pulled a beer from the refrigerator and poured it into a pilsner glass. I dropped onto the divan, put the beer on the side table.

Delilah came in and settled in a chair. I put the CD in the player and handed the control over to Rose Marie. She did her thing.

"So," Delilah said. "A parlor trick. You've been taken for a ride."

I put in the other CD. Rose Marie pawed the controller, found "Ave Maria" again. "That's a different version," I said. "Hardly sounds the same. She likes that song."

"Yeah," she said, smiling. "Right. Tell me this. How're you going to explain this to the landlord?"

"I'll work it out," I said. I looked at her. She smiled. "See," I said. "You know you like her."

"What I want is a beer," she said, getting up. "You know she could have hurt me out there."

"She was playing," I said. I followed her into the kitchen, leaned against the counter.

Delilah pushed things around in the fridge, found the last beer. She opened it. "I wanted a cat," she said, heading off into the den.

Rose Marie was on the divan, finishing off my beer. "Rose Marie!" I said. "No."

"There you go," Delilah said. "Cats don't drink beer."

"Get off the divan," I said. Rose Marie looked at me, circled, and plopped down. She covered her nose with her paw and closed her eyes. "Get down," I commanded. She ignored me. I tried to move her, but she pushed against me, worming all around—fifty pounds of drunk, stubborn woman. I gave in and sat next to her. She put her head in my lap and I switched on the baseball game. She didn't mind baseball so long as I kept my hand on her.

———

I sat in the Bronco holding Rose Marie close. She had her own way of hugging. She ducked her head, pressed as hard as she could against me. I flipped on the dome light and pulled out the blank prescription sheets. I copied the doctor's signature, wrote out a dosage of Tegretol. I slipped the scrip into the leather passport pouch and killed the light. I steered us into town and parked behind the CVS. I didn't miss a beat. Rose Marie and I strode into CVS and handed over the scrip for Keflex.

"You're not supposed to have that dog in here," the pharmacist said.

"Service dog," I said.

"Yeah, right," the pharmacist said. "For what?"

"Seizure alert," I said. "I got her from the John Fisher Center. Sheffield. Four thousand pounds just for training."

He looked at me like I was some kind of criminal.

"We're going for dinner," I said. "We'll pick that up afterwards." We headed off. "Oh," I said, turning. "We'll be at the Monkey Bar if you need us."

The Monkey Bar was the scene in town. Full of the chic hipster-duffus crowd. You know, all industrial looking. Stark, shiny, expensive. Men in suits and ties. Women in short skirts, stockings. Rose Marie and I walked right in, like we owned the place.

"I'm sorry, sir," the maître d' said. "There are no dogs allowed—"

"Service dog," I interrupted. "We'll take that seat over by the window."

"Under no circumstances—" he continued.

"You deaf?" I said. "This here's Rose Marie. You'll address her as Madam Rose."

"Yeah," he said, condescendingly. "Right. You'll have to leave or I will have the police come."

"You do that, buddy," I said. I leaned toward him. "I'll sue your ass. You heard of the ADA?"

"I don't believe so," he said.

"The Americans with Disabilities Act," I said. "I have epilepsy. This is my seizure-alert dog. Goes everywhere with me."

He looked down at Rose Marie, rolled his eyes.

"I'll bet you have a boss," I said.

"Yes," he said. "And he—"

"Will come escort us to our table," I finished. "Run along, mister. Fetch him."

He looked at me. "Stay where you are," he said.

"Wouldn't dream of leaving," I said.

The manager waltzed over. "I understand that you believe your mutt is going to get served."

"Damn straight," I said.

"Do you have some sort of documentation that will identify this thing as a working dog?"

I pulled out the letter I'd downloaded off the Internet. "This here's from Scott Harshbarger. Attorney General. If you can read, you'll notice it says I don't need identification."

He studied the letter. "I'll take my chances—"

"But I keep paperwork with me," I interrupted. "For dickheads like you." I produced the certificate.

"This is a photocopy," he said.

"The original is in a frame on my wall," I said. "You spend eight thousand dollars on training, you frame the diploma." I pulled out the passport wallet. "Here's Rose Marie's state license. My prescription for carbamazepine. Known as Tegretol. For seizures, you know."

He examined the photo. Looked down at Rose Marie. "Enjoy your kibble," he said, handing the wallet back to me.

"That won't do," I said. "We feel harassed. Rose Marie and I smell a lawsuit. Perhaps you'd like to personally escort us to our table."

He yanked the menus from the maître d's hand. "This way, sir," he said.

The group at the bar made way for us, looking down at Rose Marie. I lifted her into the booth and sat across from her. The manager handed me a menu, turned. "I don't think so," I said.

"Excuse me?"

"A menu for Madam Rose," I said.

He dropped a menu on the table in front of her. "Good enough?"

"No," I said. "Ask Madam Rose if she'd like something to drink."

"Madam Rose," he said. "Would you like a drink?"

"She'll have a pint of Sam Adams in a bowl," I said. "I'll have mine in a glass."

"Very well," he said, turning. "I hope you have a seizure-free meal."

I reached, grabbed his hand, and spun him toward us. "Now that wasn't polite," I said. "Am I going to have to take you out back?" That seemed to do the trick. A skinny prick like that doesn't want to dirty his Armani.

Madam Rose had pan-seared steak. I had Cajun gumbo. I'd begun to like the new arrangement, though I knew time was running short. That's what had turned me mean, angry. All the piss holes in the world walking around carefree, and Rose Marie suffering, dying.

———

Delilah and I always slept late on Saturdays. Rose Marie's first weekend with us was no different. I couldn't bear to crate her, so she slept on the divan. I was awakened by Rose Marie sounding off, letting out these strange noises that sounded like the adults in one of those Charlie Brown specials. I was groggy, unsure if I'd heard anything. I lay in bed, listening. She let go again, added this high-pitched squeak at the end. What the hell? Buddy'd said she would be a handful. I rolled out of bed and went to check. Rose Marie was sitting up on the divan. She looked at me like, "What? What did I do?" I shook my head, decided to make breakfast for Delilah.

I cooked up eggs and bacon and sausage. Fresh-squeezed O.J. Made the coffee and put it in this fancy white decanter. I looked in on Rose Marie. She glanced away from me, like I'd betrayed her. I brought the breakfast in on a tray and served it to Delilah in bed.

"You're sweet," she said, sleepy eyed.

"I'm sorry about the rent," I said.

"It's not that," she said. "I just wish you'd talked to me."

Rose Marie's nails clicked on the hardwood. She came into the bedroom and looked up at us.

"Hey, Rosie," Delilah said. "You've got a face only a mother could love."

"Don't say that," I said. "You'll hurt her feelings."

As if on cue, Rose Marie drooped her head, turned, and walked out. She looked back once, eyed us, and went off to scuff around in the den for a moment.

"See," I said. "I told you. You hurt her feelings."

"She'll get over it," Delilah said.

Suddenly, we both heard Rose Marie's paws scratching frantically, out of control. I saw her come around the corner, down the hall. Full speed, ears slicked back. In an instant she was airborne, in the bed with us. She bounded up and down, tail swishing. Dishes clanking, cups spilling. She flailed. Us, dismayed, frozen. Quick as a train wreck, she whipped around and swiped Delilah's bacon. I reached for her, but it was gone. As if spring-loaded, Rose Marie shot up into the air, maybe three feet. You couldn't even see her legs bend. There was no way of knowing how she did it.

"Jesus H. Christ!" Delilah yelled. "Get that thing out of here."

I held on to the tray, laughed. Rose Marie had sized us up, taken charge.

"I mean it," Delilah protested. "Get that out of our bed!"

"No way," I said. "She just wants company."

"I can't eat this shit," she said, pushing her plate away.

"I'll trade you," I said. I reached over, pulled Rose Marie close. I held her tight against my chest. "Take my plate," I offered.

Delilah reached over and lifted my plate off the tray. She raised her leg, creating a sheeted barrier between her food and Rose

Marie. I ate with Rose Marie in my lap. Each time I took a sip of coffee, her nose went wild. She sniffed the air, jabbed her front paws into the covers, and lifted herself.

"You want some of this?" I asked.

"Don't give her that," Delilah objected. "She's hyper enough."

"She wants it," I said. "She can have a little."

I lowered the cup. Rose Marie sniffed, lapped. She lifted her head, thought about it, and licked her snout. She went for the entire last half cup, till it was bone dry.

"I can't believe you," Delilah said. Disgusted, she flung the sheets back, stormed out of the bedroom and into the bathroom. I moved the tray onto the floor, pulled Delilah's pillows over, and snuggled in with Rose Marie. I heard the shower running. We drifted off to sleep.

Later someone banged on the door. I answered it. Buddy had come by to check on Rose. He wanted to look around. I let him in the house and he gave it the once-over, approved of things mostly. Suggested I keep my shoes locked in the closet, instead of on the floor. He said she'd eat the tongues out of them. It could kill her, he said. He looked in the backyard, made a list of improvements— work on putting up a fence, pick up tools, et cetera. I stayed alert, made mental notes. He said he'd check back to see how things were going. Make sure I was doing as I was told. I said I would. I said to come by anytime. Before he left I told him about the breakfast scene. He laughed. That was a mistake, he said. She'll sleep in the bed from now on. He said, you'll have to serve her breakfast. I don't think so, I replied, confidently. Over time, I was proven wrong.

———

Rose Marie and I returned from dinner to discover that Delilah had left us an envelope on the kitchen table. I unhooked Rose Marie's harness and hoisted her onto the divan. I turned on the television for her. Often she'd stare at the screen. I'm not sure what the attraction was, maybe the music. Music was the only entertainment that I knew for sure she enjoyed.

I looked around the house to see if anything was missing. Nothing. "What do you think we got?" I asked Rose Marie. "Probably a letter bomb for you. Maybe for me." I pulled up the clasp, dumped the contents onto the table. There were a dozen or so newly taken nude Polaroids of Delilah. Explicit. The poor lighting made her yellow, rank. There was a note too. "Me? or Her?" it said. And there was a phone number. She was at her friend Katie's house. I guessed the two of them had gotten drunk and taken the pictures. Now, I'm a man and like any man I have enough sense to get a hard-on. You know the joke about a cool breeze? But the circumstances were dire and Delilah knew it. She knew.

I put on Eric Clapton's "Wonderful Tonight." Rose Marie'd come to enjoy the guitar. We played it over a couple of times. Then I let her select "Ave Maria." She had begun to have trouble with the controller. Legs just wouldn't work for her. I puzzled over buying her one of those jobs with the extra large buttons, like old people used. I just couldn't bring myself to do it. That meant admitting something. It meant, in a way, giving in.

Everyone learns in time, when it comes to illness, and eventually it always does come down to that, that compromise is really only a process of letting go. I gave only a little bit of ground at each juncture, but before I realized it, I looked around and nothing was familiar. My world had changed, all in an attempt to make Rose Marie feel that nothing was happening to her. To make her feel as though she was still the same, still doing everything, self-reliant. I was only fooling myself.

I punched up Buddy on the Bell Atlantic. I told him the news. My voice cracked, kind of went out on me. "I don't know what to do," I said. Then, I just cried. Buddy was good about it, didn't say anything. He just waited for the dam.

"She'll let you know with her eyes," he said, flatly. "Bring her by," he added. "Let me have a look."

"Will do," I said.

Rose Marie and I listened to music for an hour or so and decided to call it a day. I tucked her in. Of late she'd gotten to where she wanted her own side of the bed. Her own pillow and her own covers. She'd get too hot snuggling. I didn't know whether she was trying to make all this easier on me, a little more separation every night, but the farther away she slept the less rest I got. I would lie awake and listen to her breathing. In the night I could hear her sucking, nursing. It was a part of her dreams, I'm sure. But she nursed, the tip of her tongue showing. I put my thumb at the edge of her lips and she sucked on it.

———

I had carried Rose Marie over to Buddy's once a week, so she could romp and roughhouse with other bull terriers. Bullies, as they're called by people in the know, are tougher than the rest. They play hard and'll put the hurt on another breed. Rose Marie ran along the front of the cages, the other bullies scrapping it up with her. I had a picture album tucked under my arm.

"She looks good," Buddy commented.

"She's a dream," I said. "I got these pictures if you want to look."

Buddy glanced through the pages. "You got a thing for Rose," he said. He let the last half of the album flip by quickly. "Must be a hundred pictures."

"Two hundred so far," I said.

"It's only been a month," he said. Buddy shook his head, smiled.

"Let me ask you," I said. "It's like she nurses in her sleep. I can hear her kind of . . . nursing?"

"Yeah," he said. He kneeled, whistled, and Rose Marie trotted up to him. He ran his hand over her. "She was weaned a little too early. That could be it. They all have a personality. She's sensitive. It wouldn't surprise me that's it—weaning. Her mother probably wasn't good with pups."

"Hmm."

"Yeah," he said. "She's special. Don't think I've seen one like her."

"Why'd you let her go?" I asked. I blocked the sun with my hand.

He stood. "Business," he said. "This here is business," he said, pointing to the kennels.

I studied him. "Really?" I asked. "Why give her up?"

Buddy stood there looking off, then he stared at me. "Her bite went bad," he said. "Couldn't show her. She isn't really show quality. She's got the personality, but . . . Anyway. This man brought her in and she was so sweet my daughter wanted to keep her—"

"You got a daughter?" I questioned, thinking there goes my fudge-packer theory.

"Well," he said, hesitating. "I did. She died of leukemia."

"I'm sorry," I said. "I didn't mean to pry."

"Oh, no," he said. "It's OK." He took a more reassuring tone. "Rose was her dog from the time she came in. Rose and Missy had a way with each other."

"I can believe it," I said. "Rose Marie seems to have a way with everyone."

"Not really," Buddy said. "You ever read Thurber?"

"I don't have much time to read."

"He's got some stories about bull terriers," he said. "You ought to read them. Bullies have a way about themselves. Rub some people the wrong way."

"Yeah," I said, admittedly. "Delilah's not too sweet on her."

"My wife liked them all right," he said. "She wasn't crazy about them. When Missy died it kind of put a strain on our marriage. She wanted me to get rid of all the dogs. Especially Rose."

"You couldn't?"

"No," he said. "I couldn't. Not Rose. Not at first." He glanced over his shoulder at Rose Marie. "You ever have someone die on you?"

"I've been lucky, I guess." I looked down, kicked at the tiff green lawn.

"It puts you in two places," he said. "You know like part of you wants to go backward. You want to just remember. The other part wants to be far away. Like years ahead. You don't want to feel that hole that's left in you, that's a part of the present."

"I reckon," I said. I felt bad for him, wondered if bringing Rose Marie all these times was hurting him. "It bother you, me bringing Rose Marie over?"

"No," he said. "Lord no. I love seeing her. It helps me think of Missy. It helps the remembering part of me."

Buddy got us beers and we sat in the sun and watched the dogs go. He gave me pointers on caring for Rose Marie. Show dog stuff. How they can get backed-up plumbing. How to get a thin stick, gently touch their back end and they take a shit. That's how they keep those dogs from pinching a loaf in the ring. You know, in those contests they show on cable. There's a lot to owning a dog. Buddy said dogs own us. They touch that part of us that can't speak, he said, that it's just all feeling where they're concerned. He said, it's dogs that show us how weak we really are.

———

Rose Marie woke me up panting, 3 A.M. There was a look in her eyes that I took for pleading, for fear. I watered her and she settled down a bit. She didn't like the dark, so I moved a lamp next to her bedside. I kept it burning, and she drifted off about five. That gave us both an hour.

Usually I go straight to the dock, but I had to assuage my boss, prick that he is. I took my prescriptions and, of course, Rose Marie. I strolled right through the building, past the secretary, and into Sweat's office. We all called him Sweat. He was fat. He worried over every detail. And he sweated. Thing is, we called him this to his face.

"Sweat," I said. "You're breaking my balls making me come

down here. I could be on the river by now, instead of here running papers by you."

"You know how many days you've missed?" he asked. He shuffled through stacks of papers on his desk.

"The question is, do you?" I eased down into the chair in front of his desk. I leaned back, crossed my legs. "Up," I said to Rose Marie, pointing to the next chair. She put her front paws in the seat. I bent, helped her settle in.

"What the hell are you doing with a dog in here!" he yelled, just noticing her.

"It's my seizure-alert dog," I said. I tossed my prescriptions on the desk. "These here are my running prescriptions. I got a bug. That's what the top two are for—Compazine and Lomotil. The Tegretol is for epilepsy."

"Epilepsy?" he questioned. "Since when?"

"It's a recent development," I said, with an ease in my voice. "This here is Rose Marie. She works for me, so there's no need to put her on the payroll."

"Why didn't you inform us of this change of status?"

"Change of status?"

"With your health," he said. He turned and took a book off his credenza. He began flipping through it.

"It seems a private matter to me," I said. "Didn't think you needed to know."

"Mitch," he said. "You can have seizures. You work a government boat on a river. We're not talking even a lake."

"What are you saying?"

"I'm saying I don't think we can let you keep your job," he said. He paused, ran his finger along a page.

"You're going to fire me?" I asked. I couldn't believe I'd not thought of this. "Are you aware of the ADA?"

"Yes," he said. "I'm not firing you. But we may have to put you behind a desk, or in a less dangerous setting." He scanned another page.

"Give me a break," I said. "That's what the dog is for. She alerts me when I'm about to have a seizure. I take my medication, I prepare, and I'm OK."

"I'm not sure it's that simple," he said. "First of all, I'm not sure you can have a dog on the boat."

"She's a certified service dog," I said.

"I understand," he said. "I need some time with this."

"You take your time," I said. "Rose Marie and I are going to work. By the time you have an answer, I'll have a lawyer."

"Mitch," he called.

I stood up and Rose Marie followed as I strode out of the office. I helped her into the Bronco and then found my seat. I stared in the rearview to see if Sweat had trailed us. He hadn't. What the hell had I been thinking? If I came clean they'd fire me. If I stuck to it, I'd lose the river. I sat stunned. Rose Marie lay down in the seat with her head in my lap. I stroked her grayed face. She closed her eyes and drifted off to sleep. We were both beat.

I drove us to the docks and Rose Marie came alive on the boat. I pulled us into the current and she sat at the nose of the boat, leaning into the wind and sniffing the air. It seemed to give her a charge. The early spring air was chilly, wonderful in our faces. I threaded the run-off current, took us all the way into Vermont where there was ice. Rose Marie pawed from one side of the boat to the other, looking at all there was to see—the deep, thick forest and rising mountains, the eddies of swirling water, the small islands of ice floating downstream. We passed a moose drinking, and Rose Marie barked, scratched around the deck. The moose looked up, undaunted.

I'd packed us both a lunch, and on our down-river trek I put out the spread. We each had a ham sandwich and a bag of chips. I poured her a cup of hot joe, spilled in real cream and a spoonful of sugar. She drank the coffee first. I drank with her. We studied the shore for wildlife, the trees for birds. We ate and drank and I hugged her and petted her and told her how wonderful she was and how much I was sorry for what was happening. Out here on the river I felt I was alone. I felt it was OK to let Rose Marie see me cry. I wept. I got down on my knees and hugged her and cried and asked God not to take her. But on a river you can't lie, either to yourself or anyone else, and you know the truth, that all things end.

After lunch I covered Rose Marie in a Filson blanket and she slept. I piloted the river, took note of all that I saw. I'd grown to love this job. It's a good job, tending a river. I figured the two of us would have a few more days on these waters, and I was going to enjoy it. We stayed out all day, making the docks around five-thirty.

The heat in the Bronco blasted all the way to Buddy's. Rose kept her face up at the vent. I parked in the driveway and sat for a moment. My nerves were on edge. Buddy would be straight with us, I knew, and I wasn't sure I could take the news just hanging out in the air for us to contemplate. Knowing something and being told it are two separate things.

I took Rose Marie around back and let her loose in the fence. Then I knocked at the back door. Buddy answered with two beers in his hand.

"Hey, Mitch," he said. He handed me a beer and took the photo album from under my arm. "How you getting along?"

"Minute by minute."

"I understand," he said. "Rose out back?"

"Yeah," I said.

We both settled. He put the album on the table and began flipping through the pictures, slowly. He smiled at some and looked meditatively at others.

"You've had a long run with Rose," he said. "She's an old girl now. You can really see the gray in these last few." He pointed at a close-up of her face.

"She's gotten gray," I said. "But she still has the puppy in her."

"Some keep it," he said. He hesitated. "Listen," he said. "I'm going to take a look at her. I'm going to be honest. If it's her time I'll tell you. You should know it's like losing a family member. Harder."

"I've an idea," I said. "I've been telling myself it's almost time. Just knowing it is killing me."

Buddy reached under the table and pulled out a Polaroid. "Let's go take a look."

Rose Marie was bouncing around in front of the kennels, barking. Buddy smiled. We both stepped up, but she ignored us. Buddy whistled sharply and she turned. He snapped a picture. The picture motored out and he stuck it into his shirt pocket.

"Rose," he said in a deep voice. She trotted over. "You're a good dog." He felt her stomach, held her face, and looked into her eyes. Rose Marie let him do what he wanted without objecting. Buddy put his ear to her side and was quiet for what seemed forever. Finally, he leaned up, patted her. "Good girl," he said, standing. "Go on." He pointed off. She turned toward the other dogs.

Buddy pulled the picture from his pocket, and we walked together back up to the house, without saying anything. "Sit here," he said, his hand on the love seat.

I sat next to him, the photo album spread out in front of us. He turned to the front, where there was a close-up of Rose Marie. It was a picture taken only a few weeks after she'd come home with me. Buddy placed the Polaroid right next to it. "See this," he said. And I did.

———

Delilah had always wanted me to take pictures of her. I picked up rolls of film from the CVS and brought them home. There would be twenty of Rose Marie doing anything from sleeping to digging holes and four of Delilah putting on makeup or talking on the phone. Delilah filtered through the stack, looking for herself.

"You love that damn dog more than you love me," she said.

"Look." She pointed to two stacks of photos—hers and Rose Marie's.

What could I say? I didn't understand it myself.

Delilah decided she'd try and change things. Every so often she sauntered into the living room in provocative lingerie. "Take some pictures," she said. I did. She posed in all kinds of ways. She stripped. She wanted close-ups. She spread her legs and said, "How about this?" I'm a man and I did what a man would do. I took the pictures.

Delilah became more daring. Showing up at the docks to pick me up after my day, wearing only a trench coat and stockings. She wanted photographs on the boat. She wanted evidence in public places.

The rolls came in from CVS, and there was nothing but Delilah in the nude. This seemed to make her happy. She looked at the pictures and then wanted me to have sex with her. She wanted me to take her doggie-style while Rose Marie watched. It was a thing with her, she insisted Rose Marie sit on the floor while we did it. For a long time this enriched her life, kept our relationship afloat.

But I kept taking pictures of Rose Marie on the sly. I had them developed and looked at them when Delilah wasn't around. I found myself studying them more than the ones of Delilah. Rose Marie and I took long walks and I talked with her, felt somehow a better person, sensed that other part of me, the part with Delilah, was really someone else, a ghost of my past. Delilah's demands ran thin, began to annoy me.

I took her questions to heart. Why was I taking all those photographs? I puzzled over the answers while Rose Marie and I walked. She loved fresh snow and the steamy afterwards of spring showers. It didn't matter. She was game. She took her time, went over the world thoughtfully. She sat under the swamp pinks, sniffed the air that was rich with blossoms. She paused at money plants. Gave them a serious look. She buried her face deep in their leaves and took a long time letting the breeze caress her face. Winter made her run. She plowed into drifts so difficult that I had to help her out, her belly pink with chill. She made a study of the foundation of the house, looking into windows, smelling crevices. There was a place, where the basement door met the house, she dug daily, trying to uproot the long tendon of a tree. She grabbed it, tugged with her mouth, her legs working hard. She pawed mounds of dirt away. She let out strange whines. She unearthed children's toys, the head of a spigot, a wrench. How the things were there was beyond me. I felt they were present just for her, their sole purpose was for her to find them. I let her dig.

———

Her sleep was fitful, full of long panicked episodes and desperate panting. I sat up with her and tried to comfort her fears. There was nothing I could say, but I soothed her with the sound of my voice. A few minutes' sleep, and she was awake wandering the house, tousling the sheets for a perfect arrangement. There was terror in her eyes that I'd never seen before, a real sense of bewilderment. But like clockwork, at five she settled down to rest—exhausted.

I called Sweat and told him I was meeting with my lawyer, that the river could keep itself for a few days. He tried to get me to come into the office so that we could discuss the situation like gentlemen. I called him a bigot and hung up the phone. I wanted to get Dan on the phone. We needed a doctor.

I punched up the office and Pamela answered. I asked for Beth Ann. I waited, listening to the Muzak.

"This is Beth Ann," she said. "How can I help you?"

"Hi. This is Mitch," I said. "I came in for the IV the other day." There was nothing on the line. "Mitch Philips."

"Oh, yes," she said. "How are you all feeling?"

"The infection is better," I said. "The smell's gone. But the other situation," I paused. My voice gave out and I began to tear up.

"The breathing's worse," she said knowingly.

"Yes."

"Hold on and let me get Dan," she said. The Muzak returned. There were commercials for Kaiser Permanente. "Kill a person permanently" is what I thought. Beth Ann was gone for a good five minutes. "Mitch?" she said.

"Yeah."

"Good, you're still there," she said. I could hear her flipping through papers. "You're still on Bridge Street?"

"Sure," I said, wondering why she was asking this.

"Dan says he'll come by about five," she said. "If you can be home."

"I'll make sure I am," I said. "I want to thank you guys for all your help."

"I hope we can help," she said. "You two take care until Dan arrives. He's really good."

"Thanks," I said, somehow relieved.

I put the phone down and called Buddy. I said I was going to bring Rose Marie over, and he said he'd look at her. He said animals fight through winter, they last, he said, so they can die in spring. It's a law of nature.

Rose Marie acted as though she couldn't walk. I carried her, laid her out in the backseat of the Bronco. I had bought her a CD with nothing but different versions of "Ave Maria." I put it in the boom box and sat it down in the back floorboard. I took corners carefully. With the windows down the breeze felt good, and I adjusted the rearview so I could keep an eye on Rose Marie. For a while she held her head up, closed her eyes, let the wind blow across her face.

Buddy came to the Bronco, took a look at her. He crawled in and listened to her side.

"I can't hear her heart beating," he said. "Just her lungs. She's filling up."

I shook my head, leaned against the side of the truck. I turned away, touched the back of my hand under each eye.

"I don't have a stethoscope," he said. "But it can't be long."

"I can't take it," I said. I began to cry.

"I know," he said. "That's the thing with dogs. They break your heart."

"It's worth it," I said, trying to suck it up. "Most people are just piss bags."

"I *choose* to live with dogs," he said. "And not people." He put his hand on my shoulder and squeezed.

"I got a doctor coming by later," I said. "He's a people doctor. But I want him to have a listen."

"Let me know," Buddy said.

Rose Marie and I took a ride up the mountain, to where the Summit House had been before it burned down. I lifted her out of the seat and carried her over to a large, flat boulder. We had a view of the valley, its fits and starts of spring evident in the budding trees. The place had contours of green and brown, of grass and wet dirt.

For a while the two of us sat and enjoyed each other's company. I held her in my arms, helped her to see a boat moving in the river below. Her ears perked up. She'd kept her sight and her hearing. She kept a dignified air about her, a presence, as she looked down over the water and land. She studied it for a long time, until she tired and put her head in my lap and drifted off to sleep.

———

She slept deeply, soundly, snoring on the way home. "Ave Maria" played. I remembered the details of our life. Everything came to me, specifically. How summers, in the heat of the day, I sat with her on the bed, playing hooky from work. We had a window unit that blew cool air, and I ate my lunch and we listened to books on tape. I let her have the last bite of my taco and she ate it gently. The thought made me smile. I drove the roads, letting the images recollect. I knew I was putting human thought on an animal. That I was being silly. But Rose Marie had certain ways about her, and how does a person account for that? For a dog's likes?

I knew a few things. I knew I liked Rose Marie more than I liked people. And with her going I thought maybe I'd learn to like being alone even more. Because dogs leave. They die much too soon. It was what Buddy had said from the beginning.

When I turned into the driveway, Dan was leaning against his Saab. He had a frown on his face, dreading, I could tell, his job. His stethoscope in hand. I nodded, killed the engine.

"Sorry to keep you waiting," I said, coming around front to shake his hand. "I appreciate your coming."

"No problem," he said. "I don't think there's much I can do."

"I know," I said. "I just want to know."

He hesitated. "So, where's the patient?"

"I've got her in the backseat. Sleeping," I said. "I'll help her out."

"No," he said. "Don't disturb her. I can check her there." I muscled the seat forward. "How do you turn this off?" he asked.

"Switch on the top."

He fumbled for it. "Ave Maria" went silent. Dan put his scope to her, moved it about. He dipped his head. I knew half a doctor's job was telling people what they already suspected. Dan knew it, too. The difference between good doctors and bad ones was how graciously they go about their work. It's the part I didn't notice while I was grieving; it's what I remembered later. Standing there, my heart was racing. I felt the contour of the world go flat. Everything in my vision washed out, everything a shade of gray. I knew the score. Piss bags live forever. I just wanted this to be different. Dan shook his head. "I'm not a vet," he said. "She sounds pretty bad."

"How bad?" I asked.

He stroked Rose Marie, studied her. Halted. Then he maneuvered himself out of the backseat, stood, and brushed his pants. "I don't know much about these things," he said. "I should have brought Myers. He knows heart and lungs. I'm guessing," he said. "Her lungs are almost full. I can't hear her heartbeat."

"What's that mean?"

"I can only hear the sound of her lungs," he said. "Respiratory distress. It's like congestive heart failure."

I'd known of people living quite a while with this. I knew there was treatment, and I wanted to believe there was something to be done. "So what next?"

"You could draw the fluid off," he said. "It's painful." He buried his face in his hands, rubbed. "It won't buy her much time."

"How long's she have?" I asked.

He leaned against the truck. "She won't make it through the night," he admitted, finally.

I went autopilot. "What's going to happen?"

"You'll need to do something," he said. "You don't want her to suffer. You don't want to wait this out."

"What do you mean?"

"I don't have any drugs," he said. "You could take her to a vet emergency room. They'll put her down."

"You said that was terrible."

"It's terrible for you," he said. "Rose Marie won't feel anything. You don't have to be in the room with her."

"No," I said. "I'm not leaving her. I'm not going to let her die among strangers. Can't someone come here and do it?"

"You're not going to find anyone tonight," he said.

"Then tomorrow," I said. "Is there something we can do to get her through the night?" I'd become desperate. My eyes welled with tears.

"I'm sorry," he said, looking helpless. "She won't make it."

I sat on the lip of the truck, leaned against the side of the seat. It was as though someone had shot a hole in my head, emptied it, light flooding in and washing clean all my emotions. I had nothing. Just this brilliant light burning inside me.

"I wish there was something I could do," he said. He put his hand on my shoulder. "I'm sorry."

"I'm not taking her to the hospital," I said. I held my head in my hands, closed my eyes. I searched for an image, a thought, that could get us both out of this. I tried to conjure how Rose Marie had looked when she first came home. But my head was empty. The only thing there for me was how she looked now, how she'd paced the bed terrified and struggling for air. How sleep came to her only as the result of exhaustion. The thought I had was of the dying moment.

Dan crouched. "I know this is bad," he said. "But you've got to think of her. Let her have some dignity. Let her go while she can walk and eat and . . . before things get too bad."

"You're right," I said. "I know. I need time for it to settle in."

"I'm on call tonight," he said, standing. "Phone if you need me."

I nodded. Dan steered his car out through the grass, around the Bronco, and waved as he headed off down Bridge Street. I got to my feet and turned to look at Rose Marie. She slept, her chest rising and falling with effort. I waited there for a long time, wanting to remember her. It struck me as odd, the way people take for granted each moment of every day, how we don't regard the time as special, until we know a person is dying. Then, we study their every move as though memory is enough. But it isn't. It's just a reminder of all the time we wasted.

———

I embraced Rose Marie, carried her up the stairs to put her on the bed. The door was closed. Usually I kept it shut in the heat of the summer when the window unit blasted. I eased Rose Marie to the floor. "Stay there," I said to her. I turned the knob, shoved the door wide. Delilah was on the bed pantyless, in garters and stockings, surrounded by Polaroids. Candles burned on both nightstands, on the dresser, on the windowsill. There could have been a hundred of them.

"What are you doing?" I asked.

"There was some strange man knocking downstairs," she said.

"Dan," I said. I picked up one of the pictures. Delilah with a beer bottle.

"Who's Dan?" she asked. She was touching herself.

"A doctor," I said.

"A doctor?" she questioned. "When did you start palling around with doctors?"

I stared at Delilah for a few moments. "Rose Marie is dying."

"We're all dying, honey," she said. "Why don't you come to bed and do some living?"

"Damn it, Delilah," I said. "She's dying now. Right now. Tonight. Dan said we don't even have the night."

"So he's a vet," she said. "Not a doctor."

"You're so pathetic," I said. "Move over and make room." I lifted Rose Marie and gently laid her on the bed.

"Get her away from me," Delilah objected, drawing her legs close to her body.

"Get dressed," I said. I shuffled downstairs for a beer. When I retrieved a cold one from the refrigerator, I recalled the snapshot. I ran the bottle under the faucet, wiped it dry. I stood at the kitchen sink and looked out the window.

"I'm sorry," I heard Delilah say from the doorway. "I didn't know."

"How'd you get here?" I asked

"Katie dropped me off," she said. "I wanted to surprise you. Didn't want you to see my car and come in ready for a fight."

"Thought you'd just come with open arms and legs and that'd make it OK?"

"Don't be that way, Mitch," she said. "Don't be mean."

"I don't love you, Delilah," I said.

There was a long pause. She was crying. "I know," Delilah said, finally. She sat down at the table.

I felt sorry for her somehow. Delilah couldn't understand what had happened. She was a woman I'd left behind, and no matter how I shared with her, she couldn't give back what I needed. Delilah couldn't love Rose Marie. I opened a beer for her and sat down. Maybe it was as simple as cats and dogs. I don't know. We both wanted to find a way to say what we felt.

"You wear your heart on your sleeve," she said. "When it comes to Rose Marie. It's like you're in love with her. It's like she gives you all you need."

"What's wrong with that?" I sipped my beer.

"I don't know," she said. "Maybe nothing. I just wanted to have a little part of you."

"You did," I said.

"But you changed," she said. "You let Rose Marie turn you into a different person." She drank from her bottle. "I think boys have a way with dogs," she offered. "There's something between men and their dogs."

That sounded right to me, oddly. "I guess," I said.

"It's like all those pictures," she said. "There's hundreds. Mitch, she's just a dog."

"Not to me," I said. "Not to me." I let those words hang in the air. Delilah and I sat looking off in different directions, drinking our beer. I wanted to tell her about the pictures. I wanted to explain that people can talk, they can say things, they can remember things to you. But all I had of Rose Marie was in my heart. And I could remember what was in my heart in each of the photographs. They would always be there, leverage against forgetting.

It was like Buddy said about losing his girl and remembering. I'd learned something from Rose Marie. I'd learned grief is the way things come together. The way they converge. It's what is and what was. It's those two things colliding, living on as what will never be again. I knew I could use all the words I'd ever heard and never say this to Delilah in a way she'd understand or believe. I could tell her love is what can't be said. I could articulate for her just what she meant to me. But I couldn't talk about Rose Marie. Talking was nothing but admiration or lust or both.

Delilah'd never understand the epilepsy papers or how I'd lost my job or why I had that bumper sticker on the Bronco. I'd never forget Rose Marie coming over as I was putting it on. I ran my hand across the thing, pressing it down. After I was done Rose

Marie licked it. Maybe it was the salt that'd kicked up on the bumper through the winter. Who knows?

"Take the Bronco," I said, laying the keys on the table. "I'm not going anywhere."

———

Rose Marie began to bark. I hurried up the stairs and she was on the edge of the bed wagging her tail. Her whole body swayed, as though she was young again. I carried her outside, put her lead on. The driveway was empty. I figured she'd just stand, look around like she had been doing. Instead, she kicked out and we took a long walk. She bushwhacked alongside the road, pausing for long periods of time, letting the scrub tickle her face. We made it a quarter mile up the road and back, her tail going, her breathing short and huffy.

She took to the foundation of the house, smelling. Then, to her familiar hole. She pawed at the dirt, tired. It was as if she'd used herself up. She gnawed at the exposed tree root. Pulled. She let out a whine and sat down, looking up at me. I kneeled and put my arms around her. I rubbed my face against hers, kissed her brow. Her eyes closed, and she lay down in the dirt. She slept while I kept watch over her.

This could have been a walk on any day. Rose Marie pausing at her favorite places. But I knew it wasn't. I knew I'd never see her again in this way. How casual we were, strolling along. It feels wrong, I thought, going about our business in the presence of the dying. I'll be haunted by this, always. I'll keep asking, did she understand?

———

Evening came, settled with cool, shadowless light. I walked Rose Marie out into the yard. Like always, tired and all, she tugged the leash. She headed off into some ferns a ways out from the house. She stood silently, her face caressed by the fanned leaves. I bent and took her collar off, then unhooked her harness and lead. I left her alone. I let her go. I turned and walked toward the house. A distance away, I stopped. I cracked the shotgun open and retrieved two shells from my jacket pocket. Slipped them into the breach, snapped it shut. I released the safety and stared out toward her. She had gone deeper into the ferns. But I could still see her clearly enough. She had begun to wag her tail in the old way. I paused, studied her for a moment, managed a smile. The time was as good as any.

Strong at the Broken Places

"I'M MAKING FLOWERS OUT OF PAPER WHILE
DARKNESS TAKES THE AFTERNOON."
—Julie Miller

The sky hung low, matted curls dangling, here and there, even lower. The summer had been hot, parched with fire, and now the fall was cool, and for days at a time there was no sun. I drove the winding road, a hint of mist falling, my wipers dry on the windshield. I stopped by to see Murphy every afternoon. He sat on his front porch, the windows pulled open wide, a bottle of Famous Grouse on a bench beside his chair. I steered into the driveway. The sky was dotted with rolling pigeons, spiraling up. Then, a smear against the gray, they tumbled earthward. I killed the engine, watched. There were no hawks. Sometimes a pigeon didn't pull out of its dive, though I'd never seen this happen. It's one of those things you hope to experience, just so you can know that it's true.

Murphy was reading, a collection of Hemingway stories in his palm. I knew better than to ask, but I did anyway. "What're you reading?"

"Hey, CJ," he said. He spilled scotch into an extra glass that he kept for me. "Page 274."

"Sounds good," I said. I sat down next to him, took the scotch. I'd never seen Murphy read a book from beginning to end. Each day he opened a book to a random page and perused for a few minutes. If he opened to a page he'd read, he flipped through until he found an unfamiliar scene. Murphy's memory was marvelous for certain things. He repeated the habit of opening and closing books until every sentence was familiar. Then he spent the next few days putting the story together in his mind. He always said this made the writing more interesting to him, more challenging. Murphy was the most driven person I'd ever met, the most capable.

"There any hawks?"

"Not that I could see," I said, glancing out the window.

"I'm down to six birds," he said. "There's a damn bobcat. Comes down at night." He shook his head, offered an envelope between his fingers. A tender gesture, his hand trembling.

I tucked the stationery into my jacket pocket.

"There's a man and a woman drinking and talking in a railway station," he said. "They're drinking absinthe."

"I don't know Hemingway," I said.

"You don't have to," he said. "There are people talking. There are always people talking about one thing and meaning another."

I smiled.

"CJ," he said. "I know you don't want to talk about it—"

"No," I interrupted. "I don't."

"Have you ever tasted absinthe?" he asked.

"No," I said. "I don't think they make it anymore. They make Pernod."

"It's not the same."

"That's why they make it," I said.

"They distill absinthe in Spain," he said. "And in Prague."

"It can kill you, can't it?"

"I suppose," he said. "If you drink enough of it." Murphy closed the book. He finished off his scotch. "You drink enough of this and it'll kill you."

"So what happens?" I said. "In the train station, I mean."

"Depends on who you ask—the woman or the man," he said. "I came in during the middle of an argument, so I'm not taking sides. It seems to me, though, that neither one is listening."

"What are they fighting about?"

"What difference does it make, if one's not listening?" Murphy stood, paused for his balance, then hobbled to the screen door. He pushed out, whistled loudly to the sky, to the birds.

———

Murphy called it an "affliction." He had been married, but begged his wife to go. He made life unbearable until Cathy left him one October, while darkness exhausted the afternoon. Her hair was black as a raven's wing. It hung down in her face when she cried. She and Murphy both cried when the letter arrived from the doctor. To hear Murphy tell it, it was that he thought she couldn't withstand the sight of him slowly turning into a stranger. "That's all illness is," he'd say, "a slow transition into the unfamiliar." I know all this because Murphy wrote it down, a little at a time; brief notes stuffed into envelopes. I kept them all, in a box on my bureau.

One afternoon, not long after Cathy had gone to live with a friend, Murphy decided he'd raise the ceiling. I'd come by for my drink, which in those days was Havana Club. Before he took sick, Murphy made regular trips into Canada to bring back the illegal rum. He wasn't on the front porch when I pulled in, so I walked around back to the bird pen. Finally, I climbed the steps to the back door and knocked. Murphy answered, covered in a fine, white powder.

"What the hell is that?" I asked.

"Plaster," he said. "Come in." He tried to pull the door wide so that I could see, but it hung. "Hold on," he said, slamming the door. There was a God-awful commotion, the sound of things being thrown recklessly, a scraping at the foot of the door. Murphy yanked the door open. "Now," he said, sweeping his arms like a matador.

The kitchen was empty except for an ax, some other tools, and the ceiling, which was now in the floor. Large strips of molding and sections of plaster-covered gypsum were piled more than a foot deep in places. Above, a black expanse of exposed beams and the darkened underside of stained, beaten, wooden shingles. Asterisks of light peeked through, as though it was the night sky. The scent of oak and wet cardboard were in the air. Murphy coughed. "Watch your step," he said. "There're nails in some of that molding."

"It's going to get cold in here," I said.

"Once the snow covers, it'll be fine," he said. "Help me with the table."

A small dinette table and chairs were perched in the den, just out of reach of the mess. We lifted the table and set it atop a well-planned stack of ceiling parts, in the center of the dining alcove. Murphy retrieved glasses and the bottle of rum from the cupboard. We stood at the table, its top coming to our waist, bistro-style. Amid the ruins, we drank the Añejo Reserva from aperitif glasses, the butterscotch start transforming into a smooth, vanilla finish.

"What are your plans?" I asked. I sipped and held the rum in my mouth.

"This is the last of the Havana Club," he said. "Enjoy." He tipped the bottle, filling my glass again. He freshened his own and held the dark bottle up to measure what remained. "The angel's share," he said, tossing the bottle into the rubbish.

"Come again?"

"The angel's share," he said. "In the aging process, a certain amount of the spirit evaporates. They call that the angel's share." He smiled. "It's best to assuage the higher powers."

"How much?"

"In Havana," he said. "Six percent a year. Cooler climates, two. Kind of a spiritual sales tax."

"A small price to pay," I said. I lifted my drink for a toast. We touched glasses, finished the rum.

"Have you talked to Cathy?"

"Not in a while," he said. He rinsed the aperitif glasses and returned them to the cupboard. "You want to help me clean this crap out of the house?"

"Yeah," I said, pausing. "Want to talk about this?"

"The question is, do you?" he said, opening the door. A breeze seeped inside, stirring the woody dampness. "You want to talk about the ceiling, I guess. Not the cause."

"Maybe we should just get this out of here before it gets too dark?" I suggested.

"A man lives his entire life in a house with ceilings that are unnaturally low," he said. "Look at me, CJ. I'm not short. I've a right to vaulted ceilings. I want to die in a house where there's one room where I can't reach the ceiling." Murphy bent and lifted a stack of molding. He tossed it out into the failing light. "Now, you want to talk?"

"I think you should let Cathy come be with you," I said.

"That's what I thought," he said. He garnered sections of the ceiling, leaning them against the cabinets.

"I don't know what to say," I said.

"Nobody knows what to say," Murphy insisted. "What you mean is that you don't want to think about it."

"It makes me uncomfortable," I said.

"You think I'm comfortable?" Murphy crouched, picked up some scraps. He wheezed. "The problem is," he said, "you think this is about you. You think this is about Cathy."

"We're suffering with you."

"No," he said. "You're not. Cathy may be sympathizing. Maybe even empathizing. You can't even talk about it. At best, you just feel pity."

"Now you're feeling sorry for yourself."

"Fuck you, CJ." Murphy breathed heavy over a pile of gypsum. "I'm dying. I have a right to feel this way."

"Maybe I should go," I said. Murphy closed his eyes, pinched the bridge of his nose. I felt like I could guess what kinds of things were knocking around inside him. But I didn't have his way with words. Murphy had a manner of expressing himself, which was acute, exacting. His head had always been clear. How hard it must have been for him with me standing there, seeing him like this. I might have asked Cathy to leave, too. There was no way of knowing if all this was the result of what was growing inside his head or if this was just the kind of thing a dying man does.

"Fetch a chair over to the sink," Murphy said. He dug in the utility room.

I waded through the mess, brought a dining chair from the den. I tested it on the floor, angled it so that it was sturdy. Murphy clutched a portable floodlight in one hand and a coil of orange extension cord in the other. "Let's shine some light on the subject," he said. He clamped the light to a rafter, draped the cord over the latticed beams. "Plug it in," he said, handing the cord down to me. I suspended it over the door, found a socket above the clothes dryer. "Let there be light!" he called. I punched it in. "And it was good," he said.

I turned the corner, the room was awash in a harsh, artificial light. It reminded me of what I'd seen on CNN, after an earth-quake or a terrorist bomb, rescue teams working long into the night beneath that sickly glare. I always wondered what the deciding factor was, when it just became a search.

"I don't know what I expect people to say," Murphy said, his hands on his hips, staring at the clutter. "I just hope they'll say something."

"Anything I could say just seems stupid," I said. "I feel like I have to watch every word."

Murphy looked at me, expressionless. "We need fuel."

"I just don't think you should be alone," I said. "Maybe you should call Cathy?"

"We do two things without the company of others," Murphy said. "We go to our dreams and we die." He opened the refrigerator, stooped to look inside. "We don't have much," he said. "Beer and cinnamon rolls." He reached and pulled out the two cans of rolls. He ran his hands under the faucet, dried them on a towel from the drawer. "You know," he said. "People don't even call anymore."

"I know," I said. "People get busy with their own lives. Time gets away from them." This had been true of me as well. I'd picked up the phone, hesitated. What might I get on the end of the line? I'd think. Murphy could be sleeping, or worse, in some kind of crisis. What kind of solace could I offer? From the time I was born, I'd never spent a day in the hospital. I was rarely sick—once in five years—that I could remember. I stayed up too late and mixed my drinks. I threw up in the morning, took the day off from work, and by five I was sipping a beer at the Spoke, looking at the waitresses and thinking I should call in sick for the week. I'd earned it, I thought. I'd learn, watching Murphy go down, that it's the sick people who earn their days. They should get two weeks a year of calling in well.

Murphy popped the can of cinnamon rolls on the edge of the counter. He fingered them onto a cookie sheet. "That's the luxury," he said, "of thinking you've a life ahead of you."

I opened the refrigerator, took a beer. "Beer?"

"No," he said. He peeked in the oven, turned the dial.

"I've never seen you drink beer."

"I don't care for it," he said. He spread out the second can of rolls.

"There's a case in there?" I opened the refrigerator door and looked again.

"Cathy thought it'd help settle my stomach."

"Never heard that before," I said.

He tilted the oven door, slipped the pan inside. "This'll take a few minutes." Murphy stroked his hands on the towel. "Let's gather equipage." He ducked out the back door.

The night was turning cold. There was no moon. I couldn't see a thing in the pitch dark. Murphy had a freestanding tool-shed in the backyard. I heard him rummaging and I waited, looking up at the scattershot of stars, the pearly satin of the Milky Way. Murphy appeared with a wheelbarrow, a snow shovel in the bin.

"Take this," he said. "I'll get the planks."

I backed the thing up the steps, guided it into the dining alcove. The snow shovel was heavy in my hands. The pressed metal head was rusty with use. It occurred to me that it was like Murphy to have a more difficult shovel. It was heavier than the plastic ones, but also it wouldn't break. And that's what would draw Murphy—staying power. I scooped some rubbish into the wheelbarrow and it was like I was taking my insides out. These old tools would outlast their owner and then what would become of them? A yard sale, and some strange hands would tuck them into a nook of another garage. Like all secondhand tools, they'd go unused until a grandchild, maybe someone named Dave, took them out to play. In years, these tools would be in Dave's garage. By then, there wouldn't be a soul to remember Murphy, no one to tie him to these things.

I tell all of this now, because it's what I want to believe was in my heart. I want to think I was already in mourning. But the truth is, all of this came later. These thoughts came to me after the fact, after Murphy was gone. What was really on my mind was how long it was going to take to clear out the mess and how Murphy was going to repair the damage he'd done. I was worried, but not so much about Murphy, and I was thinking about how to get in touch with Cathy. I told myself the treatments would work and that Cathy would come home and that things would be like they once were.

Murphy set the planks and we wheeled the full bin down and far out into the yard. Murphy had an idea where he wanted everything, and I just followed orders. We cleared out the big stuff first. Between runs, Murphy checked the rolls in the oven. We had cleared the alcove of the larger sections of ceiling by the time the cinnamon rolls were browned. Murphy painted the icing on with smooth, deliberate strokes. I sipped beer. The kitchen was getting cold except where the floodlight poured down and out in front of the stove. Murphy switched off the oven and let the door down so that the heat would spill out. He used a spatula to lift rolls onto plates. We stood in front of the oven and began eating. Murphy was pensive.

"So," I said. "Where is Cathy?"

"She's staying with Jonathan and Lori for a while," he said.

"That's just up the hill," I said, relieved somehow.

"It's better this way," Murphy said. "I don't want her having to take care of me like some baby."

"You're doing fine," I said. "You can't even tell there's anything wrong."

"I don't want to be pathetic," he said. "Around her or anyone."

"You're going to be OK," I said.

Murphy swung the refrigerator door open, reached in, and pulled out a beer without looking. He dug into his pocket, retrieved a knife. "There's no tenable treatment," he said. "It's inoperable." He peeled the cap off and took a long swallow.

"I've got hope."

"I've got to piss," he said. "But I know better than to do it into a stiff wind."

I scuffed another roll onto my plate. This was a conversation I'd wanted to avoid. "You coming back to work?" I asked.

"I doubt it," he said. "I've got the time coming to me."

"What will you do with all that free time?"

"You know, CJ, you're supposed to be a buddy," he said. "You should think before you open your mouth."

"I meant with no one here to talk to."

"Read," he said. "There are so many books out there."

"That's an odd thing to do with your time."

"Can you think of something better?" he said. "Everyone should die knowing something. Having learned. I spent most of my life working."

"I'd travel," I said.

"I've got a time bomb inside me," he said. "I don't want to lounge in Key West. Drink for a few days at Sloppy Joe's and then, one afternoon, slump over into a grand mal." Murphy lifted his beer and took a long drink. "Can you do me a favor?"

"Sure."

"Stop talking," Murphy said. He scratched two rolls onto my plate and two onto his. We ate the rest of the cinnamon rolls without speaking; Murphy eating, looking out the window into the dark, living inside his head.

This was as close as I wanted to come to a final conversation. I didn't want any part of a *Terms of Endearment* scene. I hated those kinds of movies, never believed in forking out money to get kicked around like that. The truth is, I guess, I've got a tender heart. I cry easily. So, I hide it. I try not to get coaxed. There's no need to be one of those red-eyed viewers rushing for the bathroom when the lights come up.

"OK," Murphy said, finally, taking the long last swallow of his beer. "You shovel. I'll roll."

Murphy cleaned his hands on a towel. Bending, he picked up a large section of gypsum and dropped it into the wheelbarrow. I took the shovel in hand, began to scoop mounds of dust and paint and plaster. Murphy was quick and precise, running the wheelbarrow down the ramp and out into the yard. He came back and left a wet stripe in the plaster dust. "It's getting damp out there," he declared. "We need to move faster."

My shirt began to stick to my back, sweat burning in my eyes. I dug into the wreckage, began to worry about the linoleum. Murphy returned from the toolshed with another shovel. "Don't worry about the flooring," he said. "It's coming up."

Murphy hustled like a teenager, scooping and running the bins of trash out into the yard. We worked with a fury. The more Murphy pushed, the more I followed his lead. When the large sections of ceiling were gone, Murphy brought in a push broom and cornered a knoll of garbage.

"You take care of that," he said, huffing. "I'll go to work on the floor."

"This floor could take days," I said. I leaned on the broom, my back tightening. I took the towel off the counter and dabbed my forehead.

"I put it down," he said. "It's good hardwood underneath. No glue. It's anchored by the stripping." He went to the pantry, pulled out a toolbox. "Just wheel that out onto the pile."

I carefully ladled the last of the plaster. I set the empty Havana Club bottle on the counter. Murphy dug at the metal stripping that separated the den and the kitchen. He wedged it up, then pulled along its perimeter. I watched for a moment, resting. He seemed to be focused on something far off in the distance. The lip of the linoleum curled as he tugged the metal back.

"Take a break," I suggested. I was winded, aching.

"I'm almost done," he said. He hammered a metal wedge at the wooden molding beneath the cabinets. It lifted easily. "Get that out of here," he said. "And come help me get this up."

"Yeah," I said. I lifted the wheelbarrow, rolled it out of the kitchen, out into the cold night. My breath hung in the air in front of me. I hefted the last binful of remains onto the pile. I stood for a moment, still, leaning on the upturned wheelbarrow. The stars were brilliant. I took the cold air into my lungs and felt a chill down my back. Cathy would be horrified if she knew I was helping Murphy do this. But the damage had been done before I ever arrived. I was just seeing this through to the end. I ran the wheelbarrow back through the grass and into the light of the kitchen. Murphy had all of the molding pulled up and was rolling the linoleum. He had the linoleum in the dining area gathered and was cutting across the floor with a utility knife. The flooring sliced smoothly, with a minimum of effort.

"Come take the other end," Murphy wheezed.

I kneeled, grasped the linoleum at the cut, and lifted. "You make the turn," I said. Murphy was gentle, backing toward the door. We worked together, as if we were pallbearers.

When we had everything on the pile, Murphy went to the toolshed. He returned with a can of lawn mower gasoline. He poured along the edge of the heap and then over the top. He dipped into his shirt pocket. "Stand back," he said. He removed two matches from the box. Carefully, he tucked one, tip outwards, back into the box. He struck the other match, the flame jumping up, reflecting his expression. He appeared grave, serious as he touched the flame to the first match. Just before the entire box lit, Murphy tossed it onto the pile, and after a fleeting uncertainty the entire heap erupted, reaching skyward with the sound of a sheet being ruffled in the air.

"Jesus," Murphy said, jumping back. Still, it seemed, he stood dangerously close to the fire, lingering, as though he might let himself burn.

"The fumes," I said loudly.

He nodded and we both backed from the fire. We stood in its warmth for a long time without talking. Embers lifted up with the wind and were carried for as far as I could see without going out.

"What's on your roof?" I asked.

"Cedar," he said.

"Let's hope the wind doesn't shift," I said.

"It's all the same to me," he said. He breathed out heavily and I could see his words in the air. "It's all the same to me."

We stood with our faces to the warmth and our backs to the chill. Sparks rose and smoke mingled between us and the stars. The fire popped, the noise of burning hanging in the air. The taste of soot was in my mouth.

"The stars are beautiful," I said, finally.

"They are," he said. "You know what you're looking at?"

"You mean what constellation?"

"You're looking at the past," he said. "The light you see left those stars maybe a thousand years ago."

"I've heard that," I said.

"I like the company of the stars. More than people, I think."

"Why's that?"

"I don't feel so alone." Murphy was quiet. "You know how long they gave me?"

"No," I said. "You never mentioned it."

"Fifteen months," he said. "Best case."

I thought about this for a while. "Do you believe in God?"

"Don't be stupid," he said, prayerfully. "If there's a God, then it's an Old Testament God. I feel like I'm paying for someone else's sin."

"So you don't think a person goes on?"

"No."

"You've got to have hope."

"Tell that to yourself when you're dying."

Murphy turned, headed back toward the house, watching his steps in the damp grass. I waited, remained in the warmth of the fire for a while longer. The bare, oak-lined kitchen was waiting, gutted. Murphy would drag the table back to its place. He would be there, sitting at the dinette table with an empty bottle of rum, his life passing rapidly, as if aging more quickly than me.

———

I can still remember the box. It was there beside his chair, when I mounted the front porch steps. The November sun hung coolly in the air. The fallen leaves were dry on the ground. The collection of Hemingway stories was in Murphy's lap. His eyes were closed, and I thought he might be sleeping. Quickly, something else came to mind.

"Murphy?" I said, afraid. "You sleeping?"

There was a long pause. "Thinking," he offered. "Afraid I was dead?"

"For a moment," I said.

"We should be so lucky," he said. "I won't go that easily."

I opened the screen door, let it close behind me. "What's on your mind?"

"Mercy killing," he said, flatly.

"What do you mean?"

"Margaret just killed Francis," he said.

"Margaret?" I said.

"Macomber," he said. "Francis, her husband, was humiliated by Robert Wilson."

"What are you talking about?"

"Francis was a coward. He gut shot a lion and then ran when the lion charged from the tall grass. Wilson took the lion. Then Margaret."

"You've been reading this?" I said, realizing what he was saying.

"That's part of it," he said. Murphy offered me an envelope and I took it, pushing it into my jacket pocket.

"What's the other part?" I asked.

"Francis redeemed himself. Shot a Cape that was on him." Murphy sat up in his chair. "But no one ever reclaims themselves from cowardice."

"You're not a coward," I said, stupidly.

"You don't know what I'm like," he said, "while everyone sleeps."

"So you think Margaret is right?"

"I think bravery is nothing but endurance," he said. "Lasting through habitual crisis."

"She kills Francis?" I said. "That seems a brave gesture."

"Like an ostrich. The thing was," Murphy said. "He died happy."

There was an awkward moment when neither of us said anything, both of us reflecting, I suppose. "What's in the box?" I asked finally.

"My ticket out of this place," he said. "Absinthe."

"Absinthe!" I repeated. "Where in the hell did you get absinthe?"

"Prague," he said. He turned and looked down at the box.

It was not a square box, but rather a round tube, closed at each end by a cap. I lifted it, "PAR AVION" printed on the side. It had come from Praha 9, Czech Republic. Murphy had removed the bubble wrap, and inside was a bottle of Hill's Absinthe, emerald green.

"You're not going to drink this stuff?" I said.

"Not yet," he answered. "I don't have a drip spoon."

"This will kill you," I said. I held the bottle up to the light. The color was soothing, magnificent. I wanted a drink myself.

"When the time comes," he said. Murphy stood, steadied himself with a cane. Slowly, he made it to the door. He turned. "But thank you for your solicitude."

Murphy was unsteady on the steps. He'd written to me over the course of a month, recounting what had begun to fail him. There was a certain unexplained numbness in his extremities. His balance was leaving him. Though his mind seemed sharp, he said it was as if at times he lived in several alternate realities, simultaneously. He floated, easily, between them. For the moment, he had no trouble separating them. I held the door for Murphy, with my hand at his back.

Murphy always knew the sky. I looked and there were no hawks. I wanted to believe that his step was sure in the grass and leaves, that nothing in that respect had changed. But, in fact, he was slow and deliberate. Each foot forward drawing leaves, their crunching rising unnaturally. I strolled beside him wanting to say something, but nothing would come to mind.

His pigeons seemed to chortle. He unlatched the pen, gently reached in, and grasped a bird. I expected them to fly. Instead, they moved about on their perch. Murphy had delicate manners with the bird, and he held it out for me to touch. With a finger, I caressed its chest.

"You'll take care of these," he said. "They'll need a lot of attention."

"Yeah," I said. "But that's a long way down the road."

Murphy lifted his hand and the pigeon took to the air, corkscrewed upward. He set all six birds to flight. We both watched them fly, tumble downward in a graceless fluttering. Each time a bird fell, I felt my stomach go out of me as if I were the one falling.

"These are good, strong birds," Murphy said. "They always pull out."

"Murphy," I said. "Maybe they get it from you."

"Strong at the broken places," he mumbled.

"What's that?"

"Nothing," he said. "It's just something I read somewhere."

I nodded.

"Listen," he said. "I've got something I want to show you."

"What's that?"

"Plans for the kitchen," he said. He patted me on the back. "Murphy's got a plan."

"Let's look," I said.

We both made the back steps and I swung the door wide for

him. The kitchen was still an oak cask, the rafters filled with cross beams and the smell of time. In the dining alcove there were several boxes and a large stack of drywall panels. I kneeled. "This is a jungle gym," I said.

"Yeah," he said. "But it's geodesic."

"OK," I said. "It's a geodesic jungle gym."

"I got plans for the stars, CJ," he said, smiling. He slapped me on the back. "I'm gonna weld that motherfucker together. I'm gonna cut drywall pieces to fit underneath, then tape and bed and paint. I'll have a dome!"

"What do you want a dome for?" I asked.

He pointed to the apex of the ceiling. Above the dining area there were no cross beams, just the rising zenith. "I'm gonna hang it from that rafter and project stars onto it. A home planetarium."

"A planetarium?"

"Is there an echo in here?" he said. "Yeah. A planetarium. I got this star projector from Brookstones. I want the heavens, right here."

"Murphy," I said. "You're in no condition for this. Welding. Drywall. Tape and bedding. How the hell are you going to get the dome up there?"

"Leverage," he said. "Don't take the wind out of this for me."

"I'm not," I said. "I just don't know if you should be working that hard."

Murphy studied me for a moment. "The day I can't work anymore," he said, "is the day I'll hit that bottle."

Murphy didn't turn away. He stared. And it looked as if tears welled at the corners of his eyes. "OK," I said. "OK. You want some help at least?"

"I'm on my own," he said. "I want to do this."

"Will you call if you need help?" I said.

"I won't need any," he said.

We stood for a moment without talking.

"OK," I said. "I was just offering."

"I'll walk you to the car," he said.

The rolling pigeons were rising higher in the sky now, their gestures making the outline of a spire. I slipped onto the seat and Murphy closed the door. He bent. "I'll be fine," he said.

"I know," I said. "You didn't offer me a drink."

"Nothing in the house," he said.

"I'll pick up some things from the store."

"I don't need much," he said.

"I want to see to it that you get indoors," I said, pointing to the house.

Murphy turned and slowly made his way inside. If I squinted, I lost sight of the fact it was Murphy. It was just an old man, unable to get around. A man just biding his time.

I dug into my jacket and pulled out the envelope he'd given me. I tore it open. He'd written,

I've never seen Prague and probably never will and that makes me sad.
I've not seen the stars in days and that makes me anxious.
I've seen some things that most never will.

I put the key in the ignition and started the car. I looked toward the house and Murphy was sitting on the porch, his head ducked, reading. It's one of the images I'll always have with me. I thought about his plan all the way home.

―――――

I picked up fresh vegetables, potatoes, steaks, charcoal, and a bottle of Famous Grouse. Murphy had asked for beer, so I picked up a case. Darkness fell before four in the afternoon, and the Christmas traffic was heavy. People were rushing to finish their shopping. I was patient. I had time. I wanted to surprise Murphy with a good meal.

Along the streets, away from the traffic, scattered houses glowed with colored lights. The ground was bare, dry, and hard with freeze. Murphy had hoped for snow, and I told him there was still a week before Christmas. He'd said he knew. I'd learned not to take anything for granted. I turned into the driveway and the front porch was dark. It had gotten too cold to sit there and read. Inside, Murphy had resorted to space heaters for the kitchen. I hoisted the groceries, leaving the beer, for now, to stay cold in the trunk.

Murphy met me at the door. "CJ," he said. "You didn't need to bring all this."

"You don't even know what I've got," I said.

"I just needed the beer," he said.

"Life's more than just needs," I said. I patted him on his back. "Let's move to the counter."

"I'll catch up," he said.

I maneuvered around him, set the bag on the counter. Murphy was using a walker. He made two steps, lifted the metal frame, and let it fall ahead of him. He had been lucky so far, according to the doctors. He had kept much of his ability. He could talk and think clearly, though at times he was slow. For me, it was excruciating. There were no more envelopes or books. He did not talk of characters as if they were neighbors. What I'd known of Murphy was gone. Other than his birds, there was nothing left for him to attend to. The bottle of absinthe, untouched, was on the counter. I let it go.

"What did you bring?" Murphy asked.

"I got some Famous Grouse," I said. "Would you like a pour?"

"Just a finger," he said. "My three-finger days are gone."

"I brought steaks to cook out."

"Neighbors have my grill," he said, working his way up beside me.

"Why's that?" I reached for two glasses in the overhead cupboard.

"I didn't think I'd need it."

"We'll figure something out," I said. I poured two small scotches. I put a glass down in front of him. "I've got potatoes and vegetables."

"Enough for three?"

"Three?"

"I asked Cathy," he said, letting the sound of her name fall like a stone.

I turned, looked at him. "That's great," I said. "Let's toast." I lifted my glass. Murphy took his. "To Cathy," I said.

"To Cathy," he said, raising his glass to touch mine.

We each took a sip and held it in our mouths for an instant. Murphy swallowed. "I've got something to show you."

"What's that?"

"Look up!"

"Christ," I said. In the dining area was a perfectly white dome. Below, something was covered in a sheet. "You did it!" I walked over to take a closer look. "How'd you get that up there?"

"Sunk some heavy duty eyebolts into the rafter," he said. "Used one as a pulley. Ran a rope through it. Hooked up the dome."

"Jesus," I said. "How'd you keep it aloft? I mean when you let go of the rope? You had to go up there and maneuver it—hook it up?"

"Tied it around the refrigerator," he said. "Leverage." He smiled.

I laughed. "So what's under the sheet?"

"The projector," he said. "I had to build a platform."

I laughed again. "You're something, Murphy."

"Pour me another finger," he said.

I splashed scotch into both our glasses. "Those heaters do the trick," I said.

"It's temperate," he said, taking his drink in one mouthful. "Turn them off, will you?"

I kneeled and fingered the switch. "When's Cathy going to be here?"

"After a while," he said. "Let's get some fresh air."

"You up for it?"

"Yeah," he said. He pointed to the trash can. "Tie up that sack and meet me at the steps."

Murphy scuffed across the floor. I knotted the trash and lifted it out of the can. I paused, finished my drink. Murphy braced himself with the door frame and I stood in front of him. He leaned into me.

"How do you do this on your own?"

"The same way I do everything," he said.

He walked with me to the trash can at the side of the house. The night sky was mottled with clouds and the smell of snow was on the air. Together we mingled out into the yard, beneath the dry, bare bones of a chestnut. The leaves crumbled under our feet. I tried to forget Murphy's condition. I imagined it was just another stroll, like any other, which we often took in each of the changing seasons. Murphy was keen on weather; he was in tune with all that surrounded him. The illusion I tried to keep for myself, of course, was transparent. Murphy had to work hard to gather each step. He wheezed, and I could see the breath leaving him. Each puff a cloud, and then nothing.

I tried not to accommodate him, wanted to be just like I was before he took sick. I needed him to ask for help, though I understood he wouldn't. Finally, he paused, looked skyward.

"Will it snow?" he asked, breathing heavily.

"Eventually," I said.

"I'd like to see one last snowfall," he said.

"You'll see plenty."

"You just can't talk about it," he said. "People don't talk about the dying enough. They try to avoid mentioning the dead to loved ones. 'Oh,' people say, 'be careful not to mention so and so. She's still in mourning over him.' "

"What do you want me to say?" I asked. "Do I think you'll live to see it snow? Maybe. Maybe you will."

"That's a start," he said.

We walked on a little further, out over the frozen dirt where Murphy had had vegetables and flowers only six months before. He had difficulty managing the walker. I looped my arm through his. Murphy nodded. "Thanks," he said.

"Are you giving up?"

Murphy looked at me, surprised. The question had come from somewhere else, from a part of me that I had been guarding for a very long time. Murphy halted. He turned in his walker, looked back toward the house, then faced me. "Yes," he said, finally He began walking back toward the house, as if what he'd agreed to was something as simple as, "Would you like ice in your drink?"

Once out of the garden, I let his arm go. I thought he'd want to make this trip on his own. A cold breeze picked up. Both Murphy and I were mute. We walked this last walk alone, together.

Cathy's car pulled into the driveway, and she met us at the back porch steps. "You're getting along so well," she said to Murphy, with a china smile that was flawed in that minute way.

"A regular Charles Johnson," he said.

"Let me help you," I offered to Murphy.

"I can do it," he said. He braced himself on the door frame, took each step one at a time. When he mounted the top step he said, "Give me that damn thing."

I placed his walker in front of him. Murphy's back was to us, and I turned to see Cathy, tears streaming down her face. I put my arm around her, held her close. She dried her face on her jacket sleeve, and we all went inside together.

———

We had each had an absinthe, our drip spoons beside our glasses. As we'd added water, our drinks had turned from milky green to opalescent. A smooth narrowness came to my vision. The stars were crisp on the ceiling. I felt strangely euphoric about Murphy's dying, as though, now, it made sense. The absinthe was a serene thing, and I think we all felt this gentle passage. Strong or not, we all knew, the world destroys us without mercy.

"The stars are perfect," Cathy said.

I turned to her. "Murphy's idea," I said. "Pretty good."

There was a long pause, a vacancy. "It's just a shell," Murphy said, dolefully. "It's paper roses."

"Paper roses," I said, "last longer than the real thing."

"But they smell of glue," he said.

"Sometimes, Murph," Cathy said, "you have to settle for what lasts."

"Nothing lasts," he said. "Everything just evaporates—desiccates."

"No," Cathy said. "It's like hunger. Some things just come back, stay."

We were all motionless for a while. Murphy leaned forward, stirred the last of his absinthe with the slotted spoon. He drank the last of it down.

I gazed at Murphy. "I've got a powerful hunger," I said. "Speaking of things that last."

"It's like an aperitif," Murphy said, looking at his empty glass. He paused. "Let's cook!" He stood, steadied himself with the edge of the table.

"I'll get the oven," Cathy said.

"We need a grill," I said. "Which neighbors have it?"

"Across the driveway," he said.

"Keep your place," I said. "I'll help you in a minute." I walked to the window and looked. "No one is home over there."

"I've an idea," he said. "CJ. Put the oven on for the potatoes. Give Cathy one of the oven racks."

I turned the dial to 450, pulled a rack out, and handed it to Cathy. Murphy headed for the door. "Where're you going?" I asked.

"Wash the steaks and bring them out," he said.

Murphy and Cathy went out the door together. Slowly, I scrubbed the potatoes and put them in to cook. I knew Murphy and Cathy needed time alone. I ran the cold meat under the faucet, laid it out on a nice platter. I salted each piece, dashed out some fresh ground pepper. I left them on the counter. I stood at the door with my hand on the knob, motionless, waiting. The absinthe had taken away my sense of time. I tried to conjure Murphy's face. Finally, I gave up hope that remembering would ever fill the hollowness, would ever be the same as seeing. I buried this thought, opened the door.

Outside, in the side yard, Murphy had turned the lid of a metal trash can upside down and stuffed it downward into the barrel. He'd poured the coals into the bowl of the cover, set them aflame, and settled the oven rack on top.

"You're a fucking genius," I said to Murphy.

He smiled. "Give the coals a while to heat," he said.

Cathy put her arm around Murphy, and we walked together back out under the chestnut. We stood, looking up for the clouds that had now abandoned us completely. There was an inky blackness out over the yard. Above, the sky glittered.

"No snow," Murphy said.

"No," I agreed.

The absinthe tightened on me and somehow I felt we had all gone weightless, as if we were just floating among the flickering points of light. I thought of the box the absinthe had come in. Even now I think of it, and how, in the end, it was larger than the one that contained Murphy's ashes.

"It's such a beautiful night," I said, the cold having given way to the alcohol.

"Isn't it?" Cathy said.

Just then, I heard a muffled noise, the sound of a pillow being fluffed. I thought of Murphy, but he was there with us. We all turned toward the house, toward the sound. As though a shotgun blast filled the space between us, I felt the concussion. The lid of the trash can rose, in an instant, as high as the roof, flaming coals reaching even higher into the limbs of the chestnut. Shards of fire drifted in the air, high up above us, and met with the stars. I felt as though we were liquefying, merging into the center of the universe. Fire burned in places, at the tips of tree limbs. Coals came down on the cedar roof, burned a pale white; others drifted down and lit the dry grass.

All that had been raised, lifted on the hot air, seemed to take the longest time to settle. In the trees, in the grass, on the roof of the house, asterisks of fire flickered like stars. Murphy lumbered forward, toward the house. Cathy and I could only watch, stunned, under the air of the absinthe. Murphy moved slowly, far out into the grass and into the darkness and the fire. It seemed as if he walked among the stars.

The
Buried
Boy

The man sat with a pint of bitter on the patio of McGuirk's, looking out on the thumbprint of the shore. The sand reflected so brightly that it hurt to look at it. He was nearly blind in this light. When I finish, he decided, I will walk out to the afternoon tide to check the feeling in my legs. He did not mind watching the young girls walk past in bathing-suit tops, the half-moon of their breasts showing. He was not an old man, only in his late twenties, only the age of some of the women that strolled the boardwalk still looking fit. But his body had aged on him.

He had grown up in a beach town in Virginia, had spent his childhood summers on the boardwalk and in the waves. He remembered the feeling of the warm tidal pool. The water was calm, tepid, and there was a piece of driftwood that floated about. His mother worried over him playing in the standing water. She coaxed him away, out to the breaking surf. The sand rushed from beneath his feet and the water treaded back. The feeling of the sand going made him dizzy, and he could not look down.

"The water is fine," his mother said. "You'll get used to it once you're in."

He worried about what he couldn't see beneath the surface. His mother held his hand. They walked out until the water was at his waist, and he saw that the waves swelled, rose up higher than his head.

"Jump!" his mother called. And they both jumped, and the water carried them up high and washed them in closer to the beach. The boy laughed. "Wasn't that fun!" she said. He nodded.

The boy's fear slowly immersed itself with each passing wave. The cold water felt good on his face, the swells pushing him about nicely. His mother let go of his hand, and they both jumped together into each wave. Far off, in the distance, he thought he could see an island. He wondered how difficult it would be to swim there. Maybe Olympic swimmers could swim there, he thought. I bet Mark Spitz could swim there. He saw a big wave moving toward them.

"Here comes a big one," his mother called. "Hold my hand." But she was too far away and the current was too much. "Jump!" she finally called.

The wave carried him for a while and left him on his feet. It was the most pleasant thing. It was like walking on the moon, he thought, the wave taking you gently over the ground. His mother was still out in the water, where they both had been standing together. The boy stood laughing.

"Go in!" his mother yelled. "Go in!"

It wasn't clear to the boy what she meant. She seemed upset, but why? The water was barely above his knees. He smiled. "What's wrong?" he called back.

"Go farther in!" she cried.

The boy waded toward her, looking out at the rising surf. This one will take me even farther, he thought. He pushed hard, wanting to make it into the surge.

"The other way!" his mother cried.

He looked up. He would not make the wave, but rather the break. He turned away, tried to high step. The breaker caught him, threw him face first. His head hit the bottom, hard. He went black for a moment, then felt his body tumble, scrape across the ocean floor. It was as though someone had taken sandpaper to his arms and legs and forehead. He sucked in water, began to choke. The water rolled him for what seemed a long time. Then he was left terrified, thirty yards down the beach. A lifeguard reached him first. His mother was crying. He had lain around the house for days, his mother putting medicine on his scrapes. She worried about infection. He was diabetic. His head ached, his injuries burned. He had gotten a slight concussion, and one of the abrasions would scar. It was still visible on his shoulder.

Clouds rose high up in the distance. It will rain later, he thought as he finished his beer. He left five dollar coins on the table, descended the steps to the street. Down the avenue there were noisy arcades, young boys and girls beginning their lifelong affair with gambling. There were tacky clothing shops and a strip casino where old men went in their guayaberas and baggy shorts. Straw Panamas, scrunched down, blocked the sun. The man did not like the bustle, so he crossed the street so that he could walk along the beach. The sand would work his muscles.

My right leg needs work, he thought. I should have gone for therapy after the injury. He had been building bookshelves. He had stained the white pine planks. There were so few tools in the house. This building notion was new. But he'd read about building shelves and was enticed by the photographs. Most of his books had been in storage for a few years. He'd finished his schooling—his doctorate from M.I.T.—not more than a few years before. But when he was done there were no jobs for him at the universities. He took a job as a night assistant on an eighty-seven-inch telescope out west. He loved the cool, breezy, nighttime work. But in the day he was free and secluded. The next town was an hour and a half away. So he decided on a handyman pastime. He thought, I'll take out my books, maybe begin my own research on UV-Ceti stars. There is plenty of free time on the small telescopes. I could do the work during full moon. So he bought lumber. He wanted to countersink the screws. His drill was cheap, with only one bit, so he used screws to make the holes. He didn't have a bench and he drilled through, easily, into his foot. At first he did not know. He bore the second hole and then noticed blood on the floor. He went to lift the plank, but couldn't. It was screwed into his foot. His drill didn't have reverse, so he had to sidestep to his toolbox, where he used a screwdriver. It wasn't until then that he took account of how much feeling he had lost.

He had been diabetic his entire life. They called this lack of feeling neuropathy. But it wasn't just numbness. It was both numbness and shooting pain. The arching pain came at night—rhythmic, sharp pulses that worked like torture. It was pain that could keep him from sleeping for days at a time. His not sleeping was the added factor in the mistake, in his drilling a hole in his own foot. The only thing that kept him sane was his night work on the telescope. It kept him from thinking about his illness, about the fact that slowly he was losing contact with the world.

His deck shoes were full of sand, he was sure, but he could not feel it. Far out on the horizon a sailboat tossed in the waves. The lifeguards had gone home, their towers having been dragged across the sand and stored near the boardwalk. He followed their tracks in the sand. He pushed hard, working his leg. For two years he had been on crutches. Several doctors had wanted to amputate, but finally he found one in Boston who could help. The doctor had saved his leg. Gulls hovered, dipped. Some pecked at the surf's edge, their black-tipped beaks coming up with food. The beach was changing hands. Mostly, the fat, old, afternoon crowd had replaced the young tan bodies. A few muscled, T-shirted boys tossed a Frisbee. Really, the young crowd had gone home to shower and dress for the seaside bars. The man knew he could find people his own age at the Sea Breeze. But he did not feel his own age. He thought of the crowd at the casino.

The man pushed on through the sand for a quarter mile. He felt the muscles in his legs tighten. I have to be careful not to push too hard, he thought. I'll walk down close to the water. So he did. The water rolled up onto the beach, smoothing the sand out like wet cement. Overhead a plane bannered across the sky, "The Sea Wok, Best Chinese in Town." Who comes to the beach for Chinese? he thought. He even laughed out loud at this. Far out on the peninsula he could see where the cheap motels gave way to condos, then to large, rich houses. At the point was a lighthouse. Its beacon was already clearly visible in the afternoon light. The man thought of how he couldn't make enough money.

The universities didn't want a sick man, a man with a disability. They asked questions and then told him they were sorry but he did not meet their needs. A night assistant makes nothing, he thought. It's only enough to live on and occasionally take a vacation such as this. There are no towns, no places to spend money near the observatory. But there are professors living in the rich houses on the peninsula, he thought. He thought of the observatory, the white domes. He had spent the better part of his life looking at the smallest patch of sky, only what could be seen through the shuttered opening of the dome. He had all but forgotten the constellations. I have all but forgotten what it is like to live in the world, he thought. Ahead of him he could see a sizable group of young people, huddled. He walked to them and stopped. They were laughing, shoveling sand.

"Did you bury him standing up?" the man asked. The boy was maybe eight, perhaps short for his age.

"Yeah," one of the girls answered, the straps of her swimsuit down, off her shoulders.

"Do you think that's a good idea?" he asked.

"Why not?" the girl said.

"The tide."

"What about it?"

"It's coming in," he said. He pointed out to the waves. They were coming in hard on the sand.

"Mind your own business, mister," the buried boy said.

The man looked at the boy. "Suit yourself," he said. He walked down the beach a little way and then decided to wade out into the surf. It was late summer and the water should have been cold. The water streamed over his feet and he felt nothing. He waded out a little farther, until the water broke at his knees. He only felt the push of the surf. The boys and girls of the group were laughing. He turned to watch.

They took photographs of the buried boy, only his head showing. They had packed the sand around him so that not even his neck showed. The man noticed that some of the boys had T-shirts on with the letters "W.W.J.D.?" They are a church group, the man thought. He knew the letters. He'd heard about it on the radio. "What Would Jesus Do?" The girls were modest, towels wrapped at their waist. A girl dropped her towel, kneeled, and kissed the boy for a photograph. The boy howled.

The man waded farther out, until the water was at his stomach, and only then did he feel the slightest tingle of the cold water. Is the feeling real, he thought, or am I just imagining? He dipped his hands in and felt nothing with them. The man could not hear the church group any longer, just the ocean and the sound of a Hood blimp that drifted overhead. The white-and-red balloon glided effortlessly, only a hundred feet overhead. What a wonderful feeling, the man thought. I would like to see the beach from there. It must look like a cuticle. It must be like the smallest sliver of the moon, but with people gathered at the cusp. It made him remember an Italo Calvino story, where people would row a cork boat into the sea, lean a ladder up, and climb onto the moon. The blimp hovered for a few minutes and then headed out over the water, toward the rich houses that stood solemn and white.

The man waded farther out, to his chest. The rising current still scared him. With each wave that came, he jumped and was carried. Really, only his face felt the cold water. The glare of the afternoon still left him almost blind. He looked upward at the blue sky and could see the scars left by hemorrhages. He had lost a great deal of sight. But he still had his sense of smell, and he loved the salt and the freshness of each wave. He tried to feel everything he could. He tried to body surf each wave, but it only made him unhappy. He wished to be a child again, to feel the pain of the breaking waves. After a while he made his way back to the shore. He lay on the sand, just out of reach of the water.

He heard a boy scream. Down the beach he could see that a wave had made it up to where the boy was buried. The sand had gone smooth and dark. Several of the older boys were working frantically with the shovel, taking turns.

"Hurry up!" he yelled. "Goddamn it, hurry up!" He was crying.

Each wave that came in carried more sediment. The water turned the sand to wet cement and the boys were working against time. The man thought about running for help. He thought, I should go for help. But then he didn't. He thought of the boys with the letters on their T-shirts. "Mind your own business," the buried boy had said.

"God, please help me!" the boy screamed. A wave rushed in and over his head. By now all of the group were working with their hands and feet. One older man was pulling on the boy's arms. The boy screamed with pain. Another wave rushed over him. He coughed and sputtered. "Help me, somebody!" he screamed. "Get me out of here."

The man did not look. He stared out at the ocean. He thought he could see an island far off on the horizon. A sailboat tipped by and he was certain there was an island. By now all of the members of the church group were yelling, working frantically. The tide was rising quickly. The boy's screams had gone wordless. They were just random noises, like the gull's squawking out over a fish kill. The man looked and could see a wake in the sand, where the water rushed back. It was like the trace a motorboat made far out in the ocean. Soon it would be gone. The tide broke heavily on the beach, the waves rushing up and over the man's legs and lap. He thought of the girl kissing the boy and the photograph. He thought of his mother holding his hand, of the scar on his shoulder. Soon the boy's yelling would cease. The tide rushed over his body, up to his chest. Still, I cannot feel the water, he thought. The tide rushed over him and he had almost no feeling.

Darkening
of the
World

Sometimes I wake myself up laughing. Dim light cuts into the room from between the curtains, where they fail to meet. I hear Pork snoring, the noise echoing down the hall. The exposed wood floors carry the sound. I don't know what I laugh about. But I recognize the voice, I know it is mine, and I lift into waking easily. When this happens, and it happens more often now, I am unable to drift back to sleep.

I listen for the sound of Pork's dachshund, Heidegger, at his water bowl, lapping water. I measure his steps, his nails on the linoleum in the kitchen, the rickety noise of his wicker basket as he settles himself down. This is winter and Pork says he can't afford to insulate and heat Heidegger's doghouse. Summer is a different story. Summer, Heidegger has a house. The house is antebellum-style, two-story, columns and balustrade. The mullioned windows open and close.

Pork is good with his hands. He built the house himself with tempered glass, double-paned, to keep in the cool air. He's air-conditioned it with the motor from an old refrigerator, having adjusted the thermostat. On cool evenings he turns the air off and opens the screened windows. He turns on the ceiling fan, made from a floor model he purchased at Wal-Mart. Heidegger can come and go as he pleases, the door to the house swings shut, a rubber seal sucking tight to keep in the coolness.

In the morning Pork stands in front of the stove in his boxers, cooking up sausage. He talks to Heidegger.

"How was your night?" he asks Heidegger. He does this in a high, unnatural voice.

I sit at the table with coffee and watch. Heidegger begins to wag his tail.

"How was your night?" Pork repeats, this time higher.

Heidegger wags his tail more, spins, darts from the kitchen to the living room. I can hear him running in tight circles. Then he does figure eights. He runs back into the kitchen, skids to a stop at Pork's feet.

"You're my love-dog," Pork says. He forks a patty of sausage and feeds it to Heidegger. What the dachshund doesn't get off the fork, Pork eats. Pork eats with the same fork as Heidegger.

"You're a sick man," I say.

Pork sits down in front of me. He looks at me.

"Not sleeping well?" he says. "Still laughing yourself awake. I hear you."

"Sorry," I say. "I don't know what it means."

"Darkening of the world," Pork says. He shakes his head, takes a bite of sausage, chews. "Darkening of the world." He gets up and goes to the stove where he has more sausage cooking.

Pork sells bowling supplies for a living, but when he was in school he studied philosophy. He sees everything in terms of philosophy. His work ethic, his dog, his love life, my not sleeping, all provide him with philosophical investigations, all come down to some kind of reasoning. He's a reasonable man. I like him. But I don't understand him.

"What do you mean, 'darkening of the world'?" I ask. I take a sip of coffee and stare at him. He flips the patties he's cooking and turns to me.

"You have fallen out of Being," he says. "Being with a capital 'B'."

"I have," I say, as if I understand.

Pork takes the sausage off the skillet and puts it onto a paper towel. He flips the patties, drying both sides. Reaching into the cupboard, he takes out a saucer and sets it on the counter. Heidegger stands at his feet, eyeing each move Pork makes. He sniffs the air.

"You work at the paper mill," he says, turning to me, "but you have stopped understanding."

Pork brings the saucer over to the table and sits down in front of me. He reaches over and takes my coffee cup. He takes a swallow.

"And this is serious?" I ask. After Pork sets my coffee cup in front of me I push it back across the table to him.

"Very," he says. "Very." He forks a patty of sausage and takes a bite. Heidegger sits at his feet.

"What does it mean?" I ask.

"You're caught up in the minutiae," he says. "Making paper. The people around you. You're forfeiting yourself, your Being toward death, your realization of your potential."

"What are you saying?"

"You need some dread," he says, finishing off my coffee. "Some real nothingness."

———

I run the barking drum and the chipper at a paper mill in Miller's Falls. In winter it is cold and in summer it is hot. It's never just right. I take the timber, cut it down to size, turn it into something usable. All day long I have nothing to think about. Today, I am considering what Pork has told me at breakfast. I consider my potential. There is not much there. I can run a few machines and I know how to make paper. Blank sheets of paper that someone else can fill up with ideas. It's not much, but without me some people would become desperate.

By lunchtime, I feel pretty good about myself. I'm convinced I'm doing something important. That without me Pork wouldn't have his books to read. Then I think, maybe I should stop. Maybe we all should stop what we're doing. Then people like Pork would understand dread. We'd throw a wrench in their notion of Becoming. Then the lunch whistle sounds and I go back to work. I need the pay.

I work all day and then come home to find Pork on the couch napping. Heidegger is curled up by his chest, resting his long nose over Pork's neck. When I come in the living room Heidegger opens his eyes, watches every move I make. It's as if he's guarding Pork, and I think if I make the slightest questionable move, he'll come off the couch and latch on to me. I go to the kitchen and get a dog biscuit. I return and give it to him, hoping crumbs will trickle into Pork's ear or something.

I switch on the table lamp at the end of the couch. It is late March and, though light is lasting later into the evening, I know it will be dark when Pork wakes. Too exhausted to eat, I climb the stairs and go to my room where I fall into bed, boots and all. I fall asleep, easily, quietly.

————

I am laughing. Suddenly, I am awake and covered in a light sweat. The room is bright, lit by moonlight angling between the open curtains. The room seems barren, vast. It's as if it is covered in a blanket of light snow. Downstairs I hear the television going. The evening news is playing. Outside my window, down in the yard, I hear muted voices. I raise myself, walk over, and look.

Pork and his girlfriend, Sheila, are standing apart, tossing an old baseball glove back and forth. Heidegger runs in the snow between them. He barks and leaps. Sheila laughs. The moonlight is bright on the snow. It casts the jagged shadows of trees all about Pork and Sheila. As Sheila throws I notice how thin and beautiful she is. Pork is heavy set. I don't see how the two of them got together. Pork throws the glove to her. She catches it and bends down. Heidegger runs to her and leaps into her arms. He takes the glove in his mouth and shakes it. Both Sheila and Pork are laughing. I open the window and feel the cold air come in. I feel the sweat drying on my skin and a chill down my back.

"Hey, guys," I yell down to them.

Sheila turns. "Strawberry!" she says. "Come down and join us."

"Hey, Straw," Pork says. "We've got a hint of spring in the air. Come out."

I shut the window and go downstairs to get my coat.

Standing in the yard, I can see out across the large lawn that fog is beginning to rise. An unnatural warmth has settled in. I walk up to Sheila and give her a hug. She kisses me on the cheek.

"How'd you sleep?" Sheila asks. I can tell Pork has told her about my laughing.

"OK," I say.

"Went for a walk in the woods," Pork says. "Snow's still too deep for Heidegger in areas. We carried him."

"Yeah."

"You should have come," Sheila offers.

"Yeah," Pork says. "You need to get away from forfeiture."

Sheila hands me Heidegger. He wriggles in my arms, leans up, and licks my chin. A bank of fog is headed across the yard, blowing toward us.

"Get off that," Sheila says to Pork. "Don't listen to him," she says, leaning into his chest.

Suddenly we are standing in the fog. Light from the moon spreads through the air. It floods out the windows of the house. We can hardly see each other for the glare. Our breath is visible, suspended before us.

"Let's go in and have a drink," Pork says. I can see his words hanging in the air.

"Let's," Sheila says.

We go inside and shed our coats. Pork goes to the cupboard and gets three glasses. He pours us each a gin and tonic. Heidegger laps water from his bowl, then shuffles into the den to settle on the couch. The three of us follow his lead.

"You laugh in your sleep?" Sheila asks. Heidegger sits between Pork and her. His head is on Pork's lap.

"I've started to," I say.

"How strange," she says. "That's never happened to me." She runs her hand down Heidegger's back. "What do you suppose it's all about?"

"I don't know," I say. "Pork claims it's a symptom of my falling out of Being."

"Pork always thinks that," she says. She takes a sip of her drink.

"It is," Pork says. "We are cast into the world of Being. We appropriate that world. If we fail to find ourselves in it, if we don't see our finite consciousness in connection to the future and the past, we fall out of Being."

"And that makes me laugh?" I say.

"Yes," Pork says. "You need a sense of dread. A sense of Being toward death. It wakes you up except in a positive way."

"Laughter isn't a good thing?" Sheila says.

"Not in this case," Pork says. "Straw has no sense of himself in the world. He makes paper. That's it. It's a gadget that has consumed him. He worries too much about others."

"Pork," Sheila says. "Sometimes you worry me."

"You think that death will motivate me?" I say. "You think I'll sleep better, won't wake myself laughing, if I worry about death a little?"

"Yes," Pork says. He holds his glass down. Heidegger lifts his head and licks the moisture that is dripping down its side.

"I won't sleep at all if I worry about such things."

"Let's go to bed," Sheila says. "Let's all go to bed before this gets out of hand."

Pork seems happy with this suggestion. He picks up Heidegger and heads up the stairs. Sheila reaches over and pats my leg.

"Get some sleep," she says. She follows Pork up the stairs.

I go to my room and undress. I slip under the sheets and lie on my back. I try to think forward, to a time when I am dead. I consider what this house will be like and who will live in it. All I can imagine is that I will die soon. That Sheila and Pork will live here. I imagine them forgetting that I ever lived here. I hear their conversations, daily, about all kinds of things. But they don't include me. I can't stand these thoughts, and I imagine what it was like before I was born. This is easier. I think of the World Wars. I think of my mother and father, both still alive. I see the house where I grew up, my mother and father living inside, having dinner and breakfast. This is easier. It helps me see how I came to be here in this bed. I think of this bed. I think of my childhood bed. Then I fall to sleep.

————

It is summer now. It has been three months and I still wake myself up laughing. Pork goes on the road selling supplies to bowling alleys during the summer months. This leaves me to take care of Heidegger. Since summer began there has been a drought, a forest fire, and I have been laid off from the mill. It is temporary, they say. Just until the timber becomes available from out of area. I don't mind. I have all day in the house with Heidegger, though mostly he stays out in his own air-conditioned antebellum. Afternoons, I doze on the couch. I have taken to reading *Being and Time*. Pork's copy is marked with notes. I can only take a few pages at a time, maybe ten or twenty a day. I don't feel good about what I am reading.

Late one afternoon I awake without laughter. From the shadows I know it must be about five. The heat of the day has just passed. I'm used to seeing Heidegger on the carpet when I wake up this late. He comes in to share the couch with me sometimes. Sometimes he stretches out on the floor just below me. He is gray-muzzled, old, and he sleeps like an old dog. He snores. But the room is quiet. So I get up and go to the window to look out. I don't see him in the yard. I think he must be in his house or down the street playing with the neighborhood kids. I decide I will walk down after dinner and collect him. He's not supposed to wander. Pork has put up a short, white picket fence—really used for garden and flower bed boundaries—but sometimes Heidegger gets it in his head to jump the fence.

I scoot into the kitchen to cook dinner. I slice and chop bell pepper and carrot, press garlic, peel and dice onion, all to make stir fry. I feel good about using my hands. All afternoon with nothing to do, I miss the mill. This is a kind of work that somehow frees me, here cutting and chopping in the kitchen. But for some reason Heidegger is on my mind. I have fed and watered him, turned on his air conditioner and ceiling fan. I stop what I'm doing and go back to the window. His windows are down. He's either cool inside or down the street playing along the creek bed with the kids. He'll come home caked in cool mud. I'll have to hose him down and scrub him with a towel. I go outside.

The heat is oppressive. It clings to my shirt and pants as soon as I walk out the door. It has been like this for weeks. The news is on the radio and television, everything about the forest fire, the heat, the disaster area we are becoming. I consider Pork to be lucky, traveling and all. He calls on occasion to check on Heidegger.

I take the water hose in my hand and turn on the flow at the spigot. I begin to water the flowers Pork has planted along Heidegger's fence row. The news has called for water conservation. But I think this little will not amount to much.

"Heidegger!" I call as I spray the honeysuckle. Pork has planted it hoping for hummingbirds. I point the water away from Heidegger's house, toward the fuchsia. The bee balm and petunias are all but dead. I lay the hose down in their bed to give them a deep soaking. I knock on the second-story roof. "Heide!" I yell. "Come on out."

His house is quiet. The air conditioner has cycled off. Inside I can hear the hum of the ceiling fan. I peek through a second-floor window, but don't see him.

"Heidegger!" I yell, directing my call with my hands. I am hoping the kids will bring him up from the creek so that I don't have to hunt them down. I hear them whooping it up down by the water. Since the drought there is only a trickle, which pools where the beavers have dammed it. I have warned the kids that Heidegger will give a beaver a run for its money, that they should be careful and keep an eye on him. Considering rabies and all, though I don't know if that's a worry, I fret when Heidegger is away. Pork says it's fine. Over the phone he says, "Let him enjoy himself, he's a dog."

Leaving the hose running on low, I decide to go in and cook up the vegetables I've cut. Cool air greets my face and I breathe in heavily. I hate to warm up the house by cooking. But my not working all day somehow builds up a ravenous hunger in me. I put some oil in the pan and heat it up. Flipping on the vent over the stove, I spill the carrots, peppers, onions, into the pan. Steam rises. I stand back from the hissing pan for a moment. While I stir the vegetables, I consider what I have read that day. Being toward death. The notion that by placing ourselves in the context of history, time, we see our beginning, our end, and the dread that arises moves us to appropriation of the world, of seeing ourselves in the world. It is a practical idea as I understand it. It's reasonable. I sprinkle water into the pan. It hisses and smoke rises. Turning down the heat, I cover the pan.

Heidegger's food is in a plastic wastebasket on the back porch. I lift the lid and fill his bowl. I leave it on the kitchen floor, step off the porch into the heat, and look toward Heidegger's house. Through a front window I gather sight of brown-black fur. Heidegger is in his house, sleeping. Going to the window, I peek inside, tap on the glass. Heidegger moves a little, then settles back in. I tap on the glass again and he ignores me.

"Heidegger!" I call as I rap on the window nearest him. "Hey, boy," I say. "Come out."

He doesn't move. He sleeps more these days, his age beginning to slow him down. Pork says it's part of the process. He says Heidegger is beginning to look distinguished. Like an old southern gentleman, he says.

Open palmed, I slap the glass. "Heide," I yell. "Wake up." I notice the glass is warm and Heidegger doesn't move. I listen. The air conditioner hasn't cycled back on. I feel the window nearest Heidegger and then the other, the opposite side of the door. They are warm. Jesus, I think, he must be hot in there. I lean over and push open the door. It's resistant, the seal locked tight. The door opens and a wave of heat pours out. It reaches up to my face, into my eyes. It's blistering, as if coming up off asphalt, with a chemical smell—the paint, the plastic frames of the windows, the rubber seal on the door. The ceiling fan is still working, but it is just pushing around the unbearable heat and smell. There is something else on the air. Something living. It is the musty scent of warm fur, urine, dog shit, all that has been baked for hours. Heidegger has messed his house, has lain in his own stench in this convected heat, the sunlight intensified through the glass, the white interior walls radiating back and forth, undulating, the energy. I catch him by his hind legs. I feel shit caked to them. I drag him out of the house, out onto the porch, and then pick him up and carry him to the lawn.

He is still breathing. Taking shallow, quick breaths, his eyes are unfocused, distant. I turn the spigot on full and take the hose from the flower bed. Around Heidegger's eyes and along his mouth and gums there is something dry and powdery. The water is cool and I pour it over his body. He doesn't resist. His eyes move, following my movements.

"Jesus," I say. "What the fuck happened?" I bathe his face with water. I wipe it away from his eyes. I run my hand over his body. It is unbelievably warm. A smell, something that I cannot describe, rises. It is sweet, sickly. "Heidegger," I say. "Oh, Heidegger."

I carry him inside the house and lay him on the couch. His body is limp. A stain spreads out on the fabric, taking on the larger shape of his body. For a moment, Heidegger's breathing slows. I go to the kitchen and get ice, wrap it in dish towels. I lay the towels down around his belly. I lift his head and put an ice pack down. He rests on it. His eyes close. He is calm. His breathing seems better.

I sit back and watch. A few minutes pass and then Heidegger gasps. He lifts his head and his tail, curling his body upward at both ends. He sucks at air convulsively, rapidly, one, two, three times. Then he lies out flat again. His eyes are wild. A mucus comes from his nose. I get close to his face, kiss the side of it, and I stare into his eyes.

He is wanting. It's as if he tries to talk. He whines and leans his face close to my lowered head. I hold his face in my hands. I stare into his eyes and for a moment I imagine I am him, that I am having his thoughts.

There is a gnawing, tugging in my chest. A beating fills my head. I cannot hear for the beating in my chest. Heat throbs, cuts into my body, as hot as the pavement on the hottest days. I feel as if I am falling. I cannot hold my eyes open. I am afraid to close my eyes. His flesh is warm against mine. I will close my eyes for a moment. The beating in my chest is easier. It becomes lighter, less painful. I take a deep, long breath. The burning in my head eases. I hear the throbbing as it eases. He touches against my face. I will close my eyes. Sleep is deep, black. My chest rises. It rises. Then falls. I am falling, without fear.

The moon is bright, near full. The lights are on in Heidegger's house and they spread out on the ground before me. The earth is soft, soggy from where I left the water on. The edge of the bee balm and petunia bed are tender and make for easy digging. I dig, exposing the blackened soil. Heidegger's body is still warm, yielding. I lay him in the ground and cover him. I go inside and climb the stairs to my bedroom. Undressing in front of the window, I can see out to where Heidegger is buried. Light cast from his house illuminates a small cross I've made from a piece of leftover clapboard. I leave the light burning. It is a comfort. I go to sleep and sleep late into the next morning.

———

Pork stands holding Heidegger's blanket. His face is red, swollen. He is silent for a moment. Heidegger is still visible on the couch as a stain, his shape outlined by the water that has dried there.

"Why didn't you let him lie in state?" Pork asks. "You could have wrapped him in his blanket."

"I don't know," I say. "I thought it would be best . . ." I don't know how to finish this sentence. Outside the window, Sheila is standing over Heidegger's grave.

"Damn it, Straw," Pork says. "You should've kept an eye out. It's a fucking machine. A compressor. You can't trust machines." Pork is getting angry. He sits down on the couch. He places his hand on the stain. "I have to see him," he says. "I have to see him."

"You can't," I say to Pork.

"I can just see him over there," Pork says. He points to an open area of the carpet. "Running those figure eights."

"I'm sorry," I say. "I'm really sorry. I did what I could."

"It wasn't enough," he says. "You could have let him lie in state. It would have been fine for a day."

I am standing up, looking down at Pork. He sits on the couch with his arms crossed. He looks at Heidegger's shape crusted on the cushion next to him. I think we'll never get rid of the stain. It will stay with us. I don't know what to do. I don't know what to say. There is no saying what one feels when it's grief that's on you. I'm grieving just like Pork.

"You're going to help me," Pork says, finally. "I'm going to see him one last time."

"I can't," I say.

"What do you mean?" he says.

"I just can't," I say.

"You killed Heidegger," he says, "you buried him without me. You're going to help me dig him up."

"You're getting irrational."

"I have to see him."

"You don't want to do that," I say, calmly. I want to comfort him.

"You're going to have to face it one day," Pork says. "You are so fucking weak." He stands up and looks at me face-to-face. "You know it?" he asks. "I've got to see him."

Pork slams the door on his way out. I see him give Sheila a hug before he takes the shovel in his hand and begins to dig. The ground is hard and dusty. The sun has been beating down all morning. It's been beating down for as long as I can remember. It's as if I can't remember anything. Pork shovels. The earth comes up in clots. Heidegger's cross is lying off to the side. Pork has pulled it from the ground. Sheila stands back with her hands over her mouth. She is red faced and crying. It's as if it's her child. Pork stabs at the earth. He kicks the shovel down into the dust. He is careful, making a much larger hole than I have dug.

Pork works for twenty minutes while I watch him from inside. I cannot go out and help him. It's just not in me. I can't imagine how Heidegger will look. I can't bear the thought of the sight of him. Pork's body is rising and falling heavily. His shirt sticks to his back with sweat. It cuts down the runnel and across his shoulders. Moisture drips from his chin. His face is wet.

I watch him lift soil from around the edges of the ground he has broken. He falls to his knees and begins to use his hands to push away dirt, forming a mound along the far edge of the grave. Pork stops for a moment. He looks up at Sheila. She kneels beside him. Pork leans over and lifts Heidegger's body from the ground. The body is swollen and rigid. Pork lifts him to his face, kisses him along the side of his head. He cradles Heidegger in his arms and rocks him. Sheila is leaning back, sobbing. Pork's large body rises and falls. He is trembling, shaking with grief. He holds Heidegger to his chest. I can see flies hovering in the air. Pork leans his head back for a moment and shakes from side to side. He heaves, bending over. All I can imagine is the smell and how it must feel having it so close to my body. I can almost taste it. It is in my mouth, watering. My stomach turns, gurgles. I breathe out a heavy sigh. Something rises, in the heaviness of my stomach. It overcomes me. I begin to laugh, quietly. But it builds from within me and I cannot control myself. It builds, rises, becomes impossible for me to silence. Pork and Sheila turn, holding Heidegger, staring blankly. I am laughing uncontrollably.

Blood
Knot

Pate came by early on a slate gray Saturday and waited for me out front in his pickup. I'd lived north, in Massachusetts, long enough to know that sour weather in April could burn off and turn beautiful. I was counting on this to happen. A duffel bag packed with waders and a vest sat next to the door, my fly rod perched against the jamb. Jess, my wife, sat at the breakfast table hunched over two spools of monofilament line, practicing a knot Pate had taught me.

I had made coffee and put a steak in to broil while Jess scrambled eggs—a real western-style affair. Jess was quiet, simply tired I thought, but I loved to work beside her in the kitchen on mornings when the air was cool and the light shadowy. The oven gave off warmth that she stirred with her movements between the refrigerator and the stove top and the various drawers. I sometimes wondered if it wasn't an image of my mother and father I held in mind, compared to this scene of Jess and me, and from the difference somehow gathered a charge, a fleeting sense of satisfaction. The coffeepot gurgled and sucked, dripping slowly. I drew up insulin into a syringe, held the vial and needle up toward the overhead light, and measured the cloudy fluid. This was ritual, something I'd done without much thought since I was a child. Jess watched.

"Get some socks on your feet," she said. "You know better."

I slipped the syringe from my arm and bent the needle on the edge of the counter. She was right. I had in recent years lost all feeling in my feet, was prone to being off balance and unable to sense the chill of the linoleum or even something as drastic as a nail piercing my flesh. The year before I'd almost lost my left leg to an infection, a simple cut, which worked its way to the bone. Since then, Jess often woke me up in the morning, bringing me a pair of clean socks she'd warmed in the microwave. But on this morning I'd been awake hours before her, first listening to her wispy breath, seemingly cajoled by gentle dreams, then rising, putting on my dungarees and a khaki shirt.

"You feeling OK?" she asked. She bent and ran her finger along the inside of her calf, gathering one sock and then the other. "Take these," she said. "They're yours anyway."

"Pretty well," I said. I steadied myself against the kitchen table and pulled on each sock. "I'm ready for this."

Jess took the steak out of the oven. She cut into the center and checked the color. "Your blood sugar's good?" she asked, lifting a bite of meat to her mouth.

"Fine," I said.

She focused on me, to see if I was telling the truth. Jess's eyes are green, clear and deep, and she can stare through the silt of the warmest, most comfortable lie. I reached across the counter and touched the back of her hand. "Pate'll be here soon," I said.

"He'll have to wait," she said. "You've got to eat." She lifted the pan of eggs and reached to turn the burner off.

"Time's wasting," I said. I put my arms around her waist from behind, held her body to mine, breathing in the scent of sandalwood.

Jess divided the steak and eggs onto two plates. "Food's up," she said, with a husky tone. I poured coffee and brought it to the table.

We ate quietly, letting the morning sounds fill the kitchen. In a few weeks warblers would return, and we'd open the windows and be pleased to hear them. Winter had been dry but hard, bitter. Jess and I had sheltered against the cold by buying new boots and sweaters and wearing silks instead of cotton thermals. We took long, hot showers together, embracing beneath the flow of water. We sat on the lip of the tub in the steam, moisture beading on the mirror and the lavatory fixtures, and talked about how happy we both were that we'd moved up from Texas, up here where it was cool and where we could appreciate the warmth when we had it. The onset of warmer days, May and June, gave us something to think about and plan for. From our front porch we could see a range of mountains, and in the spring we ate breakfast, staring off at them in the distance. Often, we fell silent, never saying specifically what kind of happiness we'd found. I think we were both trying to convince ourselves of something, attempting to make amends, wanting the stillness that gathered on the porch, in the bathroom or kitchen, to give us the sense of filling space with meaning. Still, I sensed we were edging toward something, getting close to discussing important things, situations that eventually we'd have to face.

———

A few years before, when we lived in Texas, routine lab tests, creatinine and blood work, came back with news: My kidneys were giving out.

"This happens with diabetics," the doctor said.

"How long?" I asked. Jess sat next to me, holding my hand and listening closely.

"It's hard to say," he paused. "There's medicine that will, perhaps, retard renal failure—Zestril. Though not substantiated, a low-protein diet couldn't hurt." He paused again, shuffled the papers on his desk, surveying the numbers and then studying our faces. "Five. Six years."

"Then what?" Jess asked.

"Then we'll have to talk about alternatives," he answered, flatly. "Dialysis. Evaluation for transplant."

"Evaluation?" Jess said.

"Eligibility is restricted," he said. "The procedure is risky even if all his other organs are healthy. And Jake shows signs of other long-term complications—retinopathy, neuropathy, gastroparesis."

The words cascaded, rushed over us, and seemed to cleanse or wash away any notion we had of a past. I felt new, rootless. I wanted a fresh start, at least for a few years. For a couple of weeks I talked about the possibility of moving away, of seeing places and things before it was too late.

"Like retired people do," I said to Jess.

She smiled. "Can we do that?" she asked. "Leave everyone behind?"

I debated at the dinner table and Jess became anxious for me. She left her food untouched, wiped the tabletop and stove with a damp rag, stood at the pantry and said she didn't know what she was looking for, just that she was hungry. After a month the move just came on us and we didn't fight it. It had begun as a notion, and after we looked through books of photographs, we settled on the idea that we wanted to see New England.

I took a job selling insurance for a company out of Hartford. I could set my own hours, work the western region of Massachusetts where the Berkshire hills rose up and captured streams and rivers among the valleys. Jess thought the new job would give me more free time to do whatever I wanted. She was quiet about what was going on and was scared like I was. We didn't talk about what would happen in the end. Instead, we planned summers on the Cape and off-season visits to Maine. The first spring, while canvassing insurance, I took to rivers, standing along their banks. I worked my way into the Berkshires, westward from Buckland to

Charlemont. Between appointments I'd park along the winding highway and watch the churning water, violent and gray with run-off.

There, time almost stopped for me. Standing beside the running water, I felt the urge to be in the midst of the coursing sound, leaning against the weight of the breaking flow. The need to do this was inexplicable to me except that I couldn't think of a better way of being closer to people that mattered to me than to be away from them. I could listen to myself and every word that had ever been said to me. I imagined I could sort things out and find some peace. I thought of the rill, the source that built into this gap of rushing water, and imagined straddling it, a foot on either side.

———

Across the table from each other, aware of what we weren't saying, mindful of each other's thoughts, and with silence, Jess and I questioned, wondered, about this fishing trip.

The sheers above the kitchen sink went milky with light. Jess sat with her bare feet on the edge of the seat. She hugged her knees and sipped coffee. "Eat," she said, urging me gently. "Pate's not going to want to idle."

"I'm eating," I said. "I'm not hungry." I pushed a bit of egg onto my fork with a wedge of toast.

"Eat the steak."

"There's a lot of protein."

"You've got to cover your insulin," she said, picking up her fork and pointing to my plate. "You've got to have something. It's not a choice."

"There's a choice," I said, not knowing why I was disagreeing.

"No," she said. "That's what choices come to the older you get."

This was how Jess had come to talk about my failing health. She pretended I'd lived longer than I had, as if I used up time more quickly than her. I sensed she wanted to believe that everyone's lifetime, no matter what the duration, was somehow equal. It was a careful way of thinking, and I wanted to believe she was right.

I cut into my steak and began to eat slowly, gathering hunger as I went. Cars passed along the road, the damp pavement lifting a plaintive sound to the front of the house. Jess left her steak and eggs untouched. She watched me finish off my breakfast and poured each of us a second cup of coffee. I cleared the table and stood at the kitchen sink, considering how the day was shaping up—sky the color of newsprint, dew turning slick and pearly on the chestnut out back and up higher on the hill, white pines skirted with patches of snow. On days like this deer emerged from the tree line along the top of the hill and grazed in the shag grass. Before long, trout lilies and columbine would appear.

There was a lot between us here in the kitchen, a history. Arguments over meals—what I should and shouldn't eat, the difficulty in weighing everything, measuring carbohydrates and exchanges, giving numbers to every bite I consumed. We put meals on a clock, which despite invitations to early movies or late dinner parties, we met with a constant vigilance. But still it was difficult, a battle for us and sometimes between us. I weighed all of this against the day ahead, watched the dullest of shadows begin to form, and hoped Pate would arrive soon. I was eager, in a nervous way, to get out on the water and discover what I thought I'd find—though I didn't know exactly what that was.

Jess had gathered the spools of line and was working to seat a knot when I heard the rough skipping of Pate's truck engine. I sat at the table and laced my uplanders and then gathered my duffel bag and rod. I knew he would wait outside. Of late, he was skittish around women, and I think Jess in particular agitated him. He was toward the end of an ugly marriage, and Jess was everything his wife was not. Seeing us together ran a curl up his spine. Not in a resentful way, but in the sense that it reminded him of something he didn't have. Jess understood all this and tried to be gentle with him.

"You have the creel?" I called to Jess from the front hallway.

"With your lunch," she answered. She had filled a Thermos with coffee and slipped it into the creel with a plastic bag—a sandwich, chips, fruit, and juice. "Take time to eat," she said, hooking the leather strap over my shoulder and kissing me.

"Sure you won't come?" I asked.

"Boys' day away," she said and smiled.

We stepped onto the front porch and Pate tapped the horn. "Jake," he yelled. "Sorry I'm behind." He had the windows down on both sides. I hoisted my gear into the bed of the truck where Pate had a pair of waders laid out. I didn't see his rod or vest. "You're not fishing?" I said, surprised.

"We'll see," he said.

"Pate," Jess said, heading around to his side.

"Hey, Jess." He leaned his head out the window and she kissed him on the cheek. "This boy keep you awake all night worrying about fish?"

"It's not the fish," she said.

"This'll be something to talk about," Pate laughed. "Real memories."

I slipped onto the seat and set my creel between us on the floorboard. "We shooting the breeze or fishing?" I said. "Get this junk heap off memory lane."

"You take care of him," Jess said to Pate. He rested his arm where the window was open, and Jess ran her hand along his chambray shirt sleeve. He let her hand rest for a moment before he reached out and adjusted the side mirror and then pulled the truck into gear.

"I'm no kid," I said.

"No problem," Pate said, winking at Jess. She stepped back from the truck and Pate rolled up his window, letting the truck draw backward. Jess waved and we pulled away.

On the seat between us was a Thermos and a paper sack that had a loaf of French bread peeking out from its edges. Pate reached over and pinched off a section of the bread. "Have some," he offered. "It's still warm."

"Had a big breakfast," I said. "Jess was on me about eating."

"Take it as a good sign."

"I do," I said. I let a silence fall between us for a moment, trying to collect my thoughts. I rolled up the side window and relaxed into the seat. A warmth slowly built in the cab, and I felt a twinge of sleepiness running up through my legs. I glanced at the Thermos on the seat between us. "Coffee?" I asked.

"No thanks," Pate said. "You better steer clear of that," he added, nodding toward his Thermos.

"Huh?"

"It's loaded," he said.

I paused. "Oh—" I said, slow to gather his meaning.

"Fly fishing and bourbon go together," he offered.

"You're the boss," I said.

Pate smiled. He leaned over and tipped on the heater. A sweet scent hung on the air. Beneath the bread I noticed he had brought along the binder I'd given him a few weeks before. On the cover there was a strip of masking tape, ballpointed with the title, *The Book of Timothy*.

"What's with the title?" I asked.

Pate looked down at the binder. "Saint Timothy," he said. He peeled some crust from the bread and put it in his mouth. "The first apostle to rely on absolute faith."

I nodded. The binder was filled with a collection of things—paragraphs, sentences, letters, sometimes stories. I'd started writing after I learned about my kidneys giving out.

"He missed all the miracles of Christ," Pate added.

I glanced at him. "What brought it to mind?" I asked.

"Timothy wasn't well," Pate said. "You know. Take a little wine for your stomach?"

I had heard that before, but I didn't know where it had come from or what it meant. "So what happened?"

"Timothy had memories," Pate said. "Doctrine. Liturgy. But still he'd missed out on everything—all the excitement. He wasn't even in Palestine during the forty days Christ kept popping up after he was crucified."

"So what happened?" I asked again.

"He got fed up," Pate said. "He went to the temple of Artemis. Looking for trouble. So the Ephesians clubbed him to death."

I laughed. I liked the title. I supposed, in a way, this reflected my own life. I felt I'd missed most of my family's vitality and maybe most of mine. Though none us of were saints, I imagined I'd lost out on a lot.

I'd tried to write about the silence that fell in the wake of my father's absence and the way my mother's life had spiraled away from his and inward on itself. In the few years I'd known Pate I'd recollected the story for him from every angle. When I was thirteen, my father left my mother and me. My father refused to write or call except on occasion, and his not speaking became a physical distance. It was intentional, real. But my mother, as close as we had been in proximity, together and sharing our daily life, maintained a vacancy, a disavowal of the past. She seemed to live inside herself, her thoughts never completely expressed. There was a coolness there, and I wanted to understand how it mocked the past, echoed like a slap across the face of both me and my father.

———

My father had been a fisherman. A man named Starling, a civil engineer he worked with, would come by on Friday evenings and they would pack up my father's boat with tackle boxes, rods and reels, life vests, and a cooler full of beer and sandwiches. I helped carry the boxes brimming with lures and plastic worms, the dull scent of petroleum clinging to my hands hours after my father and

Starling had pulled out of the driveway. Bass fishing at night on Lake Tawakoni was peaceful and good according to my father.

My mother and I would watch the taillights of the trailer brighten at the end of the street and then she'd say, "We're on our own, honey-bunch."

I slept in bed next to my mother, the smell of my father's after-shave on the pillow. I tried to stay awake, imagining what it was like out on the lake in the darkness with the waves lapping up against the prow of the boat. It was because of my health, my father said, that he couldn't take me along. "You could have an insulin reaction out on the lake," he said. "Then what would you do?"

I thought to myself, "Eat something." It seemed simple to me.

But next to my mother, her breathing calm, I would begin to feel distant from both of my parents. I sensed I had worked my way between them, frozen amid crevices that had formed as a result of my illness, breaching even further an invisible rift. Outside the bedroom window the air-conditioning compressor hummed. Street light cut into the room from behind the drapes, and the sheets and pillows cooled. I drifted with scattered thoughts until I fell asleep.

In the morning, my mother would cook breakfast and then sit on the front porch and drink coffee while I ate. She opened up doors and windows to let in fresh air. Neighbors sometimes visited, and I could hear their conversations lingering in through the front screens. While my mother talked, I would wander into the bed-room she shared with my father. I opened the closet where I could smell the polish of my father's shoes arranged on the floor and his leather belts that hung from hooks along the wall. I stepped into the closet and let the sleeves of jackets and shirts brush against my face, and I ran my hands up through his ties, letting them sift between my fingers. Occasionally I got down on my knees and put my hands into a pair of his shoes to feel the impressions left by his feet. I thought about what it must have been like in the months before I was born, my father just home from work, changing clothes, hanging up his slacks, while my mother sat, heavy, on the edge of the bed listening to how his day had gone. They had not bargained on my illness.

Saturday evenings, Starling and my father returned, their faces and arms wind-burned pink. Out in the backyard I watched my father scale, gut, and fillet bass on the picnic table, under the harsh glare of the outdoor floodlight. The agile movements of his hands, the tawny glint of scales, the sharp knife exposing the ruby insides, calmed me. My father caught his breath in sudden, raspy spurts, as if he were holding it in for long periods of time. We didn't talk much, and when we did my father recounted how he struggled to land his fish among the snags and drift.

What I remembered most for Pate, though, were the times my father had to return home early. There were occasions when my blood sugar went wildly out of control, and I was sick enough that I needed to go to the hospital. My mother had to call the marina where Starling and my father liked to put in and land the boat. Evenings and mornings they ate at a diner and bar called The Cozy. She called and left word that he should meet us at Baylor Hospital. In the few hours before he arrived, I drew into my mother and her soft gestures. She was quiet but hopeful, occasionally suggesting visits to the library or the natural history museum when I was better and able to leave the hospital. The time passed quickly, and almost too abruptly my father came into the room. His coveralls were still crisp, unstained, and he'd tip the bill of his cap backward and look down at me lying in the bed.

"See," he said in a way that suggested he'd proved something.

"See what?" my mother replied, angry.

He ran a rough hand along my arm, and I could feel how the sun and wind had beaten a light fever into his skin. A hint of lake water and beer clung to him. I smiled, pretending to feel fine. My mother was silent, holding something back. There was an instant when I felt secure, close to both of them, but it was diminished by what was never discussed in front of me.

"You shouldn't have gone," she said, finally. "He wasn't feeling well."

"I had to get away sometime—" he said.

"I need a smoke," my mother interrupted, looking at my father.

They stepped out into the hallway together where I could hear them begin to argue, their voices at first hushed and then sharper, overtaking each other as they moved off into the distance. I felt myself wash away from them, from their thoughts and reasons. I was alone. Outside my room, nurses bustled, telephones rang, doctors were called, but I was immersed in stillness.

This was part of what I wanted to understand. Over the years I tried to get an idea, an image that made sense, that captured exactly what it was that had come between us all—my mother, my father, and me.

I wrote at night while Jess slept, leaving typed pages on the kitchen table for her to read before leaving for work. After a while Jess suggested I get Pate's thoughts on what I'd written. She respected him and the fact he'd been teaching at the university for twenty years. It seemed odd to me now that he'd brought the manuscript along.

"What'd you think?" I asked, reaching for my Thermos.

"About what?" Pate said. He pulled a pair of sunglasses from his shirt pocket and put them on. The sun hadn't come out, but a glare was cast on the pavement as if the clouds were thinning.

"This," I said. I sat back in the seat and put my hand on the binder.

"Still working on it," he said, flatly. He glanced at me and peeled off another piece of bread.

"Yeah," I said, a bit disappointed.

"I'm halfway," he added. "Today ought to do it."

I poured coffee and put my Thermos back. I watched the road

as it began to rise and descend, weaving into the forested hills. The truck engine groaned as we climbed, mounting the first ridge where paper birches began to line the road, their chalky bark peeled away to reveal slices of orange trunk. Pate reached for his Thermos. He settled into driving and began to drink from the bottle.

We'd agreed I should fish the Westfield, a river that in its bends could be forgiving, with deep pools and easy wading. The runoff wouldn't be bad, Pate thought. Though it was an hour east, the trip would take us into the hills where the scenery was beautiful and the fishing was some of the best. According to Pate, it was a river he fished often back before he decided he didn't have time to fish, that it was more work than it was worth. I tried to conjure an image of where we were headed.

"What's with the split willow?" Pate asked. He nodded toward the creel. "You'll look like one of the Maclean brothers on the Big Blackfoot."

I laughed. "Jess gave it to me," I said.

Pate ran his fingers lightly across the top of the steering wheel. "You've never waded before," he paused.

"No—"

"This isn't what you think it is," he continued. "How's your balance? Your eyes?"

Pate knew the answer to these questions. I turned to face him, to get an idea of where he was going with this.

"Water is tricky," he said. "It can fool you. Pull your feet from under you," he said.

"I know."

"This is work," he said. "You have to read the water."

I listened. Pate had given me instructions all along, from the time I'd decided I wanted to fish. I read books and studied magazines and catalogs. He answered my questions, attempting to be clear, thorough, but without encouraging me.

"Plan ahead," he said, glancing at me. "If you get a fish on, you have to land it."

"Yeah?"

"Most people don't think about that," he said. "A fish is like a good idea. You have to know what to do with it or it's wasted."

"What do you mean?"

"You have to get yourself situated," he said, pausing to take a sip from his Thermos. "Look around and see where you are on the water." Pate looked around the truck cab as if he were on the river.

Taken by surprise, I followed his gaze thinking briefly that he was actually looking for something.

"A fish will take off, run," he continued. "You have to be in a position to handle it, to let it have line and then be able to reel it back to you. To net it and release it without fucking up."

"OK."

"Don't get your feet locked between rocks to where you're off balance," he said. "Mess up the landing . . . there's no point being on the river." Pate's tone was earnest. He wanted me to understand what he was saying.

It had made no sense that I felt the urge to surround myself with water, the rugged surface concealing, deepening an apprehension within me. Pate's suggestions came as a reminder. I faced something that, in truth, was plied with awe. I hadn't considered what it would be like to catch a fish—the difficulty of maintaining my balance while gently bringing the fish into my net, angling to then dislodge the hook without damaging the tender surface of its skin, careful to touch the fish only with river-dampened hands. It was true that I should plan ahead. The thoughts, as they came, surprised me.

———

I had spent late afternoons practicing the four-part cast, two-point control, double hauling, and shooting line. Keeping twenty yards of fly line aloft, curving in graceful loops, without creating a tangled mess is not easy. It's not the weight of the fly you're casting, but rather the line itself. I wanted to be accurate and have a gentle presentation, and so I worked at it, tossing at the corner post of the blueberry patch or the neighbor's cat if it was out. Pate stopped by one Wednesday after teaching his Milton seminar and watched.

"Any ideas?" I asked, retrieving line to make another cast.

Pate stood at the roadside, leaning against his truck. He let my voice empty from the air, paused a moment longer, and then called back, "Practice."

I looked at him and smiled. "Screw you, old man."

"Practice," he repeated as if he hadn't heard me.

I whipped the line in his direction before I reeled it in. "I've got questions," I said as I walked toward him.

"Fly, leader, line," he said, suggesting the correct order of presentation.

"The leader to the line?" I asked. "What knot do you join them—"

"Nail knot," he said before I finished. "Or—"

"I've been trying the blood knot," I interrupted.

"That'll work."

"I'm having a terrible time," I said. "My fingers just won't work."

"Jess could help you," he said. "Her fingers are probably more agile."

"She's tried," I said.

"With the blood knot," he said, "you have to use seven turns with each line, exactly. You really have to work to seat it."

I snipped the practice fly off the line and unferruled the rod. My body was stiff from the cool weather. Pate tucked his hands into his pockets and curled his shoulders forward, huddling in on himself for a moment. I reached out and patted him on the shoulder. "What's up?" I asked.

"You know," he said. *Paradise Lost.* The wife."

"Sounds like *The Inferno,*" I said.

"Or a country–western song."

"Not without a dead dog," I said. I fed the rod into its cloth slipcase and then into the rod tube. "Coffee?"

"Maybe a beer." He hunched forward and pushed his body away from the truck.

We went inside the house and I got Pate a beer. He took a seat at the kitchen table. I leaned against the counter and watched him sit quietly with his thoughts. I was worried about him.

"You going fishing with me?" I said.

"What for?" he asked.

"Show me how it's done."

"It's done over time," he paused. "A long time."

"Spring's around the corner."

Pate sat back in his chair and was quiet. "I'll go," he said finally.

I took a glass from the cupboard and stood at the refrigerator, spilling apple juice into it. I took a long drink.

"You OK?" he asked.

I nodded. "Sure," I said. Taking care of my blood sugar was a matter of equilibrium—insulin bringing it down and food elevating it. Exercise, though, could throw the balance off, and casting had been hard work. A vague weakness ran through my body. My hands trembled lightly. I sat down across the table from him. "I'm fine," I said.

Pate took a pull from his beer. He ran his hand across the surface of the tabletop. This was a gesture I'd seen him make often during the last year. We would sit at the table and he listened as I talked about how my father was faring. I'd chosen to stay with my mother after the split, but I think my father was the most in need of help. When I graduated high school he sent me a letter. It said, "Things will be different now. You're a man." After that it got to where he rarely returned my phone calls or answered letters. My mother had moved on, found solace in art openings and docent work on the weekends. She sipped wine in the evenings and took a liking to Wagner. The house thundered with music. She said to let go and try not to embrace my father's weaknesses. I wasn't sure exactly what they were, but I felt, in part, I was the source of them. I tried to locate this frailty in myself, but I was a different man. Pate had listened to me talk, gliding his hand across the table. I think my talking had been a distraction for him, a way inside his own problems.

Pate took another long drink from his beer. He seemed to be waiting on something. I let a moment pass between us. "I'm writing," I said.

"Yeah?" he said. "Good for you."

"Coming to terms, I guess."

"It's not easy."

Pate straightened the place mat in front of him. I sat looking out the window at the light flurry of snow that had begun to fall. I was uncomfortable, nervous. I felt like we'd been trying to fill the silence when we should have been doing something else. In the distance I could see a line of bare maples. They would begin to sap early if the weather didn't change. Jess would want to go to a sugar house and have pancakes.

"Listen," Pate offered, "if you've got some line I'll show you a blood knot."

I turned. "Don't worry about it," I said. "I'll go it alone first."

"Your choice." Pate stood to leave and looked out the window. "Snow," he said, surprised.

"It won't amount to much."

"I guess not," he said. "Give Jess my love."

He shoved his hands into his pockets and halted. I held the door for him. "Keep writing," he said, as if the thought had just occurred to him.

After dark I struggled at the kitchen table to shore two ends of monofilament line. I wrapped the tag end of one line seven times around the other, looped it, and threaded the other tag end seven times through the loop. It was the loop, the first line turning back on itself, that was difficult to hold. Jess suggested I figure a way to hook it on something, to keep it open. I refused, thinking I wouldn't have that luxury on the river. The knot was difficult but not impossible. I could see that. But the longer I worked the more jittery my hands became, my fingers refusing to find the tag end of the line, letting the turns come unfurled. I considered how difficult tying the knot would be while wading the open-water current.

———

Pate kept his focus on the road and continued to drink from his Thermos. The truck engine clattered as we began to work our way into a more serious grade. The hills had turned to steep, rocky cliffs with the road winding between. Occasional patches of ice hung in sheets from crevices along the natural bulwark. The clouds had begun to tatter, pockets of blue sky showing through.

"Things are shaping up," I said. I put on my sunglasses.

"Maybe so."

Pate lifted the loaf of bread in my direction, offering me some. I shook my head no and sipped my coffee. It had gone cold. We crested the top of a ridge and the road ahead curved downward, giving a view of the basin. The land rippled with color, the sun glinting off the evergreens and the sage hue of the nearly budding willow and oak. In the long silence between us we'd covered a good distance. From the look of things we were near the Westfield River, just above Chesterfield Gorge. I tried to catch a view of the river, but it was tucked deep into the land.

"We'll take a washboard in a few miles," Pate said. "It follows the river."

"How far?"

"Several miles back," he said. "Forestry road."

"Should we hike it?" I asked. "Could be muddy."

"We'll be fine."

The road hugged the curve of a hill then pressed onward into the distance, a silver thread in the sunlight. The view opened up one last time before we descended into the cover of trees. Hills splotched with evergreens rolled toward the horizon. A haze slackened in the valleys.

"Jess would love this," I said.

"You should bring her sometime." Pate put the top on his Thermos and slipped it into the floorboard. He tore off another piece of bread and began to chew.

Pate slowed the truck and turned off into an opening where the pavement quickly gave way to dirt and gravel. We passed an open gate, and the road narrowed to a single lane. The dirt turned to gumbo beneath the canopy of trees. Light spilled onto the road in patches.

"We'll take this back about two miles," Pate said. "There's a pullout."

"Sounds good," I said. I rolled down my window and emptied my Thermos cap. A cool breeze rode in the cab. I closed my eyes and listened to twigs brushing the length of the fender and slapping against the side mirror. Spruce and pitch pine filled the air with a musty sweet scent. The suspension creaked as we listed over swells and washouts. Down a ravine, two hundred feet below us, the river flowed quietly. As we drove on, the road descended toward the water, and I could hear more clearly the current breaking over and around rocks. The hum of tires on highway pavement fell silent behind us.

"You OK?" Pate asked.

"Sure." I opened my eyes and tried to catch my first glimpse of the river. We'd made it below the gorge and the water was white foam, pushing hard and fast where sheer rock faces had guided it through the shaded notch, a glacial relic. The distance we covered was also a measure of time. Around me I sensed something dark and old, a recollection, like a photograph, the colors changed, intensified and false, a memory I did not have. As the truck crawled forward I receded from the world I knew. I could smell the river water, a hint of fish luffing in the breeze. The engine noise eased. We were level with the river, and out beyond the trees I saw how the riffle had become more gentle.

Pate guided the truck into a clearing and killed the engine.

"Paradise," he said in a flat tone. He kept his hands on the wheel and straightened his arms, stretching.

I got out of the truck. Twenty yards of wooded area stood between us and the river. The sunlight had come clean from the clouds and hung in sheets out between the trees. The light was brilliant on the water. "This is what it's all about," I said, aware of being cliché. Now that I'd made it to the river, I couldn't think of what I should be saying. I went around back of the truck and dropped the tailgate. Pate slid out of the cab with his Thermos and the black binder.

"Get my waders," he called.

I dumped my duffel bag onto the soft, pine-needled ground. In the shade the light breeze carried a hint of leftover winter, icy and spry. Pate had wandered over to a willow snag and taken a seat. He gazed out over the river. I pulled my waders on and laced my boots. I was slow about it, deliberate, watching myself in a way. My thoughts turned simple. I wanted to do this right—double knot my laces, belt my waders, ferrule my rod by twisting the tip guides into alignment. Pate was quiet and patient. When I had finished, I carried Pate's waders over and took a seat next to him.

"Great day," I said.

"Could be." He put the binder down beside him and began to unlace his shoes.

"I didn't find a belt," I said.

"Don't have one."

"You can get in trouble that way."

"Only if I fill them," he said, urging his feet into each booted leg. He pulled the suspender straps over his shoulders and let out a deep breath of air. "Did you ever get that blood knot figured out?"

"I'm not sure of it."

"You know there's an easier way," he paused, then laughed. "A surgeon's loop on your line and leader. Then just run them through. Simple."

x

"Who's looking for a simple way out?" I said. "I'm learning."

"You're learning knots you don't need," he said, running his palms along the legs of his waders.

I opened my creel and reached in for an orange Jess had packed. I was a bit put out that Pate had neglected to tell me about the surgeon's loop. I hated feeling as if I'd done something wrong. I ate without talking. Pate shifted his weight, ran his hands into the waders to smooth out his shirt. He seemed nervous, fidgety, with my silence as if he realized he'd been unfair.

This was like the silence between my father and me, an impasse of wrongdoings, of talking each other into a distant corner. When I had called to tell my father I was leaving Texas, that I was going to make the best of my final years, he let the line run dead with silence. I was wordless, too. An accusation, I felt, on both our parts.

"What'd I tell you," he said, finally.

"I did what I could."

"You never took care of yourself."

"I took care of myself when I could," I said. "Back then it wasn't my job."

"You were an adult," he said. "Once you got old enough to know you were sick, you had to be."

"But you weren't," I said coldly. "You were never responsible."

He was quiet again. He knew that I was right about this. There were doctors and summer camps that children with diabetes went to, places my mother, on her own, couldn't afford. He refused to help, believing I could manage on my own.

"Jake's a smart boy," my mother would say. "He needs this."

"He's so smart," my father would say, "let him figure it out himself."

I wrote my father notes, stuffed with brochures filled with information on the summer camps. In my imagination the camps were more about having fun, about canoeing and fishing, about learning the woods. Though I think my father loved me, he wouldn't be reminded of my frailty, of what had grown between us all. He had never responded to my letters about the summer camps.

But in our silence there on the phone line, the weight of guilt was being cast back and forth, gathering power, and reaching further back into our past.

"I was a child," I said, finally. I could hear my father's breathing gather and leave.

For a long time he said nothing and then, "Good-bye."

I told my mother this and she cried. She said she was crying for all of us, but mostly for my father because, she said, he was too stupid to understand much of anything.

"I am grieving," she said, "the way you grieve for an animal that dies."

I put my arms around her and felt how small her body had become over the years. Her hair was thin, wispy, gray. It brushed my cheek. Still, her arms were taut with muscle, the runnel of her back, distinct. I knew then what I'd missed at camp, what had worked its way between my father and mother, between them and me: The fine line dividing the living and the dead, the breathing and the dying. Guilt can swell, form a swift current that runs between the two. My parents sensed the consequence of loss, while I was finally reaching the point where I felt weightless.

I had known this, but had only just recognized it in the silence between Pate and me. I offered him a slice of orange. He refused.

"There's a lot going on here," he said, finally. He placed his hand on the cover of the binder.

"Not so much," I said.

"Your father is a brick," Pate said.

"Dense," I said, "that's for sure."

"I mean you want to make something of him," he said. "You carry him around—"

"Maybe we're both bricks," I said.

"You want to be self-reliant," he said. "Hold things up on your own."

"That's how we all should be," I said.

"It doesn't work that way," Pate paused. "You have to work with what you have."

"What do I have?"

"You have Jess," Pate said, pausing to gather his thoughts. He didn't continue. He reached for his Thermos.

I thought of Jess at home working on those knots. I glanced over my shoulder at the river. "Where's your rod?" I said, knowing I'd not seen one in the truck. "Let's get going."

"Didn't bring one," he said. "Thought I'd coach."

"Time's wasting," I said. My rod was resting on the tailgate. I slipped into my vest and hooked the creel over my shoulder. "Ready?" I said, heading to retrieve my rod.

Pate carried his Thermos and the binder to the river's edge. I stood beside him as he studied the water. "It's running better than 240 per," he said.

"What's that mean?" I asked.

"Strong water," he said. "You'd better watch your step." Pate set his things on a large rock where they'd be safe. He pulled the bill of his cap down and shielded his eyes from the sunlight. "Let's walk down the bank a ways," he said. "See the flat just below this riffle?" he said, pointing downstream.

"Yeah."

"You'll want to drop a nymph out there," he said, pointing again, "and let the current carry it past those boulders that stand out of the water."

"Good deal."

"The fish are in the eddies."

Pate negotiated the rocky bank easily, each step sure, balanced. I became anxious, worried that the riverbed would be as difficult to walk on as the shoal. My stride was clumsy, an uneven gait, that was, in each moment, closer to a fall than a balanced stride. We hiked twenty yards downriver before Pate paused and took his first step into the water. I watched as he carefully moved out into the current, the water cuffing, white at his knees. He motioned for me to follow.

My first steps took me in up to my knees. Already the current tugged at my legs, the waders sucking close to my calves and the cool of the water seeping through and up into my body. Each step became heavier, more difficult, my boots and waders saturated, as I moved out into the river. Pate stayed ahead of me, giving me a path to follow along the uneven stone bed. There were places where the bottom dipped invisibly away, revealing nothing but the dark surface of the water. The sight of these deep pools caused me to pause, to study my path ahead so that I was certain I wasn't headed off onto a shelf, where I'd have to backtrack. I felt I couldn't turn around. The wading became increasingly precarious the farther I went, and my only hope was to keep moving. I took small steps, finding a perch on each stone before looking for my next foothold. Leading, Pate's motion seemed mellifluous.

"Take it slow," he yelled back to me. He was standing thigh-deep in the current, just below the riffle.

I paused. Along the bank a haze hung in the branches of the trees, spreading the light softly into the shallow water. Out farther, where I stood, the light took angles, sharp and glinting. Above us hawks glided on the air that lifted out of the gorge. Briefly, it occurred to me how much I wished Jess was there to watch from the bank, to remember this, so that she could recall it for me, like a story, and then I'd be able to make sense of it. The thought faded in an instant, washed away by the air and the light and the water coming down in a thick, warm cover. I focused on making it to where Pate was waiting.

"Let's see your fly box," he said when I finally stood next to him, unsteady, struggling to secure my feet. I unzipped a pocket on my fly vest and handed him the box.

"I got a Quill Gordon on," I paused. "Early season fly," I said, as a half question.

"You can try it," Pate said with a slight hesitation in his voice. "You'll probably have to go wet. A nymph." He reached over and hooked a March Brown on the fleece patch that hung from the shoulder of my vest. "Try this if what you have doesn't work."

I nodded.

"I'll get you started," Pate said, reaching for my rod. He dropped the fly and leader into the water and let the current take it downstream. Quickly he fed line off the reel and then with a gentle, even motion he lifted the fly off the water. On his back stroke he stripped line off the reel with a sharp yank, the sound of the reel drag changing from a click into a rich whir that settled in me a fine, comfortable feeling. With his forward stroke he let the slack line shoot outward and load the rod tip with power for the next back cast. I closed my eyes and listened to the sound of Pate's false casting, the line whispering above us, the stroke gaining power and slowing as the line reached farther out, the reel, its drag resistant, clicking, and Pate's breathing as it matched his effort to load the rod, carrying the fly out into the current. I could smell whiskey on the breeze.

"You don't want the line to drag the fly," Pate said. I opened my eyes. "Like that," he said, pointing out to where the fly was drifting on the water. "Mend the line," he said, flipping the rod tip in a rolling motion. "The fly has to look natural." He handed me the rod.

"OK," I answered. I drew some line in and began my back stroke. The fly lifted overhead in a weak loop, and in an attempt to gather more power I began my forward stroke too soon. The cast fell short, only a few yards out in front of us.

"You'll get it," Pate said, patting me on the shoulder. "Bring in some line and start with a small loop. Then let it shoot."

I had practiced casting for long enough to know what I was supposed to be doing. But the pull of the water against my waders made me uncertain, and I was afraid that shifting my strength into the cast would throw me off balance. I tried to relax. "All right," I said. I brought in about ten feet of line, letting the water pull the rest taut.

"Remember," Pate said. "Once things are in motion, you can't do much to change them. Start off right." He rested his hand on my shoulder.

I lifted my rod tip with a powerful sweep, accelerating the line overhead in a graceful arc, feeling the rod tip bow as the loop unfurled. I paused, then thrust the rod forward, sending the fly out over the water.

"Perfect," Pate said. "Damn perfect." He let his hand fall from my shoulder. We both watched the fly drift along the water's surface. "I think you're on your own," he said. "I'm headed upstream."

"Where to?" I asked, turning to watch him study the water. He was looking for the easiest path to the bank.

"To read," he answered. Pate planted his first step upstream and the current seemed to catch him by surprise. He shifted his weight against the river's tide, attempting to hold his balance, but he didn't have the resistance, and he dipped his left arm down into the water, catching himself on a submerged rock. I watched as he crouched motionless for a few seconds and then righted himself, his rolled-up shirt sleeve soaked, water sluicing down his forearm, back into the river.

I reached my hand out in his direction. "OK?" I asked.

"It's stronger than it looks," he said, looking upriver toward the gorge.

"Maybe you should go light on the coffee," I said, trying not to sound like a father.

"Work on your cast," he said, as if he hadn't heard me, as if nothing had happened. He looked off in the distance, toward the shore. "I'm fine," he said.

He began again, surefooted, hunched, wading steadily. My fly had drifted downstream below me, soaked, the line taut and pulling against the rod. I lifted the line into the air, paused, and then thrust forward, sending the fly away from me. I repeated the motion, false casting, the fly drying as it coursed through the air. With a pendulum motion, I counted the four-part cast, the rhythm, and then with the rod in front of me, a forward snap halted at one o'clock, I lowered the tip to present the fly. I watched the Quill ride the surface of the river and mended my line. I became aware only of the water, the constant change of the surface, the imminent possibility that a fish might rise and take the fly. I felt hope settle in me, high, like the peaked smell of camphor. I waited for the line to tighten, anticipated the feel of a trout struggling to free itself, the jittery pulse of its body trying to loosen the hook. Lifting the fly off the water again, I laid it out in front of me with a soft presentation. Watching the drift, I relaxed, feeling the coolness of the water through my waders and the warmth of the sunlight. The sky had cleared and the sun was directly overhead.

Upriver, Pate had made his way along a rock jetty. He was resting on a large boulder, his feet hanging down into the flow, and reading *The Book of Timothy*. I worked the slower moving water below the riffle, sometimes casting up into the rough current and letting the fly drift, slightly submerged, giving the line a slight twitch to imitate a struggling insect. I remembered what I had been told. Positioning myself, my feet steady, balanced against the current and the possible run of a fish, I located an area where the water went shallow and I could easily net and release.

With twenty or thirty casts, I exhausted the water I was fishing. I reeled in the Quill and tied on the March Brown Pate had selected. Below, the river swept down a gravelly run and then, a quarter mile farther, slackened into a bend. I decided it would be easier to wade to the bank and walk.

From the muddy lane I could see the river and judge how far downstream I was hiking. As I walked I felt awkward on land. I had grown used to standing in the river. Beneath the cover of trees the sound of the water, the sunlight, the shadows, all moved and changed with a rhythm that was soothing. A cool breeze collected in the shade. I paused, my breathing heavy, and turned. Pate was out of sight, a thick stand of birch between us. I wanted to think of Jess, my mother and father, but I couldn't. Nothing came to mind but the river. Above me in the branches birds chattered. I was alone and out between the trees I could see that I was halfway along the flat run of water. A knoll rose from the roadside, then descended to the rocks and the water. I stood at its crest, looked and saw Pate still seated on the boulder. I made my way to the rocky bank.

Cast from behind me, the shadows of trees reached out onto the water. From where I stood I saw that the run was deeper than it appeared from a distance. I waded into the shadows, the coolness of the day settling on my back, and worked my way out until I was in full light, the water at my waist. The current in front of me was swift, but I thought I could cast across it, mend my line, and find a fish along the far bank, resting in the inside eddy.

I dropped the nymph into the water. Several yards away from me, beneath the surface, I noticed that there were fish suspended above the rocky bed, ranging up and crosscurrent, then drifting downstream. They were dark, quick-moving ghosts. It wasn't the fish I saw, but their shadows on the river bottom. I cast, mended my line quickly, and far away the drift was bringing my fly into the clear water, sifted, and punched with fish. I felt nothing but the drift of the fly. I focused on my line, floating along the surface, looking to see if it would indicate the slightest change, if below, beyond my detection something was happening. On the water, shadows from the trees crept out onto the run.

I hauled line in, casting short into the quick water. In an instant I felt something, the least touch, and I drew back with the rod tip. There was resistance, but I wasn't sure if it was a fish or something along the bottom. At once, a spark ignited, ran like an electric current throughout my body. My hands trembled. I relaxed, hesitated, drew back again deciding it was a strike. But there was nothing. The fly could have drifted between two stones or maybe hooked on a frond. A trout may have sipped at the fly and I was late, indecisive about setting the hook. Thinking that I had, for a moment, gotten what I'd come for, my body relaxed, emptied, when I felt the line was slack. I leaned back against the current and paused. Around me the water beat onward and I could sense my blood, a pulse in my ears, flowing.

I was certain I had ruined this stretch of river. The fish were steady in the current, but none of them would strike again, if one had at all. Still, I lifted my rod with an abrupt tug, thinking I would try another cast into the run. With a hasty forward stroke the fly nicked the rod tip. I attempted to bring the fly back with a strong thrust, but with my next forward stroke the line lost all momentum and fell a few yards in front of me, the leader tangled around the line. I raised the rod tip and drew the bird's nest into my hand.

The fly had caught where the line and leader were shored with the blood knot. My poor casting had twisted the two together, the fly curving through tiny loops and then around and over and in between the smallest intersections of line and leader. I had created a mess that to my eye looked like the drawing of an atom I'd seen in schoolbooks as a child. I held the confusion in my hands, thinking I might try to unravel the knot. I ran my finger from the head of the fly down the leader, studying the path the thin line had taken. It was like tracing the course of an electron. The filament came together in unintelligible knots. In an instant I'd created this mess, but as I traced each entanglement back from the fly, I was dividing that instant, going backward in time. With each twist of line, each bond, I thought of how, as an extension of myself, the line, this atom, had become connected, a molecule, a knot, that ran deep in my blood. For a moment I held the line and leader in my hands. The water teemed past me and I relaxed, focusing on dark shapes that darted beneath the surface. I felt a weakness, a trembling in my arms and chest. My legs were tired. The barbed hook of the March Brown made undoing the tangle impossible. I would have to cut the leader off and tie another on.

It had gotten late. I let the current take the knotted line downstream and reached back for my creel. I unbelted the top, fished inside the plastic bag, feeling for the other orange Jess had packed. In the shadows the air had gotten chilly and, together with the cold water, had worked a stiffness into my fingers. Balanced against the current, I peeled the orange, fumbled with it, and felt a shiver run through my body. I tossed pieces of orange peel into the water and sucked the juice out of each slice. I chewed the tough pulp. A few yards from me I saw the slow-moving, dark ghost of a fish. There was a bulge on the water's surface and the trout swirled, rising and then drifting back. The fish held steady in the current. Again it tailed upstream, and in a lithe gesture sipped a fly from the surface. Rings drifted outward from this point. In the poor light, I could not see the flies riding past on the current. I stood motionless and watched as the fish drifted downstream again and then shifted farther out, midstream. I looked upward, traced the line of trees poised on the ridge that mounted behind the opposite bank. Sunlight was fiery in the high branches. I would remember this, the fish and the sunlight.

I ate the last of the orange and reached into my creel for the sandwich. When I finished, I knew I'd have to tie on another leader either with a blood knot or, as Pate had suggested, a surgeon's loop. That would take a while, but I figured I would have enough time to get in a few more casts before it was time to head back. Jess would be worried if Pate and I were late getting home.

My head hurt, a dull ache that settled behind my eyes. The constant glare of the sunlight had left its impression on me, but looking out, the river had gone cold, dark. Along the opposite bank I could see the water break frothy in the light. I studied the run, trying to detect the late afternoon hatch, mayflies or caddis.

"Jake!" I heard Pate call.

I looked and upstream he was in the water, off his feet and struggling as the current carried him down, between two boulders and then over a slight drop. Pate's head dipped under water and emerged again twenty yards from me, water pouring from the bill of his cap. He thrashed the water with one hand and in the other I saw that he was still holding the binder.

"Give me a hand!" he yelled.

Watching him, I didn't move. It was as if I wasn't certain I was really seeing him struggle. I felt calm, certain there was no danger. But when Pate called to me I realized he was too far out in the river for me to reach him. By the time he entered the run, the water level would be above his head and his waders would be filled.

"Try to get in closer!" I yelled to him. Carefully, I waded out farther to where the current ran at my chest. Fighting against the surge of water, I turned my back and leaned into the flow. There was nothing I could do to help Pate, and I knew if I tried we'd both be in trouble. "Can you get to me?" I called, back over my shoulder.

He didn't answer. Then I saw him, his boots tipping the surface, his body submerged, drifting past me, out of reach. I was able to see his face, expressionless, and his arms, paddling, pushing against the river bottom. He was fighting to get into the shallows, an eddy or shelf. Silently, he went past.

I shifted my weight, stepping sideways toward the bank. If Pate had a chance, if I was going to reach him, I would have to make it to land. Holding my rod high, each step I took was slow and balanced. My creel floated downstream from me, the strap tugging at my shoulder. The plastic bag with food slipped beneath the unlatched top and drifted away. I let the current take the creel, and I turned toward the bank and wallowed forward. In waist-deep water, I slipped, going face down into the river. Cold water filled my waders above the belt, and I could see dull light catching the shape of the tumbled bottom—white rocks worked like bone. The sound of the river was enormous, pressing against my ears. Angrily, I dug with my feet and caught the stone bottom. Pate was getting away from me, drifting farther downstream. The distance between us, the idea of it, was building up inside me, and I thought if he had just listened this wouldn't have happened. The cool breeze became cold. I floundered toward the bank, my body numb and sluggish. Evening had set in, the sky silvery, the sun hanging on the horizon.

The rocky bank was flat but then rose up into a small, craggy bluff. The washboard road ran along the edge, only a narrow shoulder between it and the drop-off. I slid my rod up and climbed the rocks on my hands and knees, digging into the soil, pulling away chunks of earth.

The lane veered off from the river, rising before settling again, close and following the bend downstream. I took to the ridge, running along the soft, crumbling shoulder, shifting into the trees where the land gave way too steeply to the water. I searched the folds of water, now completely blanketed in shadow. Sunlight was sharp against the far bank, the pale birches standing radiant. My legs tired, became clumsy in the soaked waders. Moving in the underbrush, amid the saplings, fallen branches, staghorn and fern, was difficult. The river ran thirty feet below the bluff. If Pate hadn't righted himself he would snag downstream at the bend. I took a line that carried me toward the road. I imagined what I might find when I caught up to Pate. Would he still be alive, breathing? What could I say if he was? The worst came to mind, and I didn't have a plan for getting him out, to the truck, to help. The road ahead descended toward the river, curved, opened up in the light, with no trees between the water and the muddy route.

There, in the opening, I got clear sight of the bend, the exposed, rocky shoal. A shallow riffle ran for a quarter mile, but there was no sign of Pate in the water or along the bank. Downstream, light glinted off the water. I followed the river, examining the shallows, from as far away as I could see, back to where I was standing. My breathing was heavy from hustling through the underbrush. I checked the riverbank again, first far out and then closer in.

"You looking for something?" I heard Pate say.

I turned and down the embankment, a few yards upstream, Pate was in the water, resting against a rock pile. "Son of a bitch," I said.

Pate began to laugh, a wheezy, moist, out-of-breath laughter that as it rolled built up tension inside me. I shuffled down the rocks toward him. "What'd I tell you?" I yelled. I stood over him, looking down at his limp body, his clothes soaked. His face and forearms were pink, sunburned. The black binder rested on his chest. "I told you," I said. Frustration seemed to rise from nowhere and settle along the heady, light pain behind my eyes. I had gone empty inside.

"You told me what?" Pate said with a soft, defiant tone. Water beaded on his face, dripped from his hair. He laughed again, shaking his head. "You think I planned this? You think this couldn't have happened to you?"

"It wouldn't have happened at all—"

"If what?" Pate interrupted. He tipped his soggy cap back on his head. "I slipped. My waders filled up."

"If you had a belt—"

"I don't." Pate stood up, water pouring off his body. He handed me the binder. "I'm finished," he said, bending over to empty water from his waders.

The jacket and pages were saturated, heavy in my hand. Pate walked up the bank, settled next to a boulder and put his feet up to let more water stream from his waders.

"You didn't do much," he said. "I could see you watching when I floated by."

"What could I do?" I said. "You were too far out. The current was too strong." I pointed upriver, somehow wanting to prove that I was helpless.

"There were some fish along that flat," he said. Pate cleared his throat and spit in the direction of the river. He shook his head. "I got a breath just down from you," he coughed, swallowed.

I could see on his face he was going through the event again, picturing it in his mind. I bent and began running my hands along his legs, pushing the water out the top of his waders. "I missed one." I stood up, looking out at the dark water. "Got my line in a mess."

"It happens," Pate suggested. "You have to keep your mind on what you're doing." He picked at his shirt, pulled it away from his skin, the chambray sticking close to his chest and arms. The afternoon was fading on us, and we were both getting cold.

GOOD AS ANY

"You're one to talk," I said. "You scared the hell out of me." I paused to think how I wanted to put my words together. The air was cool, hanging at the back of my throat. "You looked steady on your feet," I said, thinking of how I'd seen him wade out in front of me. I tried to conjure how he'd gone under. The idea was set against the notion I had of him. His experience, his way of speaking and moving, made it impossible for me to imagine what had taken place.

Pate stood and looked upstream. "This is a river," he said. "Anything can happen." He faced me, moisture caught in the lines along his forehead and beneath his eyes. "Deal with it."

"What happened?" I asked.

He turned and shimmied up the bank, his gait awkward, changed by his wet clothes. "It's behind us," he called down to me. "Let's go."

Staring past Pate, I focused on the pine and willow in the distance. Poised dark, a soft breeze caught among the high branches, the hillside, its depth, tree rising behind tree, appeared flat and contourless. The edges of my vision fluttered, a pattern like light on the riverbed. Pate was awash, his olive-colored waders bathed among the forest that stood behind him. A cool sweat ran down my back.

"We should be getting back to Jess," I said. "She'll worry."

"You going to make it?" Pate asked, holding out his hand.

"What was it like," I asked, "going down the river like that?"

"What's to tell?" he answered. "I'd either make it or I wouldn't. I didn't think about it. I did what I had to. Got to the surface and got air. Waited." He paused and looked in my direction.

We moved along the road in the softening light. I surveyed my body, searched the feeling in my arms and legs, the flickering of my sight, like looking for something on a distant horizon. I recalled how the trout had come to take a fly off the water's surface only an arm's-length away from me. The tremble of the rod with the slightest tension, the knotted line in my hands, came to me in a muted, half-forgotten way. Thoughts emerged, pressing outward. I resisted, wanting to stay conscious. I focused on the smallest details—a divot in the road, a willow snag, a scattering of chalk rock—concentrating until I came upon them, then looked ahead for another landmark. I measured the weakness in my muscles. The binder swung heavy in my hand. "There some of that bread left in the truck?" I asked, finally.

"You get enough to eat?" Pate asked.

"I could use something," I said. "It's been a long day."

"You didn't eat?"

"I ate."

"I saw your creel go downriver."

"Not everything."

"Enough?"

"I don't know."

I closed my eyes and tried not to think beyond the moment. But I thought of my father. I pictured his face, how he would have looked at me then, there, trudging up the muddy road. Pushing forward, hard, with each step, I struggled to keep my balance. I glanced ahead, where Pate was just cresting the hill. His movements shimmered in the barbed light that filtered through the trees. I felt as if we were within the shells of others, our bodies moving out of sync with our images. The numbness of my feet sloshing in the wading boots gave me the sense of walking in someone else's shoes. Each step seemed to empty a place inside me.

Pate waited at the top of the hill. "We're almost there," he said, taking the binder from my hand.

"I'll be fine," I said. The voice seemed to come from a far place, where it belonged to someone else. It was as if I was listening to a recording of myself made years before.

"You've got to make it," Pate said, putting his hand on my back. He laughed. "Jess'll kill me."

"You?" I said slowly. My speech was beginning to slur. The distance we had covered seemed immense. Pate paused to pick up my rod from the roadside.

"You shouldn't leave things laying around," he said as a joke. He wanted to keep me talking. "How was the fishing?" he asked.

"The time of my life," I said. I looked down the hill and tried to focus on the river. The water cut the land, a black ribbon laid between hills. Walking became a trick of balance, a quick shifting of weight, of falling forward and catching myself. My body felt like it had aged. But I couldn't tell if I had grown young or old. The only comfort was the jolt each step sent into my body.

We neared the truck and Pate ran ahead. He started the engine. I closed my eyes and smelled the exhaust.

"I've got you," he said. He put his arm around my waist and helped me alongside the truck, the cold metal against my side. I buckled onto the seat and Pate lifted my feet into the floorboard. He slammed the door.

"Where's the bread?" I called to him.

Pate slipped into the seat next to me and fumbled with the sack. He handed me a piece of bread, a small chunk no larger than my fist. It was hard and dry against my lips. I began to chew. Each bite seemed to grow in my mouth and my jaw ached. I swallowed, forcing the bread down. Pate started the truck and tugged it into gear. He swerved wide, turning out into the brush before bringing the truck around onto the washboard surface. He hit the gas and we began to ramble down the road.

"Where's the rest?" I asked, holding my hand out with what I had left.

"That's all there is," he said. His hands worked, turning the wheel, with the truck cutting through the ruts, veering from one side of the lane to the other.

"That's all?" My hands trembled.

"I didn't know you'd need it," he yelled. "I can't always be looking out for you." The smell of whiskey and river water filled the truck. I looked at him, his face pink, his hat tilted back. I watched him concentrate on the road. It was as if I didn't recognize his face or his hands on the wheel. The road dipped down below the ridge and the cab filled with darkness. I looked and the river was no longer visible. We were nearly to the gorge. The truck jerked and lifted over swells. The frame groaned, scraped, where the road bottomed out. Pate glanced at me. "Eat," he yelled.

I chewed the crusty bread and, for a moment, sensed I had stopped falling inward. "We don't have much time," I said. I leaned forward and swallowed the last of the bread.

"Hold on," Pate said. The truck heaved back and forth. I closed my eyes and leaned into the sway, feeling for a moment as if I was riding over waves.

I opened the glove box. A few maps spilled out. I reached in and felt around, hoping to find a candy bar, anything I could eat.

"There's nothing in there," Pate said.

Light spilled into the truck. The road rose and leveled out. I kneeled in the floorboard and searched beneath the seat. I felt the rough vinyl indentations soupy with river water, and the cool, greasy metal of supports and springs. Leaning forward, my face touched against the seat. I paused, the smell of something sweet and old rose from the tears in the cushioned fabric. I remembered the trout and Jess.

"Hang on," Pate said. "We're almost to the road."

I rested my face against the warm, vinyl seat. I could smell the river, the binder that was soaked and on the seat between us. I reached and felt the damp, warped cover. The cardboard was limp and pasty. I opened the cover and the pages were matted, splotched with ink that had run. I climbed into the seat and held the binder in my lap. The fibers gave way soundlessly as I tore off the corner of a page and put it into my mouth. The damp pulp began to disintegrate and turn thready. I gagged. The faint taste of orange lingered in my throat. I peeled off another page.

Through the windshield I saw the black silhouettes of trees. We crested a hill and the late afternoon sun fell across the dust-streaked glass in a brilliant, opaque glare. Pate hit the brake and leaned forward. We couldn't see the road ahead. He lowered his side window and the cab filled with a cold breeze. I closed my eyes and continued to chew. I remembered the trout. The nausea drained from me and I swallowed, the ink bitter on my tongue. Pate edged the truck forward, and I heard the shocks grating and my fly rod snapping rhythmically against the bed of the truck. And below us, the river pushed along its banks.

Winter
Island

1.

I was the first to see a pig fly. It happened the summer the heat
wave lasted for sixty-two days and more than one-tenth of the
chicken population in the state died. Their swollen bodies, unable
to sweat, would burst. The heat hung over the town and the fields
in a haze. Cows drank from fire hoses that were stretched across
the brown earth. During the day people gathered at the Village Co-
op to drink soda in the air-conditioning. At night most went to
Winter Island and swam in the river. They stood at the water's
edge, their skin dry and taut, air cooled. Above, the stars were dim.

Every morning I took the bus into Miller's Falls to work at the
paper mill. I got up and drank coffee in the dark, a small warm
breeze coming in across the kitchen table. The neighbor's house
would start to pale as the first light reached over the hills into the
valley. I sometimes thought about catching the bus but not getting
off when it stopped outside the gates, where the stacks blew a
wretched smell high up over Miller's Falls.

After coffee, I walked a mile down the highway, across the

bridge that stretched over the slow-moving river, into Buckland where I waited for the bus. The stop was in front of an old house, where every morning a lilting jazz melody came through the open windows, and the white sheers lifted up and out like the skirt of a dancer. Standing there I watched the blue-black morning sink down below the glow of the white farmhouses. Across the street from the stop was an open field where they used to grow potatoes and corn and behind it a hill reached upward, lined with trees, and beyond that was the river and the town.

Trucks loaded down with tree trunks rumbled past me along the road, headed up to the mill where later I would have to deal with invoices and direct men where to bear the different qualities of wood. But this particular morning I was early, before the trucks, and there was nothing but the beginning light and the music of John Coltrane. I looked back over the trees toward the river and watched the sky turn powder blue. Then, something indistinct emerged from the haze, began to take form. A pig glided smoothly across the sky. It had tapered wings that reached out from its body in a natural way. I traced its path against empty space and then it crossed in front of the mountains. Somehow, against the brown, jagged terrain, the pig became even more pleasing to me, as if I were seeing something that should be happening. The pig glided along for some time before disappearing below the tree line.

I was not accustomed to seeing pigs fly. I have seen a dog back into the corner of the yard and then run full speed around the house, jumping high and gracefully into the air, attempting to make it over the fence. I've seen cows, horses, and even pigs jump and bang themselves into fence posts and the sides of barns. Once, a cow managed to clear a low-standing fence. Old-timers claim it's the pesticides that are giving animals the notion that they can fly. But, in all this, I'd never seen an animal take flight.

I let the first two buses go by without getting on. I wanted to see if another pig would rise up above the trees. The sun came up over the hills and the sky began to thicken with the dull haze. Down the road heat began rising off the pavement, and I was sweating heavily when the next bus came. I'd watched the skies intently—nothing.

———

For three days I got to the bus stop early and was late for work. In the evenings I cooked meat and vegetables out on the grill and kept watch on the skies. Danna called and asked me over to her place one night, and I told her that I hadn't gotten the truck fixed. I told her the casings were still leaking, and this was true. She said she'd come over and get me when she was done with her work for the day and then bring me back home later.

In the early summer Danna worked in the fields at Simms's Farm picking berries—first strawberries and then raspberries. But the heat had done away with that, drying up the crops, and she'd found a job doing piece work. She cut and sewed patterns—stars, moons, all kinds of shapes—and sent them off to a place that used them to make finished products. Flags and pillows I guessed. During the rest of the year she taught at the elementary school in a town south of here. In the evenings, when she was not doing her grading, she liked to paint or read books about the American West, and she seemed to enjoy having me around.

That evening, after we'd put away the dishes, we rested in the dingy gold-and-brown easy chairs that sat angled across from each other, a table between them. A reading lamp in the front room reflected light off the faded, papered walls. It was too hot to paint, or read, or even talk. We just listened to the night coming on.

When Danna and I first met years before, I took Polaroids of her nude. She used them for her paintings. There are paintings of her, with wet hair, towels brushing the inside of her thighs, shadows only partly hiding the faint shimmering of her breasts and other parts, all over this valley above people's couches and in their bathrooms and bedrooms. Danna has some of them hanging in her hallway and in the unused bedroom. Even now, she sometimes asked me to take some photos. But that evening we mostly sat and let the night dwindle, the radio tuned to a jazz station.

"Do you need some photos?" I asked after we'd been sitting silently for some time.

"No," she said without looking up from her book, something on Lewis and Clark.

"I saw a pig fly," I told her.

"A pig?" she said.

"It was only a few hundred yards from me," I paused. "It was a pig."

"Where?" she asked.

"Over Simms's land."

Danna had a way of taking everything in and not reacting. It was her way of sustaining herself, she once said. Keeping all the energy that came her way, good and bad, and letting it equal itself out. She looked back down at the book in her lap and continued reading for a few minutes. Charlie Parker was on the radio, and as I sat listening with my head resting on the back of the chair, I let thoughts play in my mind.

I'd had the impulse on more than one morning to catch the bus and take it past Miller's Falls. Just sit in my seat next to the window and stare out at the half-empty parking lot, at the men going to work with their lunches and hard hats, and wait as the engine idled in front of the mill for five minutes and then the hydraulics would exhale, the doors would close, the brakes would whine, and the bus would head north and west down the French King Highway and take me away from the valley.

But I was afraid to leave. I knew that I'd miss what had brought me here. The first thing I'd do is get off the bus and make a call to Danna to let her know that I was all right. Then I'd probably call the mill and tell them I fell asleep on the bus and that I'd take the next one back and be to work by noon. And then I'd do just that.

I opened my eyes and looked at Danna. She was smiling at me. "What?" I said.

"Nothing. I'm just looking at you."

"Is everything OK?" I asked.

"Yeah," Danna said. "Something wrong?"

"We've been kind of . . ." I thought for a moment, "quiet."

"I'm fine," she said. "The heat just takes everything out of me." She smiled again. "There something you want to do?"

"I don't know," I said. I felt reluctant to mention what had been on my mind. "Have you ever thought about moving away from here?" I asked, finally.

Danna looked puzzled. "No," she said. "Not really, I don't guess."

She dropped the book on the floor and shifted in her seat so that she was facing me. A breeze came in the window and brushed a few strands of hair across her cheek. It was a damp, humid night and I thought we might get rain.

"Why do you ask?" she said.

"I don't know," I paused. "I've thought of it."

Danna got up off the chair, reached over, and turned off the radio. The light faded from the dial and for a moment Danna paused, with one hand resting on the edge of the armoire, the other on the arm of the chair. It was as if she had been caught doing something embarrassing.

"You haven't worked on a painting in a long time," I said. "Maybe we could take some time off and go somewhere together."

"Money's tight," she said. "It's just too hot to paint right now." She pulled her hair back behind her ears. Out the window I could see the moon coming up over the mountain. It wasn't going to rain.

"I know I don't really want to leave," I said. "But the urge is still there."

Danna leaned forward, resting her elbows on her knees and then her face in the palms of her hands.

"We should go," I said. "It's getting late and it's a drive."

She smiled, as if my saying this was an invitation.

2.

The first Fourth of July I spent in the valley, Stan Olszewski and I had been talking, sitting on the steps of Summit House. From the top of Clark Mountain the sky was blue, clear, and the valley sat calm below us. I had only been in the valley for six months and Stan was the only friend I had. I'd been traveling, on my way out west to visit some friends, and I stopped for the night. We met at a bar called The Spoke and for most of the night he kept a frown on and tapped his foot. He didn't talk much. Stan was a farmer then and, as he tells it now, he drank too much.

We were just getting to know each other. As we sat on the deck, he told me about his son, Jason, who was a musician, and his wife, Ashley, who had died of cancer six years before. Stan's face was expressive, it showed delight and sadness equally, with a nuance in each detail that he spoke.

"You know mornings you catch the bus right in front of the house where my son lives," Stan had said. Then he got quiet, concentrated on the view—the patchwork of farmland. Below us you could see a tractor working the land.

Stan stood up. "There's someone you should meet," he said. "She's over by the grill." He looked down at me. "You stick around."

Stan walked off into the crowd of people I didn't know. I did not meet people easily. There was always an awkwardness about me, an unwillingness to speak that I let go on too long. I'm not sure if I made people uncomfortable or if it was the other way around. But so far that afternoon, I'd only met a few of the valley's people. Stan had introduced them as the Co-op regulars. He'd said I'd have a chance to meet them soon in their own environment. I smiled to each of them before they drifted off into the crowd.

I stood up and looked out to see if I could find where Stan had wandered. Then I began walking the deck that surrounded Summit House. The building was perched on the edge of the mountain, one side extending over a steep drop. I stood at the railing. Below me, the place spread open and rolled to the west. I felt a hollowness in my stomach. I wondered if I'd ever find this place home.

I turned and walked to one of the large windows of the house. Inside it was dark. There were a few scattered chairs, and I wondered what the house was used for, if it was used at all, and what the people must look like wandering across the slick hardwood floor.

"You dance?" I heard a woman's voice say from behind me.

I turned. "Only my left foot dances," I said.

"Danna," she said, smiling, extending her hand.

"Gabe," I said, reaching out. Her hand was strong, rough. It was not like the rest of her at all. She was thin, with olive skin, and long, curled brown hair. When she smiled, the corners of her mouth crimped. Her face was so smooth it made you want to reach out and touch it to be sure it was real.

"I could teach one of your feet to be the right," she said.

"I have the feeling Stan's up to something," I said.

"Perhaps," she said. "Or maybe I am."

"Should I know you?"

"I've seen you around," she said. "Stan says you're new."

"New?" I said. "I haven't been new in a long time."

"We'll see about that," she said. "You want a beer?"

"Sure," I said. "I guess."

"Have a seat," she said, pointing to the steps. "I'll get us a couple. When I get back, the lessons begin."

She strolled away, confident and leisurely. She returned with a beer for each of us. "So what brings a guy like you to a place like this?" she asked, handing me the cool can, the tab peeled back.

"I don't know," I said. "I was passing through. I met Stan and decided to hang around for a few days."

"It's been more than a few days."

"I'm a procrastinator."

"We can't have that," she said.

"So how long have you been here?" I asked.

"All my life."

"All your life," I repeated. "What keeps a woman here all her life?"

"There's plenty," she said, looking out over the valley. She lifted the palm of her hand. "The place. The land. The wildlife."

"You like wildlife?"

"I love animals," she said. "I like to think of this place as my little paradise."

"Why here?"

She looked at me and smiled. "I've always had a fondness for it."

I looked out at the hills.

"I carry a shovel in the trunk of my car," she said. "When I can, if I see an animal killed on the road, I bury it. Everything needs a decent place to rest."

"That's nice," I said. A sense of joy built up inside me at the thought of her doing this. I imagined her bending into the work, her hands on the shovel, her thoughts on something other than herself. "So where do you live?" I asked.

"I used to have a cabin," she said. She tilted her head back, took a drink. "I built it myself."

"You built a cabin?"

"Don't sound so surprised," she said, reaching over and slapping me on the leg. "It's not that hard. I like to know things. How to do them."

"So what happened?"

"It burned," she said. "Propane. I lost everything. Now I live in a house up in the hills."

I imagined the house was rough, just the essentials, everything in its place—a chair, a couch, a few paintings, landscapes, on the walls.

"Listen," she said. "Would you like to go to dinner sometime?"

"You do know what you want," I said.

"Well. It's like this with people," she said, pausing. She looked me in the face. "Am I going to have to tempt you, or are you going to tempt me?"

Her saying this took the breath out of me. I looked at her, studied her face, the smooth and seemingly endless plane of olive skin, and then out at the blue sky. It was the beginning of a long and breezy summer.

3.

Danna often drove me home late at night, down the bending road. With the windows down we listened to the wind through the trees, and sometimes we stopped along the side of the road to take in the sound of the crickets and the frogs. We tried to imagine the constellations, pointing at all the wrong stars and making up names and telling stories about gods and heroes that never existed.

It had been five years since Danna and I met. Still, I'd spent less than a week's worth of nights at her place. She sleeps so easily, in a quiet and deep way that makes me angry. I cannot sleep. I wrestle with the quiet, and my mind gets cluttered with thoughts that don't even belong to me—problems, jobs, and people that I don't even know, will never have to know. I found this place because I wanted to get away from the city and all the people I was not fit to live with. I could not stand their lives.

So at night, I went home and lay awake in bed. As soon as I was out of Danna's presence, I felt alone in the world. I went barren inside. I was given, sometimes, to self-hatred, to feeling that I had no purpose, no feeling, no reason to live. Then, I would laugh at myself, at how ridiculous my thoughts had become. I would toss in bed, half sleeping, thinking of extremes, of taking my own life in one moment, laughing at how foolish this was in another. I would lie on my back and listen. The ceiling worked with mice running above me in the attic. They chewed on the wiring in the walls. And in the constant, delicate noise I fell asleep.

It was, as they say, a dead man's sleep—deep, black, and without dreams. When I first moved to the valley and took the job at the mill, I dreamed of directing trucks loaded down with white spruce, fir, and red maple, trees thirty yards long and five feet in diameter. We had to cut them before putting them into the chipper. I filled out invoices and kept track of the amount of coniferous and deciduous timber we brought in; and, though I never did it in real life, I watched over the vertical digesters as chips of wood were fed in by conveyor belts and dumped into the soda. Sometimes the sound of steam being blown into the digester woke me up. I'd lie awake in bed and listen for the mice, but by then they had settled down. I couldn't drift off to sleep again, so I sat at the kitchen table and looked out over the fields.

In winter, I sometimes put on my clothes and went outside and stood in the falling snow. Or I walked along the edge of the road and the deadened sound of my boots breaking through the fresh powder lulled me toward tiredness. I walked a quarter mile and then headed back to the house. The snow blowing out across the fields like ghosts reminded me of something that I couldn't quite remember, but I was comfortable with the feeling that I was the only one awake in the valley, wandering along the road like someone homeless and not caring about anything. I kicked the snow out of my boots and left them just inside the door. The fluorescent light over the sink flickered and dropped a cold green hue over the kitchen linoleum, and I rattled pans getting the kettle out to boil water for tea. I drank a cup of hot tea in the den and looked at the oak wainscoting, as if the patterns in the wood were some kind of cuneiform. Then I slipped back into bed and, as I warmed, I was able to sleep.

But my sleep now was empty and useless. I sometimes lay awake all night, or if I did sleep it wasn't like rest at all. After weeks of this, my body would give in and I'd drift off into a rigid slumber, pressing my body into the bed and pillows.

After a rugged, tiresome night I would go into work the next day and face the truckloads of trees, which weren't perfect and seemed to be getting smaller each year. It wasn't like my dreams at all. The grade of wood was almost always mediocre, and the number of different kinds of trees we were getting was fewer. I ran computer projections, which told us what time of the year we got maximum yield and what time of the year we could plan major repairs to the equipment. There were several weeks when trees came to us no bigger around than a man's thigh. Those we ran through a barking drum and kept in storage piles. That was what we were doing now, mostly, with the drought and a few forest fires taking out a lot of timber. There was little for me to do but sit up in my office and look out the window at the slow growing stock of pulp wood.

———

Sometimes after work, when the truck was running or if I could borrow Danna's car, I drove out along Cave Hill Road, which cut along the height of the mountains that looked down over the valley, and stopped in at the Co-op. It was set in an opening snug against the road, and people gathered there from the surrounding three towns and talked.

The Co-op was an unpainted clapboard building with a corrugated metal roof. Along the front there was a porch with benches and an ice machine; posters were stapled to the walls for lost animals and used cars for sale.

But inside it wasn't what you'd expect. Finished pine floors ran the length of the building, except toward the end where it opened up into a high ceiling room with a terra-cotta tile floor and tables where you could sit and read the paper while having coffee. Set in the gable, a fan-shaped window let light fall in on the books and papers that were laid out on a long table, and the late afternoon shadows cut across the paintings and the stained glass hanging on the walls. Danna had a still life on the wall. They wouldn't hang one of her nudes there for everyone to contemplate while reading about the outside world. All the local arts and crafts people got their chance to display their work in this room.

The store itself had three tiers of Plexiglas containers running along one wall. They held all sorts of lentils, beans, and nuts. The shelves were stocked with all-natural foods and there were fresh vegetables stacked in a refrigerated bin next to the register. In one corner there was a shelf lined with videos for rent, and next to that was a paperback book exchange where people could trade off their books for ones they hadn't read. I'd been through most of the books that seemed to circulate.

A group of regulars collected at the Co-op every afternoon: Horace Felder, the store manager; Marv Houston, the owner of the Co-op; Frank Simms, the Sheriff; Stan, who now owned cattle; and, though not lately, Clifford Simms, Frank's brother and the owner of the berry farm where Danna worked summers. Frank called him Cliff; everyone else called him Simms. There were more that came and went, but it was a sure thing to find these men standing around drinking sodas and talking on the front porch or, if it was too hot, inside in the air-conditioning.

"Gentlemen," I said as I walked in and the door shut behind me.

"Hey, Gabe," Horace said, standing at the register ringing up candy and drinks for a couple of kids. They giggled about his harelip. This never bothered Horace. He just smiled, accentuating the flaw.

Stan, Frank, and Marv were sitting around a table off in the side area. Stan was shuffling newspapers around on the table, looking for something to read.

"What's the news?" I said to Stan.

"This is all old news," he said. "Paper's been sitting around here for months."

"How are you?" asked Frank. Frank didn't wear a badge and he didn't carry a gun. His family had been living in the valley for generations and because of this, people gave him respect. When he had to go out on a call, he went in regular clothes, and whatever it was that was going on stopped when he got there. Only strangers might give Frank trouble, but not many people came and stayed long enough for that to happen.

I got a Coke and sat down at the end of the table. "I'm fine," I said to Frank. Marv was busy going through some business mail and looking at his books. "Business holding up?" I asked, trying not to disturb him.

"Yeah," he said. "Fine."

"Wow," Stan said. "Look here." He pointed to a news article. "Last spring a college professor and his buddy almost died fishing the river down below the gorge in Westfield. One almost drowned and the other one saved his life, then flipped out. A diabetic, it says."

"Now there ain't enough water in that river to carry a fish," Frank said. "I took a trip down that way last week to do a little checking on some things. River is almost dry that far south."

"Say, Frank." I paused and took a sip of my drink. "How's your brother?"

"Cliff's fine," Frank said. "But he's taking things kind of hard."

"Danna's not been down to work," I said.

"He's lost most of his berries," Frank said. "Drought's killing him."

Stan and Marv agreed. "He's been in a few times," Marv said. "His truck was full of all kinds of things. PVC pipe, plastic sheeting, rope. Trying to save the last of his crops, I guess. Took some vegetables, some meat, and a couple of chickens. On credit."

Horace walked in and began sweeping the floors. "He's really quiet from what I can tell," he said. "I offered to come by and help out. He said stay away. Kinda put me out."

Frank shook his head. "He can be that way."

"Anything unusual going on lately?" I asked.

"What do you mean?" Frank asked.

"Like around town," I said. "Any trouble?"

"Not really," he said. "Why?"

"Get some current papers in here," Stan said to Horace, interrupting. Then he looked at Marv and raised his eyebrows.

"I saw something odd over at Simms's place the other morning," I said to Frank. "While waiting on the bus," I added.

"I got books to do," Marv said, picking up his work to go. "All you people yakking."

"See you," Frank said to him.

Stan and I raised our hands to acknowledge his leaving. He usually left us this way, in the middle of a conversation, and went into the back to take care of business. The door opened and Neal Barrett, my boss from the mill, came in.

"I'm pretty certain I saw a pig flying over his land," I said to Frank.

"He's been down," Frank said. "Acting kind of funny."

"I hear he may lose the place," Stan added. "Mortgaged out."

"I don't think you saw a pig," Frank interrupted. He took a sip from his can.

"No," I said. "It was a pig."

"Flying?" Frank said.

Stan was looking up from the paper at both of us. He didn't seem to mind the idea of a flying pig. He got up and got another soda from the refrigerator. Horace had rung up Neal's purchase and slipped it into a bag.

"See you at work," Neal called to me as he left.

Stan looked at me and shook his head, smiling.

"Cliff comes down to the island sometimes and swims at night with us," Frank said. "He didn't say anything about it."

"I'm just saying what I saw."

The late afternoon sun was coming through the high window, sharp across the room. A dark shadow hollowed out Danna's painting that hung above the table, and it showed dust that had collected on the glass and the beveled edges of the frame. I stood up and wiped a paper napkin along the frame.

"We'll see," said Frank. "I'll keep an eye out." He got up and threw his drink in the trash. "Well, it's time I got home for dinner. I'll see you gentlemen at the island around nine."

"Sure thing," Stan said.

I nodded good-bye to him. Stan looked at me for a moment and then began looking through a more recent newspaper that Horace had dropped on the table in front of him.

"You coming out for a swim tonight?" Stan said over the top of the paper.

"I don't know," I said. I finished up my Coke and from the light that was coming in the window, I knew I should be getting back to Danna with her car.

Danna and I didn't usually go out to Winter Island in the evening to swim, though since the heat wave, it had become the custom of the Co-op regulars to gather and wade in the shallow water of the river. Everyone talked and swam in the pale dusk.

"Take care of your cattle," I said to Stan as I headed out the door.

"Trying," he said, smiling.

———

On the way home from the Co-op I decided that Danna and I might go out to the island for a change. Maybe swim. Or have a beer and socialize a little. The flying pig had been on my mind. Some company would do me good. But when I pulled in the driveway at Danna's, she was standing over the barbecue grill.

"It's the last of the steaks," she said as I walked up.

I took in a deep breath. "Smells good," I said. Standing behind her, I put my arm around her waist and kissed her on the cheek. Fresh vegetables were cooking, wrapped in foil, and Danna was brushing sauce onto the meat.

"Want to go down to the island tonight?" I asked.

Danna closed the lid on the grill. "We can," she said.

I followed her over to the side of the house and watched while she ran water from the garden hose on the platter she'd brought the steaks out on, the blood washing clean. She put her thumb over the nozzle and sprayed water out over the flower beds.

"This place is going to dry up and blow away if we don't get rain," she said. "Too damn hot."

"What'd you have in mind for tonight?" I asked, knowing she didn't really want to go swimming. She seemed settled in for the night—watering along the foundation of the house and the hedges and then showering the grass.

"I've been thinking," Danna said. She paused for a moment and settled back on her heels. She handed me the platter and reached down to turn off the water. "About what you said last night." She straightened up and put her hands in the back pockets of her jeans. "I'd go with you. If you were asking."

My first inclination was to say, "What about the pig?" "What do you mean?" I asked instead. I tried to sort out what we'd discussed the night before.

"Go with you," she said. "Wherever . . ."

"I can't leave," I said without thinking. "I've got the mill." I held the plate out in front of me carefully, as if I were offering hors d'oeuvres.

Danna rested her arms across her stomach. "You could move in here then," she said, taking the platter from me and starting off toward the grill.

She walked away and I imagined her smiling, not because she was happy or hurt by the fact that we'd never talked about this possibility, but merely from the relief of having said how she felt. I followed her over to the grill and stood there while she put the steaks and vegetables on the platter.

"This valley is no place to stay," she said before putting the lid down over the fire.

I said, "I'll think about it."

"Let's eat," she said. She looked at me and for a moment it seemed something had been decided. She was saying good-bye, I thought.

4.

This summer was different than any that had ever come to the valley. The skies were cloudless and the heat was being beaten and lifted upward from the depths of the earth by the constant, harsh sun. The raw dirt along the edge of the fields was hot to the touch, and I wondered if the molten core of the earth wasn't eating its way up through the mantle and the crust.

Stan had the fire department come out twice a day to hose down his cattle. He'd already lost a few. They crumpled down under the blankets of thick air and he knelt beside them with a bucket of water, rubbing their faces with wet towels until their eyes became distant and dry and he couldn't watch them any longer. When we talked about this, Stan's own eyes seemed to tear up.

I felt bad for him, and I mentioned that the Harpers' chickens had started exploding. They had a place not far from the Co-op, up higher where the air was cooler. Still, in the midday sun, the chickens walked around pecking at the ground and then suddenly exploded. It was like the muffled sound of a tire blowing out.

Sometimes when I had to spend money to get my truck fixed or something else came up, I stole a chicken from Harper. I made chicken and dumplings or fried it, and I'd have dinner for a week. But now they were losing more than ten a day and, with them falling over dead, it didn't seem right to pilfer. I told Stan about taking one of the dead ones home for dinner.

"They're no good for eating," I said. "All blown up inside. Their parts spilling poisons."

"That so," he said, trying to hold back a laugh.

We looked at each other, started smiling, and then we both laughed. It was just me and him sitting across from each other at the Co-op during the middle of the day. I was drinking a beer and Stan had a glass of iced tea.

"You seen that pig again?" he asked. He took a sip of tea.

"Not since the one time," I said. "I've been watching for it."

Stan frowned and began to tap his foot. This was something I'd seen him do before when he was trying to figure things out.

"Seen Simms?" I asked.

"Not in a while," he answered. He had both hands around the glass of tea. Moisture ran down the glass and beaded up across his knuckles. "You and Danna ought to come down to the island and swim sometime."

"We will," I said. "I've been trying to get her to go. Maybe this week."

"We'd all love to see you," Stan said.

I finished up the last of my beer and fingered the corner of a newspaper that was on the table between us. A headline said that we'd had thirty-nine days of drought. Another headline said to expect rain soon.

"What do you suppose that pig is all about?" I said.

"Don't know," he replied. "Don't know."

———

Danna's piece work was not bringing in much money, and I was beginning to skip days at work. Part of it was that I'd grown to hate the work, but also there was the flying pig and my not getting enough sleep.

For almost a week straight after I told Danna and the others about the pig, I got up early and went to the bus stop. I stood in the changing colors of late dawn, listening to clear jazz melodies, and watched. By ten o'clock, a hot blast of air took up and a white cloud settled in over everything. I'd give up for the day and walk home.

I called in at work and they knew I was lying. I told them it was personal, that I wasn't sleeping well and that I'd be more dangerous than useful. Then I'd take off my clothes and sleep; the sheets damp with sweat and brilliant in the afternoon sunlight.

One afternoon I woke and there was nothing but shadows in the room. I pulled on my dark jeans and a long-sleeved green work shirt and went into the kitchen to get my boots, next to the door. There were a couple of windows that looked out over my front porch and beyond that, farmland reached all the way to the river. I sat down at the kitchen table and laced up my boots, pausing for a moment to notice the stillness and the emptiness of the land. Rows of corn stretched for almost two miles, and I'd not seen a person tending to them in weeks. I got my fly rod and vest.

It was a cornfield where, when money got tight, I would go to catch fish. A dirt road extended along the edge of the field, and about a quarter mile down from my house it curved out and disappeared behind a group of trees that jutted into the harvest. I walked on the hardened edge of the road, and once I passed the group of oaks, I headed up a row of corn for about two hundred yards. The tall stalks reached up over me, and I pushed my way through the sharp, tough leaves. The field was full of screaming crows that lifted up into the sky as I walked. I could see them hovering above me, maybe fifty or a hundred.

The row emptied into an opening where the wild grass hung low to the ground, except near the edge of a slough. A stream ran north out of the river, making a crooked path across the field, and pooled at a spot the farmer had hollowed. He used the water for irrigation. No matter how low the river got, somehow the pond was always there and full of trout.

I kept low to the ground, not scaring the fish, and came up behind a patch of thick, tall grass. Once I got in behind it, I could stand and cast over the reeds, the orange line curving high and gracefully in the blue-white oval made by the surrounding corn and sky.

I started on top of the water with a pale-colored dry fly—a Light Cahill. At first the brookies just cut the water, pecking at the surface. Then one took the fly down and I set the hook, lifting the fish out of the water cleanly, high up into the air. I watched the trout glide over my head and land behind me in the dry grass. I caught a second, larger brown trout this way. It was a sight to see the fish cutting through the blue sky, and I felt a kind of pride in doing this. I'd only be able to fool maybe two more, and they'd have to come on a wet fly, so I slipped back from the water's edge and tied on a nymph.

I was looping the tippet back through itself when something appeared out over the top of the corn in the south field. A half mile out over Simms's farm a pig surfaced, coasting quietly across the sky. Caught in the powdery blue, it almost appeared to be swimming at the edge of an ocean's surf, its legs moving back and forth, its head held high.

It wasn't like before. The pig didn't take an extended arch across the sky, but instead flew in a long, straight, gentle path above the corn. It floated along for more than a minute before it slowed and dipped easily below the corn.

———

A few nights after Danna and I talked about going to swim at Winter Island, I cooked trout in olive oil and lemon, with slices of onion, and we sat on my front porch and listened to a breeze shuffle the dry leaves above us.

"It makes me think of a painting," Danna said. "Sounds like dancers walking around, their skirts rustling together."

She leaned back in her chair, her plate resting along her outstretched legs. She hooked her thumb on the arm of the chair and worked her fingers like a musician—each finger moving slightly ahead of the next in a gentle wave. I'd noticed her doing this when she took a break from sewing, or when she sat back from a painting.

The evening sunlight was spread keenly across the fields in front of us. "You want to go to the river tonight?" I asked.

Danna stared out at the long rows of dry dirt, fence-posted with corn, with the wind pushing tickle grass along from fields miles down the road. I could smell dry pine in the air. She turned toward me, letting the breeze pick up her hair, and fingered it back. It wasn't as if she had an answer she was afraid of giving, but more like she had no answer at all.

"Stan's been asking us to come down," I added. I leaned forward and put my plate on the wooden railing.

"We're going to have to decide," she said, "what we're doing. Are we staying, or going, or what?"

"I know," I said, sounding like I was almost pleading. "We should go to the island tonight. A little company . . ." I sat back and we were quiet for a moment. A few crows cawed out in the corn-stalks, and I began to settle things in my mind. I wasn't coming to any conclusions, but I was certain that I'd have to now.

Danna reached over and took my plate from the railing and set it on top of hers. She held them in her lap, looking down at the dusty floorboards of the front porch. "OK," she said and then lifted herself out of the chair and went inside with the dishes. Something was perfect about the way she did this, and inside she must have known it. Danna knew how to get things done, even in the way she got out of a chair or left a conversation or strolled from a porch; it was clear she had her ideas settled.

Through the front screens I heard water running in the sink and the ring of dishes and silverware being stacked, rinsed, and placed on the drain board. Out to the east I saw smoke rising up from a faint ridge of mountains. A fire was burning in the Skinner Range, and in these conditions I knew it might be real trouble, but I didn't react the way I thought I would, or the way I should have. It seemed too far away to worry about. I sat back in my chair and watched the smoke rise, spreading across the sky in a gray haze, and I waited for the sun to settle down, to light the horizon on fire.

———

Winter Island lay a quarter mile upriver from where the bridge cut through the smoky evening heat. As we crossed over the water, a cool draft washed through the cab of the truck and I slowed down. Glancing out along the banks I could see the cottonwoods and crack willows had been scorched, the outer fringes of leaves tanned. The heat hadn't broken in over a month, and everything in the valley was brittle, on the verge of sparking up into an inferno. The smell of fire was settling in on us from the Skinners, thirty miles to the east.

Over the bridge, we took River Road up a few hundred yards and parked alongside an open field. We sat for a moment and Danna rubbed her thighs, chestnut and flat against the seat, the cuff of her shorts pinching a pale, thin line across her legs. She took in a deep breath.

I hesitated. "We can head across the field and then shimmy down the bank." I glanced over and noticed that behind her sunglasses Danna's eyes were closed. She was breathing easily, her collarbone rising and falling beneath the straps of her tank top. I leaned over and kissed her shoulder.

The field was beginning to cover in sun-bleached rye grass and, as we walked, the dirt didn't give way under our feet. The underbrush was dry and full of leaves almost like it was fall. We crossed into the darkness cast by the surrounding mountains. The shade of trees became indistinct and, as we stepped out onto a shoal that bridged Winter Island with the bank, it felt as though I was stepping onto something more solid than the land itself.

Ordinarily the island wasn't a place anyone would go, with its thick brush and a heavy line of white oaks, surrounded on one side by the broad, slick water of the river, and on the other side, hewed from the bank, by a shaded and deceptively wide channel. Old-timers in the valley said King Philip—before he jumped to his death, from the top of a nearby mountain to avoid capture—had once hidden here to escape from Indian mercenaries who had been hired by the English to kill him. But now, in the heat and drought, the island had a sandy beach that reached far out into the river, narrowing the current at one point to less than thirty yards.

Danna and I followed a trail, which I'm sure had been hollowed out during the drought, over the crest of the narrow spur, and as we cleared the line of trees we could see Stan, Marv, and Horace standing together on the beach. Marv's wife was sitting in a lawn chair out closer to the water with a few blankets spread out and a couple of coolers. Even farther down the beach, Laura Dawkins and Sheila Houston stood alone, knee-deep in the water. Sheila was Marv's daughter, but Laura was on her own. She moved here from California and lived in a small cabin up in the hills.

"Good to see you," Stan said as Danna and I walked up. He shook my hand and leaned over and kissed Danna on the cheek. Stan had always seemed fond of her, making a point to ask how she was when he saw me, and usually when she stopped in at the Co-op, he'd stroll up and ask about her painting or how teaching was going.

"Marv's wife is over there," Stan said to Danna, pointing down the beach to where she was sitting. "Or not," he corrected. "You could stay and grace us with your charm."

Danna smiled. "Here is fine," she said.

Marv and Horace had been talking but were glancing off downriver.

"What's the news?" I asked them.

"We were just chatting about Simms," Marv said.

Horace was quiet and seemed to be thinking.

"Seen him lately?" I asked.

"Horace has," Marv said. "He was just telling me about going out to his farm," he paused. "Tell them about it." Marv clapped Horace on the shoulder. Horace was quiet.

"Simms's been doing some welding," Stan said, finally. It was clear they'd all been going over this for a while, attempting to make sense of something.

"Birds," Horace said. "He's been collecting up scrap metal and welding together these big birds."

"Did you talk to him?" I asked Horace. Danna edged toward me and I could feel her leaning against my arm.

"He wasn't around," Horace answered. "But his fields have been turned over."

"Looked like his potatoes were coming in fine," Horace suggested, then there was a pause.

"That's not his money crop though," Stan added.

"There's about ten of those birds standing out in his fields," Horace said.

"How big?" I asked.

"Ten. Twelve. Maybe even fifteen-foot wingspan."

"Jesus," I said. I tried to imagine what the birds must look like sitting out on Simms's land. "What do you do with something like that?"

No one answered.

"Frank is up in the Skinners," Stan said. He looked over his shoulder toward the east and then back at Danna. "Could you see it from up at your place?"

"We came from Gabe's," Danna said. "We saw the smoke."

"Kids are in there camping," Marv said. He turned and headed toward the cooler. Like at the Co-op, Marv left us for more important business.

Stan called to him, "Get me a cola."

"Looks like them kids may have set it accidentally," Horace offered. He had his hands in his pockets, hunching over a bit and kicking at the sand. He was even more lanky in the failing evening light, and the shadows caught his almost-white blond hair and his harelip, making them seem more severe than they actually were.

We all stood without talking. Marv came back with a soda for Stan and handed Danna and me each a beer.

"Sounds like Simms is in trouble," I said to Stan. "What's he doing with the birds?"

"He's not been down to swim since I saw you at the Co-op," Stan said. He looked downriver in the direction of Simms's land. He raised an eyebrow, and I thought something crossed his mind that he didn't want to share. It was as if he understood some terrible event was happening but he could not, or would not, find the words to confess what it was.

I felt left out, agitated. Even at the Co-op, I seemed to be on the fringe of things, not quite a member of the group yet. I sensed both Danna and I had stepped into the middle of a longer, more important conversation.

"I missed working the crops this year," Danna said, aiming her beer away from the group and pulling the tab back. "I look forward to getting out there and forgetting that there's anything else but dirt and berries." She took a drink and was about to continue when we heard Marv's wife call to us.

We all looked up. In the distance I could see two black silhouettes slicing through the deep blue and purple sky, tall white clouds piling up far off on the horizon behind them. I felt opened up by this, the sight of pigs creasing through, and then suspended above, the tinge of white haze that had been hanging over the valley for weeks. Marv, Stan, and Horace watched as the pigs moved in our direction and then made a slow sweeping turn, gliding along the surface of the evening sky. As they bowed around the corner, the pigs lost speed, tipped their wings in an off-center curve and, for a moment, appeared to plunge earthward. Danna stepped up beside me and gently reached around to rest her hand on my hip. We stood there and I couldn't hear anything but the sound of water and, for the first time, I could smell the riverbed. I breathed in heavily, and it occurred to me that from their height the pigs could see the fire burning in the Skinners. It was a thought that made perfect sense to me. The pigs took another turn, dipped and then caught momentum, headed away from us, until they became too faint to see, disappearing into the difficult light.

"Son of a bitch," Stan said, pronouncing each word exactly.

A feeling settled in on me, like the dark shadows that were cast out on the water. I felt it run up my legs and into my stomach, and it spread out in my head, a calm feeling, warm, that began to push thoughts out of my head, leaving impressions behind. Danna and Stan, all of them, looked out over Simms's land.

Sheila and Laura yelled, pointing at the sky in the direction where the pigs had disappeared. Stan looked around at Horace and Marv. "That son of a bitch is flying pigs," he said. "Did you see that?"

"There's no way that counts," Marv said as he tossed his can of beer out onto the beach. "That's not for real."

"To hell it doesn't." Horace swung around and looked down the beach toward Sheila. "Hey, Sheila," he called. "Thursday night OK?"

Sheila turned, shot the finger. "Not if a million pigs fly," she yelled.

"It's only a matter of time," he said. "Keep your calendar open."

"Noo'ho. No way," Marv replied. "Simms's bound to be up to something."

Stan pulled a pack of cigarettes out of his shirt pocket and thumped one out, jabbed it into his mouth, cupping his hand around the flaring butt. "Goddamn it," he said, tossing the cigarette away.

Danna leaned over and kissed me on the cheek and then turned away from where we were all staring. Her hand fell from my shoulder. She headed off up the beach toward the tree line where before we'd descended to the island. I glanced at Stan and wondered what was going through his mind. He scuffed his right boot along the sand and dug his other heel in, then shifted his weight and did it the other way around.

"What's going on?" I asked after the silence had gone on for too long.

Stan looked up from where his feet were working and stared as though he was able to see through me, off into the distance. "Long story," he said.

"I want to know," I said.

"Pigs fly is a common saying 'round here," he said. "Don't mean anything." He lit another cigarette, took a long draw and exhaled. "You better go look after Danna."

"I guess I should," I said. I stood for a moment feeling awkward, torn between wanting to stay and wanting to see about Danna. "I'll check in with you later," I said.

I found Danna sitting in the truck, her expression blank. She stared out the front window, seemingly focused on the road.

"You OK?" I asked.

"Yeah," she said. "I'm fine."

"What's wrong? Why did you leave?"

She turned and looked at me, silent for a moment. "It wasn't that I didn't believe you about the pig," she said. "I don't mind the idea of a pig flying. I mean I saw it, too."

"What then?"

"It's the others," she said. "You heard them."

"Yeah," I said. "What's it all about?"

"It's about a lot of things," she said, turning away. She stared at the rearview mirror. "Everyone's going to start calling in debts. They're just beginning."

"Just beginning what?" I asked. "It's a joke." I reached over and ran my hand along her thigh.

"Fighting," she said. "They'll ruin everything fighting. Fighting over who owes who what. They'll ruin everything they have."

"This is some kind of joke," I said. "We'll get to the bottom of it."

Danna looked at me. "The bottom of it," she said. "We'll get down to the ugly part of it. This drought. The pig. This is just the beginning. People find a way to make things ugly."

5.

I stood at the bus stop, the morning light tinged with gray smoke from the fires that burned in the Skinners. The clapboard house behind me was hushed and the curtains hung motionless. This was the first morning I could remember not hearing the music filtering out, awl-like, and cutting into my drowsiness. I didn't look toward Simms's land, or the sky. A frustration built inside me about what happened at Winter Island the night before. I felt regret already, even though nothing bad had really happened. Maybe this was all coming from Danna's gestures toward me and how she appeared to step back from the geography of the evening, as if she was determining different things from what everyone saw.

The bus wheezed to a stop in front of me and I got on, trying to forget that I was heading up to the mill. The driver had a radio propped up against the window beside him, playing news about the fire. He pulled the cantilever doors shut and glanced into the large mirror above his head.

"The fire's out of control," he said as he steered the bus back onto the road.

I looked up toward the mirror so that I could see his face. "I haven't heard much about it," I confessed. His eyes were carved into his face, dark crevices stretching as far as the bridge of his nose then rising into an ashen, bony expression. Even in the mirror I could see the finest lines running along his forehead, and he seemed to be concentrating more than I expected a driver to be, as though getting the bus along the bending road took more than clutching, shifting gears, braking, and working the wheel.

"Moving three hundred feet a second in some places," he began to explain. "Summit House on Clark Mountain burned. They're saying people were in it."

"How'd it start?" I conjured up the image of the Summit

House, flames reaching up and down the white gables. A sadness crept up on me.

"Don't know," he said. "Sheriff said on the radio a minute ago that kids are in there. In the woods somewhere. Camping."

The bus rattled and creaked. We slowly made the sharp corners and began to climb the headland toward the mill. I watched out the window. The bus made a short descent into a curve and then the road leveled out and began to parallel Miller's River. The water was slow and pocked with sun-baked rocks. In years past, the river ran fast along this stretch, making riffles and eddies, but now it lagged westward where it met stronger currents and flowed down past Winter Island at an almost imperceptible rate. I imagined what this riverbed looked like dry, and I thought about walking along the knotted bottom, traveling from the mill all the way to Winter Island.

As the bus strained, rising up the last bluff to the iron mill gates, I could hear Frank's voice on the radio, talking about bringing in smoke jumpers to try and retrieve any possible survivors from the Summit House. It occurred to me how small the valley actually was and how I'd managed to remain isolated from it, having only the few acquaintances at the Co-op and the fewer connections they brought to me. For most, even the notion of missing people summoned faces and, I guessed, produced worried telephone conversations. Still, I wasn't disconnected from what I felt happening, but instead a high, resonating tightness built up behind my forehead, dizzying, and I couldn't escape the static hum, the impression that I was somehow forgetting something that I never really knew.

"This going to hurt you?" the driver asked as the bus pulled to a stop. I was confused. "Making paper," he added.

I'd been worried about the pigs and what was going to happen with me and Danna, and it'd not occurred to me what the fire could do to the mill. I looked out the window and saw a few men gathered around in groups in the parking lot. "Probably," I said, without giving it much thought. As I shuffled down the steps into the already hot air, I could tell the oxygen was thin and tired; the fire was breathing heavily off to the west.

Walking across the parking lot, I stared up into the ash sky and anticipated that the drought and the way people were acting and the circumstances at Simms's farm would take a turn for the worst. I enjoy precision and that was exactly what seemed to be leaving the valley—my life—as quickly as excitement can turn into disaster. All morning I shuffled papers around in my office and waited for the phone to ring, expecting my boss, Neal, to let me know how many men we'd have to lay off. When the last truck pulled in lightly loaded with thin red spruce, I called down to have it cut and stored, and then I got on the phone to find out what was happening.

The fire had taken out about fifty percent of our scheduled reserve, meaning that until some shipments could be arranged from farther north, we'd have to lay off about twenty men. I sat in my office and looked out over the grounds, down toward the river, and knew that if I didn't make some decisions word would be out before lunch, and rumors would take over.

The bulk of the cutback would come from my department, and I'd have to be in on the decision about who to let go. I wouldn't have a say in all the choices, which made it worse. I would be made to look into each of their faces and see the different responses. I'd had to do this before, and though it was always presented as a temporary situation, only a few men ever reentered the iron gates, and I swear it was possible to detect—at the corners of the mouth, where the eyebrows come to meet at the bridge of the nose, in the direction they chose to stare as you told them—whether they were married, how many children they had, the children's age even, and if they rented or owned a house.

I read the employee roster, first putting pencil marks next to the twenty most recently hired, then again, putting ink marks next to the men who weren't carrying their load. Sometimes they were the same names, but mostly not. I recalled previous layoffs, the familiar ozone scent of the mimeograph machine running our own paper over the hot barrel, spitting out a list of names that met with a line of men, holding their own hard work in hand, heading out the gate to find another way to make a living.

The phone rang and I expected it to be Neal asking me to come down to his office and go over our lists. "Gabe," he said, flatly, "you'd better get down on the floor."

"What's up?" I asked.

He breathed into the phone. "Trouble."

A crowd had gathered in the cutting area, where we do small jobs, light saw work and such. There was a lot of commotion, a group of the men bellowing, and I figured it had something to do with the impending layoffs, maybe a fight, so I headed over and yelled, "Hey, break it up! Break it up!" The men were standing shoulder to shoulder, but turned to let me through.

Price and Henshaw were in the midst of an argument, which seemed to be building energy, charged by the other men's jeering. Henshaw had been hired on about two years before, was in his midthirties, and was bulky with what seemed like weight on the verge of turning into muscle. He walked with a limp and was the quiet type who did his work first and then, in the late afternoon, before heading home, spent a few minutes socializing, usually reminiscing about bass fishing back home in the South. I couldn't imagine what would get him started in on Price.

"What's this about?" I said, standing at the front edge of the other men. Neither one of them looked at me.

"You owe me," Price said to Henshaw. "Pay up." Price stood straight, leaned back on the heels of his work boots.

"Naw—"

"Price," I interrupted, "what's going on here?" I took a step forward so I could look him in the eyes. He was stubborn and carried himself as if people should defer to him. Partly, he'd earned this right by working at the mill for forty-three years, operating every point on the line, and now, only a few years before retirement, he carried a clipboard and inspected the machinery.

"Stay out of it," Price replied to me. "Boy owes me some money," he added.

"You're gone, old man," Henshaw yelled. "Don't do shit around here." He began to edge sideways a few steps, back and forth, hooking his thumbs in his back pockets nervously. By now the men who had gathered were quiet.

Price stepped forward. "I'll show you what I can do."

"Cut it out!" I yelled, but before I got a grip on Price's arm he slipped a punch at Henshaw, and his elbow clipped me under the chin. Henshaw leaned away from the blow and caught Price off balance, gracefully putting his boot against Price's rib cage and shoving him away. Everyone clamored and I felt a course of heat rush through my jaw.

Price had toppled into the pile of spruce that had been brought in earlier. It was cut into eight-foot lengths and it scattered as he floundered, trying to regain his equilibrium.

"Goddamn it," I yelled. "That should've been cleared out of here by now."

Henshaw was poised, waiting for Price to come back at him. He mumbled and stared hard into Price's eyes. His body seemed to take on an unrecognizable definition.

"Clean that out of here," I barked, at no one in particular. "Break this shit up!" I yelled.

"Son of a bitch owes me," Price said flatly. He stood up holding a section of spruce.

The pain in my jaw spread like a wildfire up the back of my neck, settled behind my eyes and cheekbones. I stood uselessly to the side, watching as Price made a deliberate action out of stepping on the foot pedal of the saw next to him, kicking the blade into motion. The sound of the blade turning, making an incision in the air, quieted the men's voices. Price kept his attention on Henshaw and without looking ran the spruce into the saw blade to cut it short for a billet. The moment was quick and simple. The flange caught the sleeve of his coveralls and took his arm into the cut.

Blood peppered across the men's shirts and pants as they gyrated out of the spray. Price's howl mounted above the whine of the blade—it mangled wood and flesh—and rose up into the metal beams and into the corners where the corrugated roof met the cinder-block walls, seeming to join with a chorus of similar wails that had lingered there from past accidents and remained to lament and resonate with new, untrained anguish. I called to Henshaw to get an ambulance and he quickly headed off for a phone.

Beneath the saw, Price was moaning and reaching over to feel where his arm had been. I found myself listening for the echo of his scream, wanting to hear it again so that I could memorize every nuance and how each wave of pain overtook the next and then faded away. I imagined the first moment of Price's experience contained the same kind of longing and mysterious absence.

As I bent down over Price, I noticed the separated portion of his arm leaning upright against the rung of a nearby work stool. I gathered sawdust and began to pack it down over the wound just above his elbow. Blood had already begun to turn the dust into thick paste. Price wasn't crying out. He was on his back, shifting his weight from side to side, moaning. I kept my thoughts on his separated arm, wondering if I should leave him and attend to the limb.

I glanced up toward a line of windows that looked out over the floor from the upstairs offices. Neal was looking out on all of this and hadn't bothered to come down and help. Even with the distance, I could make out his facial expression, drawn and disinterested, seemingly lost in thought. Maybe it was a form of panic. I'd heard of cases where people watched something terrible happen and, maybe out of fear of somehow being held responsible, walked away without lending a hand. I motioned for him to come help and pressed more sawdust around Price's stump. I took my belt and cinched it just above the cut, tightened it with a grapple.

"Somebody get something to put his arm in," I yelled to the group of men who had begun to scatter and were now silent again. A few had stepped away and I could hear them getting sick.

"Got it!" I heard Henshaw say from behind the crowd. "Ambulance's on the way," he announced as he wedged between two men. "They said put it on ice."

Henshaw kneeled next to the arm and then fingered the edge of a black trash bag he'd brought from the break room. I watched him studying the arm, trying to decide how to handle it. Carefully he reached down, clutched the wrist, and slid the ragged appendage into the bag.

———

"Gabe, I need to see you," Neal said after the ambulance pulled away, and the men had begun to drift back to their work areas. It was hard for me to imagine discussing which men we'd let go after a morning like this, and I saw how unkind Neal could be when on our way upstairs he said, "That solves one of our problems."

Neal shut the door and I settled into a chair across the desk from him. Cool air blasted out of a window unit that had scattered paperwork across his desk. My dismay must have been apparent. He stared directly at me for a few moments and then his focus changed. "He'll be fine. Don't worry about it. Price was a few years from retirement. Now he'll go on disability and by the time we have to decide to let him go he'll have retired." Neal lifted his palms into the air, as if making an offering. "Not a problem," he added carelessly.

"Not a problem," I repeated, just to hear again how careless the words sounded.

"Not a problem," Neal echoed as he shuffled some papers around on his desk. "We do *have* a problem though."

"Twenty men," I said. "I know."

"Fifty percent of reserve—"

"Nineteen," I interrupted, "with Price on disability?"

"Doesn't leave much to keep track of," Neal continued, putting down the papers he was holding. He swiveled in his chair to get a look out over the floor. Two men were cleaning up the saw area and moving the cut spruce. "We can keep it down to fifteen," he continued.

"Not if it takes a month to get the shipment," I said. "What about getting something from down south? In the Smokies?"

"By cutting the higher salaries," Neal paused.

"You're talking about cutting those with the most time here," I objected, remembering the feeling I got when I had to look someone in the face and tell them the news, imagining what the news must sound like across dinner with the children listening and the wife bearing down hard to keep from tearing up. I didn't want to have to tell the men who I'd known the longest—the few I'd had beers with and talked to at the company picnics—that they didn't have a job. "What about south?" I asked.

"It doesn't work that way, Gabe," Neal said. He reached, touched the pens in his shirt pocket. "You know that."

"What are you saying? Let the old timers go?"

"No—"

"They can't find new jobs."

"I know—"

"Then what?" I said. I leaned forward and studied Neal's face. Crevices surfaced across his forehead, emerged between his eyebrows; his eyes almost closed.

"We're letting you go," Neal said. He looked up and his face was fixed, cold. "You know you have a job when things pick up," he said.

"You're cutting me," I said. I looked directly at Neal, wanting him to see what he could in my eyes, hoping something was there. "On what I make, you're cutting me?" I said. "That won't save you anything."

"With you and a few others . . . we—"

"Right!" I shouted. "A few company men."

"You know yourself this is better," Neal explained. "Three or four men keep their jobs this way. You've been needing a break anyway and you'll get severance."

"*You're* cutting me," I repeated. "There's no *we* about it."

"Yes," he agreed. He was about to say something else but then paused. I could hear water dripping off the condenser inside the window unit, and I sat noticing how the dampness had furrowed the prints on the wall and the paperwork on Neal's desk.

We both sat back in our chairs and looked down at the men who had just finished cleaning up the floor and changing the saw blade. At first, I couldn't distinguish the impact of Price's accident from the weight of the news Neal had delivered. I felt fragile, but then I began to consider what Danna and I had been talking about. I turned and smiled at Neal.

"I'm sorry," he said, a bit puzzled by my expression. He stood up and walked closer to the window. "Your friend Stan. They think his son was out in the Skinners when they caught fire." He slipped his hands into his pockets. "No word yet."

6.

Stan picked me up outside the gates. When I slipped onto the seat beside him he offered me a soda out of a cooler that was between us in the floorboard. My head felt swollen inside, the pressure spreading from behind my eyes and settling throughout now. I reached into the cooler and got some ice for my jaw.

"I heard about your son," I said, worried about how to bring up the subject.

"I'm sure he's fine," Stan said. He kept his eyes focused on the road. "He's probably out of town on a gig."

"What have you heard?"

"Just that there was a dance up at Summit House. It could have been any band." Stan glanced at me. "Why the hell were they dancing up there anyway?" he said. "With the fire and all?" He focused on the road. "They don't know that the people *didn't* get out."

"Was Jason supposed to be out of town?"

"I don't know," he said. "He's so busy. He doesn't tell me these things."

"Does he have a roommate?"

"Yeah. But he's not around either. We've tried calling."

On the surface Stan didn't seem worried. "Looks like you had it out," he commented. "Was that before or after you called?"

I didn't feel like explaining the events all over again just to include the part about my getting hit, so I pretended to be lost in thought and in a way I was. Heat blasted through the open windows of Stan's Cadillac. The glass had fallen down inside the doors and couldn't be rolled up.

"Neal's just doing his job as he sees it," Stan said after a while and then apologetically he added, "He just seems to enjoy it more than he should."

"He didn't make any sense, Stan," I said. "His reasons—"

"May not have anything to do with work," Stan interrupted.

"What do you mean?"

"He's scared of what's happening. Scared of you."

"Of me?"

"You're in tight with the old-timers. Means you have the momentum to carry you through the changes happening here. Or at least Neal thinks so. I'm not sure if any of us do."

I didn't feel a part of the regulars. I wondered what angle Neal could be vying for and how he thought getting rid of me would help. I leaned back and closed my eyes, feeling the speed of the car through the floorboard and the wind in my face.

Stan turned on Jackson Hill Road, which creased drumlins until it met up with Cave Hill Road. As we passed along a range of dry brome and timothy grass, I wondered if the friction of the moving car might not spark a fire. Anything seemed possible. The midday sun was merciless, lifting a haze even this high into the hills. Even though I knew where Stan was taking me, I sensed that I needed to say something, so I asked where we were headed.

"I figure you need some time to cool off before you give Danna the news," Stan said. "Frank's supposed to stop by the Co-op with stories about the fire. He's been out there the whole time fighting it and talking with the news people. I don't know which is worse for him."

"You've known Price a long time?" I asked.

"As long as I can remember," Stan paused. "He drinks down at The Spoke. When I was drinking I'd see him down there every evening after work. He talks a lot of smack and gets in trouble with people."

I thought about Henshaw for a moment, about what I'd seen that morning. Then my mind went back to an image of Summit House burning.

"You sure you're OK about Jason?" I asked.

"I'm sure he's fine." Stan reached down and pulled a cold drink out of the cooler. Resting the can between his legs he reminded me, "You know you catch the bus in front of his house."

I remembered the silence that had lingered out at the bus stop.

"I can't believe Summit House," I said. I tried to forget the burning gables, remembered a pristine image of the house filled with people, dancing and drinking. I knew that in the early eighteen hundreds some men had decided to build the house on Clark Mountain where people could go to dance and drink without a hassle. Even through Prohibition you could go to the Summit House on Saturday nights and get Jamaica Spirits, St. Croix Rum, Holland Gin, Spanish cigars, or anything else and dance to jazz or blues. I thought about it a moment and then asked, "They sure there was a dance at Summit House?"

"Jason's a hell of a musician. Just put out a record," Stan said. He pulled the tab on his drink and took a sip.

I thought of people dancing, men in hats and women with the breeze catching the hem of their summer dresses and lifting them in time with the music; familiar grace notes bringing smiles to the faces of the regulars. A few times I'd made the trip up to Summit House, but only in the afternoon and only for the view. Danna and I would sometimes put our faces up to the windows, using our hands to cut the glare, and try to imagine what the evenings were like inside. We kept telling each other we were going to come up for a dance sometime. Now, I felt nostalgic for something I'd never known.

As we drew closer to the Co-op I could tell Stan had something else on his mind. Maybe it had to do with the way everything was going, perhaps the cattle he had lost, but I believed if it wasn't his son it was strictly about the pigs we'd seen over Simms's farm. Stan was the kindest man I'd ever met. He seemed to grieve for the life he lost out on while he was a regular at The Spoke. These days he made up for it with an even temper and what he called a "judicious use of time." But the incident at Winter Island had him on edge in a way I'd never seen before. I felt as if Stan wanted me to ask about what had gone on at the island between Horace and Marv and him—the dry, quick looks they exchanged, which came from knowing something; the way the evening fell apart awkwardly like a party that had lasted too long, deep into the morning. There were questions for sure, but they seemed too difficult to even contemplate at this point.

We pulled into the parking lot and Stan cut the engine. He leaned back in his seat, taking in a deep breath, and gazed at something off in the distance, past the Co-op, just as though it was invisible and he was seeing through it. It seemed as if he was deciding between two parts of himself.

"I'm going to get some air," I said as I opened the car door. I stepped out onto the caliche and felt the heat rise up through the soles of my boots. "You sticking around?" I asked. "Or coming in?"

He pushed the car door open with his foot. "Let's go hear the news."

"What was all that about last night?" I asked when Stan stepped up beside me. "I mean between everyone. After the pigs."

Stan shaded his eyes with one hand and looked at me. For some reason he didn't want to make it easy on me. "Let's go inside and see."

We stepped into the cooler air and saw Horace standing in the checkout stall, looking toward the alcove where Marv sat drinking coffee. Land survey maps were spread on the table in front of him. Marv looked up, but kept his finger on the map. His shirt sleeves were rolled up his forearms and he wasn't wearing an apron. I could see a hint of sleeplessness in the dusk below his eyes.

Stan got a soda from the refrigerator. "News?" he asked, walking over to where Marv was sitting.

Marv looked a bit puzzled by the question. "Nothing about the dance at Summit House," he said apologetically. "Frank'll be in shortly I guess."

"Simms ain't been in," Horace added. He looked at Stan in a way that made me feel I had walked in on a conversation I wasn't supposed to hear.

Stan sat down in front of Marv and glanced over at the renderings. "A bit warm for coffee."

Marv quickly looked up at Stan and then leaned in over the fine lines and deliberate numbers, the velum crackling under his elbows. Stan eyed me and smiled. He opened his drink.

"Don't matter either way," Horace said as he headed off to the back room.

I wasn't sure who he was saying this to or what it meant. Marv studied the diagram for a few moments and then let out a deep breath. "What are you doing here?" he said, as if he'd just noticed me.

Before I could answer Stan spoke up. "Neal's making a point.

The fire and all." He paused and took a drink. "Cutbacks," he said, looking directly at Marv.

Marv stared at me as if he was trying to read something in my expression. "Don't take it personally," he said. And then, as an afterthought, "I'm sorry for you and Danna."

"There's work," Stan said.

I studied the still life that Danna had painted. It was beginning to look as if the blistering afternoon sun that poured through the window high above was taking the color from out of the shadows, flattening out the full curves of the fish and onions, taking the reflection off the bottle of wine. The entire room seemed to have taken a beating. The tile floor and the walls looked brittle.

"What's the map for?" I asked.

Marv pursed his lips. "A little boundary line dispute," he said.

Behind me I heard the door open and immediately the smell of charred Staghorn followed. I turned and saw Frank looking ruffled and weary. His shirt and pants were smeared with soot and ash.

"It's a hell of a mess up there," he said, his voice unsteady. "Whole damn place is burning."

Stan stood up and slid his chair toward Frank. "Have a seat," he said. "What are you drinking?"

"A beer," Frank said, sitting down hard in the chair. "Stan, there's no news about Jason. We haven't found him, and there's no evidence that his band was the one playing."

Marv slid the surveys off the table and began to roll them up in his lap. "You been up there all night?" he asked as he palmed a rubber band down the roll of paper.

Stan handed over the beer and Frank was quiet. He opened it and took several long drinks. When he swallowed he sounded thick inside, full of smoke. "Red spruce is going down fast," he said, looking at me.

For years spruce had kept the mill going, and he understood immediately what this meant for me, but it was more than that. Frank had a good sense of how a fire like this could affect the entire valley, changing the shape of the land and, afterwards, the way people think about life. Looking at him, I could see he was afraid.

"Everyone that was at the Summit House is dead," he said. "No telling how many. On the other side of Clark we found a dozen bodies floating in Cranberry Pond. They made it that far, but the fire was burning too hot. Sucked the air right off the water."

Frank looked up at me and then down at the floor. I conjured the images of a wildfire out of control, impressionistic shades of red and black, chaotic and thrashing scrub brush and trees, animals bolting, human arms, legs, scrambling for safety.

"The ground's so hot," Frank said, "that you can't step on rocks larger than your foot. They build up pressure inside and explode like land mines."

"How long do you think it'll burn?" I asked.

Frank raised his shoulders and shook his head again. "C-130s and Chinooks have been working all morning. Fire jumpers dropped, too. They say they've got it under control, that it'll be whipped soon. As long as the wind doesn't kick up."

He finished his beer and got up to get another out of the cooler. I had the feeling he was tired of talking about the fire. I suspected reporters had been bothering him all morning, and he needed time to absorb all he'd gone through. While Frank was talking, Horace had come out from the stock room and was sitting on the counter at the register.

"What's this about a flying pig?" Frank asked, sitting down. "Scuttlebutt made it all the way up into the Skinners."

Stan looked at me. "It's what I told you about before," I offered. "We saw it again last night. We were down on the island. A couple of pigs took to the air."

Frank glanced toward Stan. "Over your brother's place," Stan said.

"Anyone go check with Cliff?" Frank asked.

"Haven't seen him since he was by here a while back," Horace said. Horace had been keeping quiet. He smiled and then looked back over his shoulder toward the aisles of groceries.

I glanced down the aisles myself. The collection of medicinals—hawthorn berries, shavegrass, yellowdock root, and others—that lined the inside of the front wall struck me as odd. Maybe for the first time I realized that in a place that worked the people so shrewdly, where people rend the ground hard or get a living off the land, these rewards were too delicate; they made the effort look too easy.

"I think he's got something to do with it," Marv offered. He held the roll of survey maps up so that Frank saw what they were.

Smiling, Frank said, "Whatever gave you that idea?"

"Simms has hit hard times," said Stan, "but then it looks like we all have."

We all sat motionless with the hum of the refrigerator measuring the time.

"Pig's flown the coop," Horace stated flatly. "That's the way it is."

"It ain't," Marv erupted. "I'm a man of my word, but this ain't a flying pig—"

"The land wasn't yours to begin with," Frank interrupted. "Hold on now," he added, raising his hand up in Marv's direction. "I'm not saying—"

"You should have said something years ago," Marv said. "When I put the damn thing up."

"Simms's brush hog wasn't worth shit," said Stan, looking toward Frank.

"A flying pig is a flying pig," Horace said, reaching across the register. He picked a newspaper off the rack and sauntered over, dropping it on the table between Frank and Stan.

"You borrowed it for a reason," Frank said. "It was worth that much."

"Yeah. And Marv's fence has been there long enough—"

"Stan," Frank interrupted. "Everybody owes—"

"Nobody," Horace said. "Nobody's getting in the way here. I got mine coming."

"Everybody," Frank continued. "This is just the surface. We go calling in all our debts, somebody's going to get hurt."

The hum of the refrigerator buoyed in the air. Marv looked at Frank and then toward Horace. "You think Sheila's going out with you?" he said. He smiled and stood shaking his head. "My daughter'd as soon date a pig," he said.

"Marv!" Frank yelled.

Horace took a step toward Marv. "That's a threat!" Marv yelled. "You men saw it." Marv looked around the room at each of us. "You're fired!" he said, pointing at Horace.

"Nobody's fired," Frank said. He looked at Marv. "You're lucky I don't help him kick your ass."

"You're a fine one to talk," Marv said. "It's your brother. You in on it?"

"No," Frank said.

"You're in on it," Marv said. "For three feet of property."

"Don't be stupid," Stan said. "We need to calm down."

"Your daughter's word is as good as yours," Horace said to Marv.

"Shut up!" Stan yelled. "All of you shut the fuck up." There was a calm. The motor of the refrigerator cycled off and there was just the ticking sound of its cooling. "Frank's got nothing to do with this. This is Simms's doing. What for? I don't know. But my guess is it's working. Look at you people." He looked around the room.

For the first time in all of this I'd begun to get a glimpse of what might be happening. As long as I'd known Horace, he had been trying to get Sheila to go out with him. Horace, though, was pasty and thick legged, with blond bucktail hair and a harelip. In just about every way he was a contradiction to Sheila. It occurred to me too, that for years I'd seen a rusted-out brush hog in the shag grass bordering Stan's pasture.

"What's the score here?" I asked, frustrated. I wanted answers.

Frank pushed his beer along the tabletop. "There's no reason to get nasty, Marv."

Stan added, "Those plans you got in your hand—"

"I'm running your place here," Horace interrupted. "I keep this place . . ."

"Tell a story of their own," Stan continued.

"Let's all shut up," Frank said. He turned to Marv. "Keep your fence and your porch."

"I'm an honest man," Marv said. "It's straight and narrow with me."

"It's three feet," Frank said. "Let's cool it."

"It's a matter of honor," Horace began.

"No it's not," Frank said, slapping his hand down on the table. "Something's going on here and none of us knows what it is." Frank leaned up and put both his hands palm down on the table. "Horace. It was you that went out and saw Cliff a while back. He was building some birds?"

"Yeah," Horace said. "I guess that's what it was."

Frank looked across the table at Marv. "And you think he's somehow responsible for the flying pigs?"

"Who doesn't?" said Marv. He looked around the room at each of us.

"Gabe. You saw the first pig, didn't you?" Frank's voice had taken on a flat tone. He had given up personal involvement and was now doing his job.

"That morning at the bus stop. About six weeks ago," I said. "And then when I was out fishing."

Frank pushed his chair back and leaned over, resting his elbows on his knees. "Well, plenty of others saw them," he said. "They're flying for sure. Can't say more than that."

"Maybe you best see Cliff," Stan said. He ran the palm of his hand across his forehead and then down over his eyes and mouth as if he was wiping sweat.

Frank drank the last of his beer and gently raised himself out of the chair. "I'm going to get a shower and a nap and then head back to the fire. See if it's all under control. I'll check on Cliff soon as I can." Frank's standing up whisked the smell of scorched earth into the air. "You boys stay away from there."

———

Stan loaned me money to buy a chicken. There were so many dying that Harper couldn't keep the ground clear of them. It looked like maybe a dozen had burst just that afternoon.

Heat convected off the dirt and gravel, climbing visibly in streamers toward the sky. I waited and watched while Harper tried to pick out a bird that would last all the way home. They were haggard, pecking at the earth like oil wells, their beaks bending downward and kicking back up, dry.

By the time Stan dropped me off at home, a tenderness had crept up on him. His thoughts, I decided, seemed to have shifted from the pigs to the trouble he was having with his cattle. He didn't mention it, but I knew that the fire trucks that had been available before were now busy in the mountains and that his herd was on its own for water. Stan was soft for his animals and could be found in the evenings walking among them out in the fields. I think he talked to them sometimes, though he'd never admit to it. We passed along Cave Hill Road, and Stan's attention drifted from the pavement. He occasionally let his eyes follow the landscape, studying the hills for something. I was reluctant to look, afraid that if I did I would see parts of the valley being erased.

With my eyes closed I imagined the distant rim of mountains becoming watery along the edges, the muted colors melting into each other, then dissolving, touched by a gauzy cloth, absorbed. Slowly the entire countryside vanished, leaving a blank parchment. Against the glare of the afternoon sun my eyelids shimmered red, and the hot wind beat against my face, the car speeding through this flush vision.

———

When Stan's Cadillac disappeared into the tack River Road took between my house and farmland—through corn, potatoes, tobacco—

I was left alone with the thoughts that I'd managed to keep pushed out of my head for most of the day. I was without a job and I had to settle things with Danna.

As far as work was concerned, I had felt a part of things as long as I was there, faced with the wood and the men, but once I got beyond the gates my life took on another quality. Only my dreams and then later my sleepless nights kept me connected to this world. In the dark, my house, cooking with life late into the morning, the mice skittering in the ceiling above my bed, the wind creaking through the rafters, anchored me to this place. Danna, too, wove this all together, made me believe that as insular as I felt, I was still threaded through the tapestry of the valley.

I sat on my front porch, looking out at the smoke that hung over the Skinners, and let these thoughts come apart, wanting to know what I might find that I could explain. My jaw ached. Without a job, leaving the valley might make sense. But Danna's ideas seemed to be changing. At the island I'd sensed she might want to wait this whole thing out—the pigs, the fire, the heat. This was home to Danna and she had fallen in love with it long before she ever met me.

7.

That evening Danna fried up the chicken and I grilled corn. She had come over while I was sleeping and found the bird trapped beneath the upside-down trash can where I'd left it—the bottom half rusted away. Her arms were ropy, and she snapped the neck of the chicken. It must have been this that woke me. From the bedroom I could see her bring the ax down and then begin to work the feathers loose. I'd seen her do this at the picnic my first summer in the valley. When I met her, I remember how the roughness of her skin surprised me. Working the berries had done this to her hands, Stan said.

I was shucking the corn over the kitchen sink when Danna came in and stood behind me, resting her hand at the back of my neck. Her palm felt cool on my skin.

"Stan called and told me what happened," she said. "I'm sorry."

A looseness filled my body, and I wanted to be mad at Stan, but the truth was I felt relieved. Danna put her arms around me from behind and rested her face between my shoulders. The warmth of her body felt comforting.

"Don't be mad at him," she added. "He thought it'd be easier on you."

"Stan's one to talk," I said. "His son's missing. Maybe dead. His cattle are dying."

"I know," she said, quietly. "The fire's all but out."

I imagined Frank walking the steep embankment below Summit House, looking for bodies, for Stan's son, wary of stones that could erupt and send fragments cutting through the air. The last burning cinders could catch wind and blow up again into a full burn, which meant there could be as much as two weeks of work ahead of the firefighters.

"There's other jobs," I said, leaning away from Danna and running a light stream of water over the corn.

"If you need one," she said. "Well's almost dry, isn't it?" she asked reaching over and turning off the spigot.

"Yeah," I answered. I shook the corn above the sink and then spread it out on a towel. I leaned against the counter, "Bottled water is coming in at the Co-op."

Danna turned her back to the sink and rested her hands along the Formica edge, her fingers splayed, her head tipped, as if she had a question. Dull light scattered across the floor from the bay window, the room was getting dark. From the window behind Danna I could see all the way to the highway, where a set of headlights moved slowly along. She leaned over and kissed me.

"Let's cook," she said.

I wanted to talk, but couldn't find the words. Loneliness was the only word I could gather, and I knew it wasn't right. Ruts sliced through my mind, dividing my thoughts from my words. I couldn't say anything. The kitchen floor was the color of snow in moonlight. I wrapped the corn in a towel and carried it outside.

From the grill I watched Danna through the bay window, moving about in the kitchen. I shuffled the coals, their centers glowing and, toward the edges, turning powdery. Danna worked from the countertop, battering each piece of chicken and then turning to drop it into the cast-iron skillet. Through the open window I heard the grease crackling, and I imagined Danna's fingers, long and precise, covered in flour, dipping each leg, breast, thigh, into the hot grease. I closed my eyes, feeling the heat from the coals rise to my face and the cooler night air settle on my back. I wondered what it was like to be up in the Skinners, what it must have felt like to be in Cranberry Pond with the last sheet of air slipping off the water.

I shifted the coals again and then stepped out into the yard where I could see stars beginning to appear in the sky. I stood under the horse chestnut that shaded the west side of the house in daylight and listened to the rustle of wind through the branches. A feeling of rushing toward something coursed up my spine and tightened in my forehead. Along the horizon I could see the weak glow of individual fires burning in the Skinners. I watched them for a while, waiting to see if they'd go out.

Danna stepped out onto the porch, and I could sense her watching me. "What's keeping you?" she called.

The absence of Danna's voice hung in the air for a moment before I turned around to face her. "Coals are just now hot," I said.

"Chicken's ready," she said. She put her hands in her pockets and started over toward the grill. "It's in the oven keeping warm." She pulled up a lawn chair and sat down in the glow of the fire.

I put the corn on the grill and took a seat next to her. She stared off at the fires and then down at her bare feet. By now even the

234   GOOD AS ANY

glow of the sun had dipped below the horizon, and we were sitting in the light of the kitchen window. I leaned forward and held my face in my hands. "You OK?" I asked, the muffled sound coming through my fingers.

"I should be asking you that," she said. She rubbed her hand along my back. "It's been hard on you."

"I was ready to leave the mill," I said. I combed my fingers through my hair. "There's a lot though that I can't figure."

"The pigs?"

"Not just that," I said. "Stan, Marv, everyone. Simms."

"This place has a history," Danna said. "It's not for everyone to know."

"Frank said to stay away from Simms's," I paused. "Like he knows something."

"Frank's doing his job," Danna said, and she stood up and began to turn the corn. There was a certainty in the way Danna moved, a decisiveness that made me feel she was more able to cope with the world. I saw it in her painting and in the way she handled fabric and scissors, needle and thread, and the careful strength she used on rough berry vines—always getting what she wanted from them. Sometimes this filled me with a kind of inadequacy. It was a part of knowing I could never be as sure of myself.

"I want to see Simms," I said, finally.

Danna sat back down, and I stared for a time hoping to be able to read something in her expression. Sweat had gathered under her eyes and her cheeks shimmered in the firelight. "It's small events that ignite into bigger ones," she offered.

I didn't know what she meant by this. It sounded like a warning. Leaning back in my chair I felt tiredness, an aching throughout my body. I felt exhausted in the way I had over the last few years when, on long sleepless nights, I sat on the edge of the bed, certain I was on the crest of sleep.

"What about us?" Danna asked, flatly. "What are we doing?"

"I don't know," I said.

"You could stay at my place," she said. "We don't need two houses."

I thought about it for a moment, considering if I'd ever get used to the quiet of Danna's house. "Do you want to stay here?" I asked.

"In this house?" she said, looking away from me toward the kitchen window. "Or in the valley?" she continued.

"In the valley," I said.

Danna paused a moment and then she frowned. "I love this place," she said. "I've known it a long time. But I don't know if I'm going to recognize it soon." She dabbed her palm along her forehead and then pushed a few strands of wispy hair back out of her face. She let her feet glide along the top of the grass, the blades grazing the soles. Then she stopped and leaned forward with her arms crossed, wrapped around her waist. "I don't know," she said.

I could smell that the corn was burning. Tendrils of smoke drifted upward in the light that came from the house. Danna stood up and picked each cob off the grill with a delicate stroke, tossing them out onto the driveway. "This'll be no good," she said.

I wanted to say I was sorry for having let dinner go. Instead, I settled back in my chair. "What was it like here before I came?" I asked.

"Like it is now," she said. "I mean the way it was before the drought. How it was for you when you came."

"Did you ever think about leaving then?"

"I doubt it," she said.

I knew about the valley from talking to the old-timers, from the guys at the Co-op, from the men at the mill, but I never really discussed it with Danna. We talked some, but it was mostly about the future and what we might do. Danna looked tired now. The heat had taken a lot out of both of us.

"Stan ever used to call on you?" I asked, jokingly.

Danna smiled, answered honestly, "A few times."

I was surprised by her reply and how she gave it. I'm sure the smile left my face.

"Nothing serious," Danna said, laughing a little. "A peck on the cheek."

"No," I said, as an apology. I raised my hand as if to brush away my expression. "I didn't mean anything by it. I meant—"

"It's OK." Danna reached over and touched my hand.

This was the first time I'd felt awkward with Danna since we'd first met. I reached to hold her hand between mine. Though it was early, it felt like it'd been a full day. "We should go to bed," I said.

"I don't think I can sleep on this," Danna said, "not tonight."

"I know," I nodded. Sleep seemed far off to me—even farther away than a decision—out beyond the mountains, I imagined. I had this notion of a place, of rough territory, where I could sleep safely out in the open, under dark skies dusty with stars, the barren landscape seductive, ghostly. I don't know where this image came from, but at night I sometimes conjured it and tried to imagine I was there, hoping to fool myself. Looking out over the cornfields, to the Skinners, I wondered if this place wasn't turning into the place I imagined.

"Let's get ready for bed," I said. I put my arms around her shoulders, held her. "We'll decide," I said.

Her body relaxed and she said, "Yes."

———

I opened the bedroom windows and pulled back the sheets while Danna put away the chicken and turned out the lights in the rest of the house. I sat on the edge of the mattress and stared at the window, wanting to see into the solid darkness that was beyond the rusty screen. In the bedroom, overhead, two bulbs pushed shadows awkwardly around the room. A breeze stirred and the sound of crickets and peepers was in the room. I slipped off my jeans and boots and lay back on the bed with my eyes closed.

Danna came in and I listened to her taking her clothes off. She turned out the light. We were quiet for a while, and I leaned over and turned the radio on low, hoping we could get some of the jazz we'd grown used to hearing. Instead, there was news about the fire. I let it play.

"I'm sorry about dinner," I said, rolling over to face Danna.

"It'll keep," she said. "We'll have some for lunch tomorrow."

"I think I'll go down to Simms's in the morning."

Danna turned on her side to face me and adjusted her pillows. A recorded interview with Frank ebbed lightly in the background.

"You think you'll find something there?" Danna asked.

"I'm not sure I'm looking for anything."

I tried to see Danna's face, to get an idea about what she was thinking. Above us the mice were beginning to go to work, skittering around in the ceiling.

"How can you stand that noise?" Danna said.

"It helps me sleep," I answered. I thought of telling Danna about the place I imagined when I was trying to get myself to let go of the waking world. I reached and put my hand on Danna's shoulder, then rubbed her neck. "I don't think we should leave the valley," I said, at last, regretting my words almost as soon as I'd uttered them.

Danna took a long time in answering. "If that's what you think," she said. There seemed to be more she wanted to say. Frank's voice continued in the room. I rolled over and turned the radio off.

"I'll keep doing the piece work until school starts," she said, softly.

My decision appeared to satisfy Danna. I could sense her relaxing, beginning to fall asleep. As her breathing softened, she began to drift away from me. The room began to widen with moonlight, and I could see Danna naked on the covers, her shape emerging like a ghost. I closed my eyes and listened for the mice.

8.

Horsetail clouds leaned across the sky, reaching over the rim of mountains in the west. The earliest of light gave the grass along the road a luminous sheen. I hadn't slept, and as I walked beside the fields they appeared white, almost covered in snow. It was a trick of light, that and a lack of sleep, which erased the contour of everything, making it seem glassy. Tears formed at the corners of my eyes when I yawned. In my arms and legs, I felt the confusion of being both rested and exhausted. They were similar feelings in my experience, and I had become intimate with both of them over the last few weeks—possessed with the loss of this place and possibly of Danna and relieved, somehow, that I was free from work at the mill.

Danna was sleeping back at the house, a whisper of air in the pale sheets, the room almost cool, lacking daylight. I had slipped from the bed without waking her, and now as I strolled along the road, my thoughts centered on what I might find at Simms's.

Looking out over the fields, the tree line and the mountains in the distance appeared threadbare. The place had been beaten, drawn. The color steeped from the soil. What I could see resembled a memory—in the way vivid events transform themselves into flatter, gauzy images that, over time, slightly lose their effect, making the loss seem even more troublesome. I recalled the first day I spent in the valley, and with the land like it was now, I couldn't distinguish the difference between what was in my head and what I was seeing. But I felt the difference. How time had changed the two places. It was the gulf between what a person said and what was meant. What I had said to Danna the night before was that we should stay, but what I meant was, I don't think I'll ever belong. A wild place is like that, inviting and then remote and cold. I could feel this like a deep note trembling in my bones, could see it in the muted hue that lifted with the dawn.

I'd been to Simms's a few times to pick Danna up from work.

But as I made the last half mile I began to notice how everything appeared to have forgotten itself—a twist of weeds beside the road, a few stands of willow trees, and a blunt, open sky. Crags, it seemed, on the face of the landscape drew me into the smallest places—the culvert alongside the road, the brittle pavement nudging the dry shag, gravel skirting off from beneath my boots and shedding the ground in a powdery cloud. Dry, without even the slightest hint of moisture, the air was so still that it seemed absent, evaporated. There was nothing to carry the usual sound of morning. It was as if the world hadn't taken shape, that light had found it hunched and formless, resting the way I imagined things did in the dark.

Already, heat radiated off the blacktop. The warmth forced a chill along my back. Just up the road I could see the top of Simms's barn, a Quonset, over the line of trees that jutted out across the field. I thought I wanted to see for myself what his fields looked like, what it felt like to see the ground beaten thin. I wasn't all that familiar with Simms. We talked a bit when he came by the Co-op. He was quiet, often focused, it seemed, on something that wasn't in the room. Because of this, there was a lot left to be said and people, the regulars, talked about him in his absence. I hated this and mostly I'd leave the room. I guessed, now, that I'd missed things I needed to know. Looking out over the countryside, sunlight draped in like a sheet. I could smell a sweet pollen floating on the white radiance. As I approached Simms's, the pavement, the soil, the trees, seemed to be raw, cut open, the drought emerging upward from out of this tract of earth. It was as if I was coming close to the point where things were born into the world.

Simms's land lay bare all the way to the river—flattened turn rows. Crows, cut and angled from metal the color of primer, wings reaching outward, spanning twelve feet or more, hovered, their bases hidden below them in the shadows that led westward. A breeze had picked up and tufts of cottonwood drifted upward, moving against gravity, over the rent dirt.

I tried to imagine I was happy. I closed my eyes and listened to the leaves scuffling in the branches, raspy and gaunt. I held on to this for a while, listening.

From where I stood, I could see into Simms's Quonset. The doors spread wide revealed a darkness cut by flashes of light and a denser patch of darkness that moved silently. Looking out on this—the half-dozen sculpted crows, the shadowy figure of Simms that seemed to be working outside the world—I felt that my lungs were collapsing, the heat tugging at the last of my air, the wet tissue walls coming together and drying out. Sweat burned my eyes. I hung back for a moment, surveying the situation, and then kicked out toward the barn.

Simms must have seen me coming. I stood just outside the shadow of the Quonset, looking in on the dimness. Simms bent, worked the oxygen and acetylene regulators, then hooked the torch on one of the cylinders. He stood for a moment and stared in my direction. Then he slipped his gloves off and flipped the welder's hood up. His face was smudged with black residue.

"Welding?" I said, as a kind of greeting.

Simms was silent. In the dark his eyes looked white. They were as clear as a spring creek. Icy. "Expected the others," he said, then paused. "Not you."

"Frank's been down?" I asked.

"And Stan and Marv," he said. He tugged at the zipper of his coveralls.

"Heat must be killing you," I said. I could see that beneath the black jumpsuit he'd sweated his shirt through. "Hotter than hell."

"I do OK," he said. Then for no reason he smiled. It was unexpected, and in the shadows it appeared to magnify something within him. He was both young and old: he had his way with the world.

"I thought I'd come down and see how you're doing," I offered. A burning had begun to rise up from my chest into my throat. I kicked at the dirt. "With all this heat and the farm and everything."

"Well, I'm making these crows." Simms turned and looked upward at the looming wingspan of the sculpture he'd been working on. He raised his hand, "Cut those pieces individually, then lap welded them."

I nodded.

"They're more like grackles, I reckon." Simms stepped forward and looked away, out across his field.

Sudden hunger cut into me. It was as if I'd not eaten in days. Then that feeling twisted itself in my stomach and turned into something worse. I was surrounded by the sound of this open, scorched space, the still air, the sun hooked to the pale sky.

Simms scrutinized me for a moment, then let his gaze fall on the ground between us. "You come about the pigs," he said, not as a question.

"Yeah," I replied. I paused, almost deciding to let it drop. "Have you seen them?"

Simms grinned and stepped farther out of the Quonset, out into the crescent of light that hugged the barn's shade. The welding hood kept his face shadowed. "If'n a pig was to fly," he said, "it'd have its reasons." He fell quiet and stared at me, never turning his eyes away from mine.

"I guess," I said, uncomfortable with Simms standing an arm's length away, expressionless.

"I never seen one take to the air of its own accord," he concluded.

Simms turned and headed back into the Quonset. I edged forward into the shade, followed his motions in the dark. He slipped out of his coveralls and wiped his face with a towel. I began to expect something from him. A tingling pushed down through my arms, through my chest and legs. It was a notion carried like an electric current. Out of the dark, a low rumble, a scratch and ping, rolled, as Simms draped his soggy clothes over the bird's wing. Then he emerged carrying a couple of sodas in one hand, and with the other hand he fiddled with the perch of his baseball cap.

"You'll dry out," he said, and with a swift punch from his one hand he released a single can into the air without dropping the other. "Cheers," he said.

The gnawing in my stomach eased some after a few sips. He had something to say. I could see thoughts scratching around in his head, him considering which words to draw on. Simms looked out on his field, the churned soil, burnt dry, brown, and leveled, the crows holding fast as if above russet clouds. The metal birds had lost their long shadows now that the day had gone white hot. Out along the perimeter of his land, Simms's tractor sat idle, as if abandoned midplow, and behind it a small mound covered with a tarp. A sheen, a white dust, settled on the trees, on the sculptures, and on the Skinners. With the cottonwood floating, it was possible to squint my eyes and imagine it was a winter scene, complete with snow.

"Thirty years I tilled that dirt," he said, finally. He fingered the bill of his cap, lifted it slightly. He turned to me. "You ain't been here near that long. You don't know shit about this place. There's time in that dirt out there."

"I've an idea," I said, trying to agree with him without revealing how foolish I felt coming here and how little I really understood about the place.

"Danna's worked my berries longer than she's known you," he said. He focused on me, raised an eyebrow. "What's it you want out here?"

I hesitated, not sure how to take his question. "We've seen pigs flying out here," I said, finally. There was a long silence.

"I do God's work," he said, halting to take a swallow from his drink. He turned and faced his field. "This time every year, until now, that's been green. Rich with berries. Now there's them crows I made. All of them together," he paused and turned to look at me. "That's a murder out there."

"That's just bad luck," I said.

"No," he said. "No it ain't." He took a swallow from his can. "That's a sickness," he said, "that'll turn to death."

"What do you mean?"

"Well," he said. "Soon, it's just going to be houses in that field."

"No," I said. "I don't think so."

"You can't stop something like this. They call it progress. Shit."

Simms tossed his empty can into the shade of the Quonset and headed out to the spent field, the crows. I took a drink. Simms was headed out toward one of his sculptures. He expected me to follow. I trailed behind him, the dust rising from his footsteps. I walked with my head down, the glare of the sun clouding my sight of Simms. He seemed to hover above the ground in the hazy dust.

Simms stood in the shadow thrown by the large wing of a sculpture. "I can sell these," he said. "People will want them."

I stood beneath the head of the crow, its face looking outward, heading forward toward something, I guessed. It had a mind of its own, it seemed, a mind something like Simms's. I stared at Simms. "Who to?" I asked.

"There comes a time when you been someplace long enough that you don't see it anymore. It's there. You count on it, sure. Like your body. It ain't until something goes out that you miss it, until it's noticeable." Simms lifted the bill of his cap and wiped his forehead.

I reached up and stroked the weld, caressing the face of the bird. I kept quiet. Simms was trying to get at me, at something I couldn't place.

"I reckon you owe somebody something. I reckon everyone owes." Simms pulled his cap down and then reached up and slapped the wing of the sculpture. The sound built, rolled out toward the tip of the wing, resonated like thunder between the hills of the valley. It was a sound I'd not heard in a long time. "You're looking to belong to something," Simms said. "Stay long enough and you'll own it all." He turned and headed out toward his tractor.

"Danna and I are thinking of leaving," I suggested to him.

"Come on," he said, motioning for me to follow.

We headed into the dusty field. The farther we moved out into the flattened turn rows the more foolish I felt. I wondered if Danna knew I was here and if she had called Frank. With the sun bearing down, the sky the color of steel, and nothing but the sound of a few insects in the dead grass along the edge of the field, I felt like Danna and Frank should know where I was, that if I didn't return soon they should come see about me. I knew I didn't really belong to this place.

Simms pulled up at the tractor and stood leaning against the back tire. I stood a few feet back from him. The air here felt thin, and turning back toward the large crows I imagined we had come to another place, an alien landscape. We each stood catching our breath by the tractor, out along Simms's fields, where down the steep embankment we could see the slow current of the river, the shallow water moving along the bank.

"This place looks like hell," I said, still breathing heavily. I kicked at the dirt. "You kind of look like hell."

"You should know what it's like to be me," he said. He placed his hand on the top of the tire. "It's where you are when things happen that makes you start owning a place. Lose them and you lose part of yourself. Part of your mind is gone, your memory erased." Simms stopped and bent down, resting his hands on his knees. He breathed heavily.

I nodded, pretended I understood what he was saying. "You've lost your share," I said. I felt like I didn't have a right to be talking, the field barren under my boots.

"Like that river out there," he said, standing erect. "It's been there always, seems like. You count on it lasting long after they bury you."

"It will," I said.

"Maybe," he said. "Maybe it will."

"We're all in the same boat," I said. "You've got to hang on."

"I don't feel like I got a boat," Simms said. He pointed to the river. "Soon we won't need a boat. The rules are changed. We got new rules now, Gabe."

"We all have new rules," I said.

Simms studied me. "Listen. You came here wanting to know something. You and all the others. I didn't say squat to them." He pulled his cap down and raised a hand to shade his eyes. "But you got to start owning something."

"What's all this about owning?" I said. I was rattled. I wanted to understand where he was coming from, what it was he thought I was going to own and owe.

Simms walked back behind the tractor. "I'm going to show you," he said. He reached down and pulled back the tarp.

Beneath the cover was a handmade contraption, a collection of PVC pipe and black plastic sheeting corded together to make a kind of flying machine. This was the material that Marv had seen in the back of Simms's truck the last time he'd been to the Co-op. He had fashioned a set of wings, scaffolded the skeleton of a large bird, and spread the plastic over the frame. At each joint, the wings were held together with the plastic, clutched with a fine filament, and pulled taut. Still, it was loosely constructed, the plastic torn in places. In its center, beneath its wings, I could see a heavy leather harness that Simms had made to fit a pig. I thought Simms was trying to fabricate an explanation, rather than come up with a cause. It had never flown. It could never fly.

"Look here at this," Simms said. "It's a work of art."

"Art?" I questioned. "When did you turn to art?"

"That's what they call progress, ain't it?" he asked. "A sign of civilization? You tell me."

I kneeled to look at the glider. What I knew of Simms was what I'd heard or seen of him at the Co-op. He dropped in like the rest of us, but not as often. I understood that he was a hard worker, tending to his place after the field hands left for the day. Simms had a sense of duty about him, a propriety. I'd heard him say more than once, "I do God's work." The word God, lilting high in the rafters of the Co-op, with everyone waiting for it settle. Now, seeing him, I was surprised by his gestures; the way he moved, talked, dressed. He wore clothes with lots of pockets and he kept his pockets full.

He had tools to fix almost anything on the spot. The wings were one of those tools.

"This thing doesn't fly," I said.

"The hell it doesn't," he said. "Get that tractor going and it sure enough puts a pig in the air."

"It's too heavy," I said. I reached down and felt the edge of the wing. I lifted the tip of the glider to check its weight. "It's too flimsy. It won't bear enough weight."

"The air resistance holds it together. It flies like a dream," Simms said, slicing his hand through the air.

"I'd have seen the tether."

"In this haze?" he said. "You're lucky to see the pig."

"What are you up to?" I asked, finally.

"Debts come due," he said. "I'm calling them in. I'm going to make them pay."

"What are you talking about?" I said. "People around here are your friends."

"I'm paying," he said. "I'm paying with everything. All these empty fields. Damn it. It's time it starts paying me. You think a heat wave like this just happens?"

"I think it *has* happened."

"Bullshit," he said. "It's people not taking care. People like your boss, Neal. Clear cutting timber. Poisoning the river. Folks worrying over petty little problems. Not paying attention to the place that loves them, lets them live, gives them food." Simms spit, kicked at the dust. "You're half right. It ain't me flying the pigs. It's people. People calling home what they're due. I'm just a means."

"You think making crows will solve things?" I asked, not even entertaining the idea that he was responsible for the pigs.

"It's a means to an end," he said. "Others will come."

"Then what?"

"It ain't for me to say," he said. "Others, like you, will come." He pointed at me. "You didn't belong to this place, the way it *was*. But things will change. You might belong then. But *I* won't. I'm making it so I get my share. Things change. You have to make them change. I'm a creator. We all have to do what we are meant to do." Simms paused. His face was slick with moisture. He wiped his hand across his brow. "I think I'm going to take myself down to the river and swim in it. I need to cool off. I want to feel that water."

"You think I believe you're flying those pigs?"

"Think what you want," Simms said. "I don't give a damn."

I reached down and lifted at the edge of the wing. "This is supposed to be the cause of all the stir?"

"You'll tell the others what you want. Don't matter what I say."

I shook my head, looking out toward the river. Rivulets streamed down my forehead and burned my eyes. I felt a tear roll down my cheek.

Simms stood up straight and began to head back toward the Quonset. "I'm going down to the water." He swept past me. "I want to be let alone."

9.

Danna was awake and waiting for me in the kitchen, sitting with a cup of coffee and a rifle. I went to the sink where she had run some cool water. I rinsed my hands and then lifted water to my face.

"You'd better conserve," she said.

"Nice welcome," I said. "You planning to do me in about last night's dinner?"

"We've got to talk," she said. "It's Stan."

"Stan?" I said. "News about Jason?"

"His cattle," Danna said. "He's made a decision."

"What do you mean?"

"They're suffering," she said. Danna looked out the bay window, out across the tops of the dead corn rows. Quietly, tears began to run down her cheeks. "Stan came by this morning," she said. "I told him you were out." She wiped the tears with the back of her hand. "He'd have come for you."

"He wants us to come help him?" I interrupted.

"Yes."

"How could he ask you?" I said. I sat down, across the table from Danna. I toweled my hands down the front of my jeans. "You can't do this."

"I'm OK," she said. "Someone's got to be there for Stan. We all go a long way back together."

"But you—"

"I'll be fine," she said. She tried to reassure me, reached across the table and stroked my forearm. "It's better me than someone else. I think he's gone to get Frank. Frank's coming, too." She took a sip of coffee then traced her finger along her lip. "You want some?"

"I'm too beat for coffee," I said. I leaned back in the chair. "Simms has got something going on down there."

Danna sat, staring at her coffee. It was as if she was putting everything together, every jagged piece of the puzzle. There were no surprises anymore, it seemed. I watched her, waited for her to respond, to register this new information. "What's that?" she said.

"He's got these sculptures he calls art," I said. "They're these large birds, crows. And he says he's been flying the pigs."

"He says?" Danna asked.

"He can't be," I said. "He's got this contraption." I drew out the shape of the wings, the harness, in the air with my hands. "It could never fly."

"If he says he's doing it—and somebody's doing it—then why not Simms? It makes sense, if anything here does."

"Danna. No, listen." I rested my hands on the tabletop, tried to assure her. "What he showed me won't fly."

"Then he's doing it some other way," she said, anxiously. Danna shifted in her chair, faced the window. She looked down the road, toward Simms's place. "What difference does it make?"

"A lot," I said. Then I thought about it. "None, I guess. I just need to make sense of all this."

"There's no making sense of what comes. It's nature, it's God, it's whatever it is you believe in. Whatever it is, it's showing us that we don't control things. Or maybe we do. Maybe this is our doing. This heat. The pigs. Maybe we're doing all of this and we don't know it."

"Danna, look. None of this is our fault."

"Then you explain it."

"I can't."

"Well, I can," she said, taking a sip of coffee. "We have to go down and shoot Stan's cows. That's enough for me. That's what I know. That's all I can take right now."

I was exhausted, like she was, but I was also longing to sleep; to sleep with my eyes closed, to feel the world that was becoming drift from me and leave me in the wild place I'd dreamed for myself sometime ago. A part of me wanted to leave the valley behind. Danna wanted to understand this place; she was continuing to embrace it.

"Are you sure you want to do this?" I asked. "Is this the right thing to do?"

"Stan says," Danna paused. "He says it's the right thing. It's the humane thing."

"Jesus," I said. "His son and now his cows."

"We don't know about his son."

"We don't," I said. "But we've a good idea."

"Don't talk like that." Danna stood up and went to the sink where she poured out her coffee. "We're supposed to meet Stan. It's about time."

"I need a gun, I guess."

"Stan's got a pistol for you," Danna said. She pointed to the rifle.

"I have to use that. I just can't be that close to them. I'll have to do it from a distance."

Her words seemed to fall. Danna was hunched, tired. I had never seen her like this, and I was beginning to realize I might not ever see her like this again. For whatever reason, the worse things were getting, the more she was becoming a part of this place and the changes that were rapidly overcoming it.

"I love you," I said.

"I love you, too," she said, faintly, without turning away from the window.

"I'll be outside when you're ready." I stood up and slowly walked out the door.

The heat hung in a dense cloud out over the valley. I opened the door to my truck and sat on the edge of the seat, my legs dangling. Everything—the seat, the door handle, the steering wheel—was blistering hot. My lungs tugged at the air. The breeze was heavy with a scent, something smoky and sour. I felt sure that it would rain soon. I was startled by the sound of Danna putting the rifle in the bed of the pickup.

"We should go," she said, slipping onto the seat beside me.

I turned and closed the door. "Shouldn't we wait?" I said. "I mean, shouldn't Stan wait? I think it's going to rain."

"Stan says they're too far gone." She rolled down her window. "They're suffering."

I clutched and turned the ignition. "It seems like such a waste." I put the truck into gear and wheeled out over the grass and then back onto the driveway.

Stan's place was a few miles up River Road, the opposite direction of Simms's land. I took it easy, letting the hot wind come into the cab. We passed Holmes Park that lay at the base of a ridge of mountains, to the west of the river. The road held close to the range that ran north for a few miles before shifting west, away from the straight bearing that the pavement held. Along the road the trees were blighted, bare. Leaves clung to their bases in piles. It could have been autumn if not for the heat. Looking out east over the river I could see clouds building, rising high like the beginnings of a thunderhead.

"Looks like we might get rain," I said, pointing.

"Too late," Danna said. She put her hand on the seat between us. "I'm sorry."

"Sorry?" I asked. "You don't have anything to be sorry about."

"I know you want to leave this place. The valley."

"I said I'd stay."

"I know what you said." She slid closer to me on the seat. "But it's not what you want."

"How do you know what I want?" I asked. I felt a deep sadness rise, build up.

"I don't," she said. She rested her hand on my thigh. "But neither do you. It's as if you have some abstract notion of what a place should be. Now that things are going badly, this place is failing you. Your idea."

I looked out at the mountains. They drifted away toward the west. Farmland ran alongside the road. "This place," I said, "is becoming something. I don't know what it is. It's like the mice that run in my ceiling. They'll also be gone soon, feels like. It's as if everything that I love about this place is changing. You're changing—"

"I've got to. People change so that they can survive."

"Let me finish. I think you're in the middle of something. Coping, I guess."

"I will. You're right. But so will you." Danna shifted in her seat. She nearly faced me. "Either you're with me or you're not."

"I want to be," I said. "I want us to be somewhere together. But I'm not sure this is the place."

Danna looked out at the road ahead. We were a quarter mile from Stan's. "Why?"

"This place is poisoned," I said, "from the way it used to be."

"But not yet," Danna said. "Not completely."

I slowed the truck. "This place was perfect. Now it's a disaster area."

"I don't know what to say," Danna said. She looked out the side window, toward the east.

"This place, when I came here, was beautiful," I said. "It's becoming—"

"I don't know what's happened," Danna interrupted. "It's like if there was lightning out there now. We'd see it at different times."

"Danna," I said. "This is not science class."

"What is it then?" she said. "Are we breaking up?"

"I don't know," I said. "I mean no. I just feel like we could find somewhere else to go."

"I can't leave this place now," Danna said. "Not after all that has happened. I can't walk out on the people I care about."

We pulled up beside Stan's fields, and I stopped the car just off the shoulder of the road. Stan was standing out among his cattle smoking a cigarette. He dropped the stub, stepped on it.

"I don't know if I can stay," I said. I cut the engine and we both sat, not moving.

The air seemed to have thickened even more. I could hear Stan's boots crunching through the dirt. He was headed toward us. Danna reached up and touched her hand beneath each eye. She looked at me and then leaned over and kissed me.

"We should go," she said.

"Danna. Gabe," I heard Stan call. "Thanks for coming."

I looked toward Stan as he was coming up beside the truck.

"God," he said. "You don't know what this means to me." He had been crying.

"I'm sorry," I said. I opened the door and the sound of the creaking, rusty hinges lifted upward, hanging in the air.

Danna got out of the truck and hugged Stan. "Stan, I'm so sorry," she said. "I'm so sorry."

Stan looked out over the field. "It's got to be done," he said. "I'm guessing they've lost eighty percent of their water."

We began walking as a group out over the clotted earth. The grass was all but gone. Above us the sky had gone gray, both with smoke and clouds. Stan pulled a pistol out from his belt.

"This has got some kick," he said. "You'll want to be fairly close."

I took the gun. "Is Frank coming?"

"He called. He'll be late," Stan said. "We should go ahead."

"Any news about Jason?" Danna asked.

"None." Stan directed us to a grassy patch, where he'd left his rifle. "Frank said we got rain coming in from the east that should help them with the fire. Help's also coming from the outside. He was coordinating that and then he was going down to find Simms."

"Son of a bitch," I said. "He could've come here—"

"I told him to go," Stan interrupted.

"He should have come," Danna said. "There's no excuse."

We stopped and Stan picked up his rifle. "He's got business to attend to. It's his job." Stan held his rifle balanced over one arm and looked up at the sky. "Been almost two months without rain."

"I can feel it coming," Danna said.

"Me too," I said.

"I've separated the cattle out," Stan said. "What I've got in this pasture is what we're doing. They're in the worst shape. Mostly dairy." He pointed off toward another pasture. "Those I'm hoping will hold out for the rain."

I studied the field. There were probably twenty head that we'd have to shoot. Stan handed me a leather pouch. It was heavy in my hand. "Here's more for your gun," he said. "Get within twenty paces with that pistol."

Stan turned to Danna. "We're going to start at the far end down there," he said, pointing upwind of where we were standing. "When Gabe starts at this end, some'll run our way. They're awfully weak. So some might not run. Still, the smell will get in the air. We don't want to make a mess of this."

I saw the gun tremble in Danna's hands. Her fingers were holding tight to the barrel stock.

Stan looked at her. "You don't have to do this. Gabe and I can go alone."

"No," she said. "I want to help. I can help."

"OK," Stan said. "Let's you and me get in place down field, and Gabe, you wait until I signal you."

"Will do," I said. As Stan turned I patted him on his shoulder. "I'm sorry, Stan."

Stan didn't turn or answer.

Holding back, I watched Danna and Stan head away. He put his hand around her shoulder and I heard the muffled sound of his voice. Danna put her arm around his waist and leaned her head on his shoulder. I was envious, because in some way I felt they shared something that I didn't, a collective experience of the past. They had known each other longer than I had been in the valley. And now they would share this. I figured the value of what two people lose together somehow has more weight than the value of what they manage to keep. They had lost just about everything at least once.

I headed out toward my end of the pasture. There were two cows together, and then farther away, downwind, there was a group of eight. I decided I would take the first two, then shoot what I could of the others as they ran past. Stan and Danna could handle the rest. Above us the sky was like dirty muslin. The heat was scorching and the thought of adding to it, of firing guns, of hot metal, of opening flesh, seemed unbearable. Across the field I saw waves of heat rising, Danna and Stan shimmering. Everything was calm. Then Stan waved his hand high in the air.

Standing twenty feet from the two cows, they looked at me, their eyes distant and glazed. I lifted the pistol, took aim, and squeezed the handle, pulling the trigger. My eyes were squinted, blurred from sweat. The cow fell, a muted thump in the dry dirt. The second cow darted downwind, toward Stan and Danna. I turned and pulled the trigger a second time. The cow stumbled, fell to its knees, and lowed a wide and high scream. I fired again, aiming at its head, and it fell gently, leaning over onto a patch of burned, dry sod. The shots I'd fired echoed back to me, it seemed, from high up. They reverberated and bounced in a stunning, piercing way. My mouth went dry.

Suddenly it was as if a thunderstorm had broken loose. I looked toward Danna and I could see a puff of smoke emerge from the barrel of her rifle, and then the punch of its report rang in my ears. Stan fired. The cattle toward their end of the pasture began to scatter. But with a slight shuffling sound they each began to fall. The guns fired, then there was a moment of metal against metal, of cartridges kicking out of the chamber, and then another loud shot that reached me and echoed again and again. The mountains to our west were carrying the sound of this killing for miles. I wondered if cattle from far away could sense what was happening, if they weren't also becoming agitated, ambling out toward the farther reaches of their pasture. I reloaded my pistol and walked toward the group of eight.

I whistled to them, clucking with my tongue. A burning built up in the back of my throat, and I thought I would be sick. One cow, hoping, I guessed, that I'd brought water, nosed toward me. I raised the pistol and fired. I saw in an instant, blood course down its forehead, its eyes wild and then suddenly dull, as it fell with a hushed grunt. There was a quiet moment. A cloud of dust rose and then settled back down on the cow. The other cows scattered, ran in the direction of Stan, who had come up closer to where I was standing. A sickness rose up into my chest and I closed my eyes. I could feel heat rise off the barrel of my gun, reaching up from my wrist and around my arm. My palm was sweaty and the gun was slick in my hand. I stroked the back of my forearm across my forehead and, looking, somehow expected to find blood.

Again there was the long and drawn-out thunder. Each shot fired was like a punch, hitting me in the stomach, the chest, the head. I kneeled down, felt a cool sweat break out over my body. An excruciating tightness pulled deep in my stomach, and I began to vomit in dry and bitter heaves. I could hear each cow as it hit the ground, Danna and Stan's rifles firing, echoing between the silences, the almost inscrutable blow of flesh against earth.

I opened my eyes and there, three feet from me, was the last cow that I'd shot. The one that came to me, hoping I would spare it misery. Its eyes glassy, its legs crumpled beneath its gaunt body. The smell of manure and blood and opened flesh was coming off the breeze. Flies had already begun to light, frantic and careless.

Stan and Danna began to fire again. The shots echoed. I stood up from my knees and looked toward them. Smoke drifted in the air and I smelled gunpowder. Stan took aim and fired one last shot into the skull of a cow that was downed but not dead. It leaned over lazily. I listened to the report echoing westward through the mountains, a long and hollow voice. And then, finally, there were no more shots.

Out across the ground I could see the bodies of dead cows, scattered. Danna was hugging Stan. Then Stan turned and faced toward the river, where most of the cows lay. Danna headed up toward the truck. Watching her walk, I noticed that Frank had pulled up behind my truck and was standing along the edge of the field, his rifle in hand. I began walking toward him.

With each step, a sense of returning to the world emerged. It was as if during those few minutes, I'd gone completely numb. Even my sickness had come forth, somehow, from my lack of feeling. Seeing Frank made me angry, and the closer I got the more rage I felt. I felt it for myself and for Danna. I didn't want her to have to take part in this.

"Where the hell were you?" I said as I got closer.

"I had work to do," Frank said.

Danna pushed past Frank without a word. She put her rifle in the bed of my truck and slid into the cab.

Frank watched her get in. "I'm sorry, Gabe," he said. "I wanted to be here. But we got the Guard coming in. And I had to check on Cliff."

"Simms? You could have done that—"

"It needs to be done," he said, holding his hands out in a questioning way. "It's long overdue."

There was a long pause.

"Simms isn't flying the pigs," I said.

"I don't know what's going on," he said. "He wasn't at his place."

"He said he was going down to the river," I confessed.

"I thought I told you to stay away from there," he said.

"I know."

"I'll take care of him," he said. "You stay away." Frank took his cap off, kicked at the ground. "Listen. You better stay up here by the truck. I've got some news for Stan."

"Oh, no," I said. I felt the pistol, heavy in my hand. "God."

"It wouldn't be right for you—"

"I know," I said. "I know."

"You go comfort Danna. It looks like she's pretty upset. You better tell her the news."

"Yeah."

Frank patted me on the shoulder and headed out to talk with Stan. I went to the truck and slipped onto the seat by Danna.

"You OK?"

"I don't know," she said. "Where was Frank?"

"He had business," I said. "Listen. There's some news—"

"Oh, God," Danna said. Stan was on his knees in front of Frank, his body shaking. "It's Jason . . ."

"Yes," I said. I leaned over to put my arms around Danna.

"No," she said. "Not now." She covered her face with her hands and began to cry. She kept repeating his name. "Stan," she said. "Poor Stan."

"I'll go with you," she said, finally. "I can't take this any longer."

For a moment I believed her. A rested feeling rose up from my chest and finally, after so many days of not sleeping and not knowing, I was satisfied. And looking out over the field, the dead bodies of the cattle, I wanted to believe her. But it was impossible. She would never leave.

10.

I stepped out of the shower, the smell of gunpowder still on my palms. I was worried for Stan. The images of the cows, each of them as they fell, were still fresh in my mind. I toweled off and slipped into my jeans. My thoughts were muddled, my head tight like I'd been drinking. I felt I needed to sleep, to let this world fall away for a few hours. I was tired of Marv and Horace and Frank. Price and Henshaw, too. Everyone like them. I was exhausted by their petty debts, their greed and spite. Simms was right: Someday everything comes due.

Danna was sitting on the front porch drinking a beer, looking out over the fields and the burned Skinners. I got a bottle for myself, strolled onto the porch. Clouds continued to build in the east, towering.

"You OK?" I asked.

"I'm OK," she said, softly. "OK as I'll ever be."

"Mind if I sit down?"

"It's your house," she said, the words pointed. She hesitated. "I didn't mean it that way."

"You haven't seen any flying pigs have you?" I said jokingly.

"It's no joke," she said.

"I know," I said. I sat down next to her. I reached to hold her hand, the roughness gone from a season without berries.

"If you give me half a chance," she said, "I could make you want to stay."

"You," I said, "are the reason I have stayed."

"But I'm not enough?" she asked.

"It's not you," I said. "It's this place. It's like what you said when we first met. This place was paradise."

"It's still the same," she said.

"It's not what it was," I said. "The more I know of the valley the less I like it."

"Seems now you know less."

"Maybe," I said. "But it's the people that have ruined it."

"You can't spend your life running from people."

"No," I said. "But I don't have to know all of them. Everybody knows everybody's business around here." I let go of her hand. "That makes them think it's their business, too."

"What about me? What about Stan?" she asked quickly. She turned and looked at me. "Are you saying you don't want to share our lives?"

"I'm saying I can't stand to live with more than a few people."

"It's called community," Danna said. "It's what holds people together when things get rough."

"Maybe," I said. "But I don't want to have to hurt for someone else."

"If something happened to me," she said, "you don't want to have to mourn? Is that what you're saying?"

"I can't take this," I said. "It's like I know all the wrong stuff. The ugly truths." I leaned forward and put my face in my hands. "I love you, Danna. I want to be with you. I just don't think here."

"Then you love part of me," she said. "That's not enough." Danna took a sip of beer. She stared off into the distance. "Belonging," she said, "means taking all that bad stuff, making it your own. It means loving in spite of all the ugliness."

"I never said I wanted to belong."

"If you stay someplace long enough," she said, "it's not a choice."

I looked at her and I knew she was right. I hurt for Stan and his losses. I had a fear of leaving. The sense of uncertainty that comes with moving was on me, and I understood it would dissipate if I just gave in and stayed. It felt easier, safer, to stay. I had loved Danna. Now, I'd grown to depend on her. The constant noise of her breezing through the house, her sleeping beside me in bed. She was a comfort and that, in the end, is what love comes to. A house without her presence would be unbearable.

"I know you're right," I said. "It's just not what I counted on."

"You should be glad," she said. "Things would be boring other-wise."

We sat peacefully drinking our beer, caught up in our own thoughts. The wind had picked up and the stalks of corn bent in the fields. The dry leaves above us were raspy. I noticed up the road, Frank's car moving quickly toward us, a tail of dust rising.

"Frank's on his way," I said, standing.

"Yeah," she said.

"I'm going to check in with him." I shuffled down the steps, descended the hill to the road.

Frank was pushing it, driving fast. I waved my hand and the pitch of the engine dropped. Frank slowed, pulled to the side of the road, and idled. He had one hand on his shotgun, holding it steady. His face was flush and slick with perspiration. His sheriff's badge was pinned to his shirt.

"You seen Cliff?" he asked. "Coming along this road?"

"No," I said. "He said he was going to the river. I took that to mean the island."

"I just came from there," Frank said. "No sign of him."

"It was early when I saw him," I said. "Check his Quonset?"

"I'm headed there now," he said.

"Need some company?"

"You stay clear," Frank said, sternly. "I mean it this time. Stay away."

"What's the worry?"

"This ain't just about the pigs anymore."

"Those pigs aren't his," I said.

"Never mind the pigs," Frank said. He looked at the pavement ahead of him.

"What's this about?"

"Not supposed to say," Frank said. He shook his head.

"Frank," I said. "It's me."

"You didn't hear this," he said, pausing. "That fire wasn't an accident."

"Simms started it?" I asked.

"I don't know," he said. "That's what I aim to find out."

"I can't believe he would do such a thing."

"There's a lot you don't know," Frank said. "You just take care of your own. Anybody asks, you don't know anything."

"Yeah," I said. I bent, leaned my elbows on the car door. "Be careful, Frank."

"Will do," he said, pulling the car into gear.

I stepped back. Frank gunned the engine, dust lifting up. I turned and made my way back to the porch. I sat down and was quiet, thinking over what Frank had said.

"What's wrong?" Danna asked.

"Nothing," I said, lying. "Frank's concerned about Simms. Wanted to know if we'd seen him."

"What'd you tell him?"

"Not since this morning."

I leaned back in my chair, picked up my beer. I took a sip. It'd gone warm. I reached and held Danna's hand. She smiled.

"I could use some new pictures," she said.

"Yeah," I said, smiling back. "I could do that. When?"

"Maybe later," she said. "When the light is better."

"Want a fresh beer?" I asked.

"Sure," she said.

I went inside, pulled the caps off two bottles. It seemed to be cooler, the drapes ruffling in the breeze. I thought of the heat wave and how long it had lasted. We were due for a break, for some rain.

Danna sat with her eyes closed. I placed the bottle down next to her chair. "I don't want to fight," she said, without looking at me.

"I know," I said. I took a long drink. I leaned back in my chair, closed my eyes.

Danna and I both were quiet, letting everything settle in. Then, there was a gunshot, the piercing answer bouncing through the hills of the valley. It came and went and then returned to us again.

Danna leaned forward, startled, looking down the road toward Simms's.

"What was that?"

I closed my eyes. "I don't know," I said.

"That was a gunshot," she said.

"It was nothing," I lied. A weight settled on me. "Don't worry about it."

11.

Fried chicken sat on the table between us. Danna and I had both eaten all we could and slid our chairs back from the table. We had been quiet all through dinner. Outside the window, evening was settling in across the hills, the river, and into the cornfield.

"Simms wasn't flying the pigs," I said, finally.

"It happens in a place like this," Danna said. "It can happen. Anything can happen. It's like an idea run wild, no matter what sense it makes."

We let this thought linger, lay between us for what seemed the longest time. The overhead light was off and nightfall crept into the kitchen. Danna stood up from the table and unbuttoned her jeans, slid them down her thighs and stepped out of them. She unbuttoned her work shirt and let it fall to the floor.

"Let's go for a swim," she said, heading out of the house.

Night settled in on the valley with a coolness we'd not felt in months. Across from the house, Danna pushed out through the corn and I trailed behind her. The clouds that had heightened were gone. The moon was near full above the mountains to the east, and I could see her in the light, her naked body glowing and being cut by the frantic shadows of the stalks. She began to run and I lost sight of her, but the sound of her body tearing through the columns of corn grew.

She waited for me at the edge of the river. I heard her breathing, her whole body rising and falling in the light, with the water running slow and black. As I got close I saw thin lines of blood tracing the curves of her shoulders and arms and across her breasts, cut like a road map into her skin by the leaves on the corn. I wanted to say something, but I didn't. Cars crossed the bridge upriver from us with the sound of tires clapping over the gaps in the pavement.

I imagined her like this in a painting; standing next to the river, the moonlight seeming to come from within her, glowing through the miles of passages cut across her body. She was like an old painting pressed behind glass to prevent the cracks from expanding, to hold in the color.

"Come on," she said, making a few gentle steps into the water before diving in.

She surfaced and hung in the current about twenty yards out from me, kicking water up with her feet. I untied my boots and slipped my pants off. Cool air came up off the water and brought chill bumps to my skin. I felt something very large and empty open up inside of me, like the land gleaming in the white light and running away from us on both sides of the river, or the highway carrying along for miles between unlit houses. Danna called to me again.

"The water's fine," she said.

I dove in and swam without opening my eyes. The water was colder than made sense and I lost my breath. Danna laughed when I came up for air.

"It's fucking cold," I yelled.

"You'll get used to it," she answered. "It's fine."

She swam upriver and then turned onto her back, floated in rippling water. The river was down. I imagined how we were barely floating above the thick, moist bed that had not been touched maybe since the beginning of time.

Above us, the moon seemed to grow colder as it rose high into the sky. The water turned metallic. I drifted along with the current until I could only distinguish Danna's black silhouette rolling and gliding as she went under and came up.

Fear began to grow inside the hollowness that filled me, and I couldn't place where it belonged. I thought of the bottom of the river and began to kick my feet outward so that I wouldn't touch whatever was there. I kicked wildly and began to head upstream toward Danna.

"I can feel the eels," she called.

Energy ran inside me like wires sparking, giving off colors and humming. I dug into the water and pushed myself toward her and, as I came up for air, I saw the moonlight catching her shoulders and face, just beginning to bridge itself across the water.

"I can feel them touching my legs when they swim past," she said.

I didn't answer. I was full inside with something I couldn't understand. I didn't want to touch bottom and I tried to hover in the water facing Danna.

"What's wrong?" she asked, and she let herself float toward me. Her body carried and I felt her legs brush my waist as she washed into me—her legs around my waist, her arms stroking my back, she kissed me. Below us the eels swept by and the water cut into the valley, moving slowly and churning up the fine sand from the bottom and carrying it away.

We pushed toward the bank and then stood listening to the sound of the water. I was glad to be out of the water, to be in the air with the corn rustling in the fields up the bank above us, the crickets and frogs scratching along the edge of the river. In the light I could see blood beginning to draw down from the cuts that ran over Danna's body, and I bent down and kissed her breast. A metallic taste settled deep in my throat, and I began to lose the feeling that I had a body. A cool breeze moved through the field, and I wanted to forget the river.

"Let's go," I said. I took her hand and we made our way up the embankment and between the rows of corn toward the truck.

We drove up into the mountains, our naked bodies a pale green from the light of the dashboard. I still felt something trembling inside me, a faint echo of the river's dark water and whatever it was below the surface. I wanted to say something to Danna about what I'd felt in the river and about what I was feeling then, with the cool breeze blowing in the windows and our bodies drying to the vinyl seat of the truck.

Pinebluff Road curved and forked several times into smaller roads leading into the hill towns. When we turned corners our clothes—shoes, pants, belt buckles—tumbled around in the back of the truck. I turned off and headed up a dirt lane that climbed past a few small cottages and then ended at an opening that looked down over the valley. I parked the truck so that we could swing the tailgate down and see the river and the town below.

Moonlight caught the water, setting off embers, and the courthouse and church glowed and reached above the black streets that were spotted every now and then with a streetlight. The fields looked as if they were covered in a light dusting of snow. Danna and I sat on a blanket in the back of the truck and looked out over the valley. The air seemed thin, even with the breeze picking up in small drafts.

I saw a chill running through Danna's skin, the thin lines dried and set across her body. The night had become cool, and we both began to shiver. I put my arms around her and kissed her lips and her shoulders. I lay her back on the blanket, kissing her breasts. As I kissed her, it was not like her at all. I smelled and tasted the river, and it was as if I'd gone under and touched bottom, the cold rocks where no one had ever been. I listened to her heart beating, her blood flowing, her breathing.

We made love, Danna looking up at the night sky, the stars and the darkness between them. As I moved inside her I watched her body, still and blue in the moonlight. She was motionless and solid, her skin taut from the river water, her hair full with the dusty smell of corn. The truck creaked and I heard a loose belt buckle scraping against the metal bed of the truck. The breeze moved through trees, and a single hawk called out as it hunted on possibly the last convected air of summer. Down below us the river moved silently, and the houses stood dark. In the distance, on the other side of the mountain, the French King Highway carried cars along, almost without sound.

12.

A cool breeze washed into the kitchen. Through the window, to the east, we watched anvil clouds tower. It had begun to sprinkle, rain sparsely beading on the window. The night before, I'd stood at the edge of the cliff where King Philip had jumped. People, I thought, cling to the world because of their losses. I turned, went back to the truck. I drove home and slept with Danna, the mice working in my ceiling. It was a sound I would miss. With the first pale of dawn, Stan had knocked on our door. We poured coffee and ate toast. Later, Frank stopped by on his way to attend to his brother's place.

"It was him or me," Frank confessed, his hand on a coffee mug. He shook his head. "There wasn't a choice."

"You do what you have to," Stan said. He looked beaten, his face gone ashen. His eyes were swollen from tears. He took a long swallow of coffee. He'd lost everything.

"Can I get you more coffee?" I asked.

"Sure," Stan said.

I brought the pot to the table, poured for Stan, Frank, and Danna. There was fried bacon on a plate that sat untouched. The wind picked up, the blowing rain hitting the glass in sheets. I lowered the windows. We sat for a long time, looking out at the cornstalks nodding, slick with the first rain in two months.

"What will you do?" Frank asked, finally. He looked at Danna. She shrugged her shoulders, glanced at me.

"Stay," I said. "I guess. Move my stuff to Danna's."

"Lot of people went belly up," Stan said. "Leaving for something new."

"I figure I'll put Cliff's place up for sale," Frank said. "People been trying to buy him out for years. That's beautiful land near the river. It could bring a price."

The rain came heavier, running in waves down the glass. Wet leaves blew from the trees, filling the air. They came to the window, touched like handprints, then dropped away.

"Some storm," Stan said.

"About time," Frank said. "Just too late for most of us." Frank sipped his coffee. His face pinched. "Stan," he said. "What are you going to do?"

"What do you mean?"

"I mean with everything the way it is," Frank said, "I thought you might be thinking of leaving."

"This place is home," Stan said.

"It's not what it was," Danna suggested. "Not for any of us."

"Anything that is lovely," Stan said, "is easy to lose."

"I guess that's true," I said. "Everybody wants it."

"Everybody wants to give it away," Stan said. "Beautiful makes a good gift."

Rain milled the window and roof, the noise filling the house. The clouds turned dark and a dusky light settled between us in the kitchen. Lightning flickered, thunder rolling through the hills of the valley. We heard a quick pop, a jagged bolt slapping the ground, and a crack of thunder shook the house. Everyone ducked.

"Jesus," I said, excitedly.

"That hit out in the field!" Frank said.

"We should get away from the windows," Danna suggested.

Lightning struck again. The rumbling echo shook the house. We picked up our cups and headed into the den. We settled and listened to the storm. In the distance I heard what sounded like a roofer, hammering.

"What the hell is that?"

"Don't know," Frank said.

The pounding grew, surged toward us. Through the front windows we could see the trees bowing frantically in the wind. The house creaked with each gust. Rain lipped in breakers, out of the gutter.

"Look at it overflowing the drainpipe," Danna said.

The battering creeped toward us, and then we could see out the window—hail. It fell, the size of marbles, then golf balls, then baseballs. The pounding grew so loud that we could barely hear each other scream. We stood at the window.

"We should get to the basement," Frank said. "This could come through the roof."

In the field, cornstalks were being flattened. Mounds of ice were building—a blanket of white stones. Above, I could hear the roof creaking under the constant drumming.

"This way," I yelled. I held the door open. They shuffled down the steps, their feet beating in time with the hail. I pulled the door closed, dipped into the cool, musty darkness. I fumbled for the pull cord of the light. I found it, tugged. There was nothing but darkness. "We lost power," I called.

"We should huddle under something," Frank shouted. "Near a weight-bearing wall."

The muffled thump of stones broke through. The ceiling had splintered, and hail pelted the carpeted floors above us. Dishes, furniture, window and picture frames, all shattered in the falling ice.

"Jesus," I said. I thought for a moment. "There's a work bench by the center wall."

Stan lit a match. We got a brief glimpse of the clay-floored cellar. Frank blew out the flame. "Could be a gas leak," he said.

I took Danna's arm, led everyone to the table. We crouched in the dark, the hail slacking, bouncing from the living room floor, off walls and tables. I tried to locate in my mind where each stone hit. I pictured the destruction that rested over our heads. Slowly, the falling stones ebbed. Every few seconds a palm-sized fragment of ice trickled through the shattered roof. After a few minutes, an extraordinary calm settled on the house. We couldn't hear the rain or the wind. A stray chip of wood fell, now and then, breaking glass.

"Keep your seats," Frank said. "It won't be safe for a while."

"How long?" Stan said.

Frank didn't answer. A fetid scent lifted from the damp clay. I felt the tickle of spiderwebs against my cheek. Danna leaned into me, her face tucked against my neck. "I can't take this," she said. "I want out of here."

A large, heavy piece of ice pounded above our heads. It was as if it had dropped from the sky, clear and unhindered, to the living room floor. The wood beneath the carpet fractured.

"That's what I'm saying," Frank commanded. His voice was loud, as if to speak above the now dissipated hail. His words trickled into the quiet, unanswered. We all sat motionless, waiting. In the distance, there was a low hum. We listened as it grew.

"Any ideas?" I asked.

"Yeah," Frank said. "Listen."

"What?" I asked.

"Shut up," Frank said. The sound turned to a deep, resonate rumble.

"What is it?" Stan said.

Before Frank answered the civil defense siren pitched its call above us. We all knew what it meant. The noise swelled.

"What should we do?" Danna asked.

"Stay where you are," Frank commanded. "Keep low."

Danna crouched, leaning closer to my chest. In the room above us, the wind kicked up scraps of wood. The joists loosened, squeaked as gusts of air gathered and battered the house. The roar seemed to reach from a distance, then distended. The pitch was deafening. The brick wall behind us vibrated, mortar dusting from the crevices and falling onto the table and into our hair. I could feel the growl rising up from the clay, resonating deep in my bones. I held Danna tightly, covered her with my arms. The noise mounted. It held near, oppressive. Above, it seemed as if furniture knocked against walls, rose, and lifted out of the room. The wind seemed to have whipped the room clean of everything. I could only hear the whistle of empty space. The roar held steady for several minutes. The wall behind us buckled, a few bricks tumbling down around our feet. I thought the house might fall in on us. The outside cellar doors beat against the lock. They vibrated, a booming drumbeat. Dust coursed through the air, and I had to close my eyes. The cellar doors beat harder, the clamor pounded in my ears. The reverberation grew and then, suddenly, it was gone. I felt the air sucking out of the cellar, and it was as though all the sound dissipated. I opened my eyes and light poured into the basement. The doors were gone. And then, in an instant, the rumble became distant, the house left still trembling.

The civil defense siren wailed above us, coming and then going. It was as though all the other sounds of the world had been taken by the tornado. We all remained huddled. We didn't move or talk. We waited.

"It missed us," Stan said. The words hung empty in the air.

"Careful," Frank said, finally. "Don't move. Everyone OK?"

"I think so," I said. I could feel Danna's body shaking, tears on my arm. Stan sat next to us, his eyes still closed. "Stan?" I said.

"Son of a bitch," he said. "Can we get out of here? I need a smoke."

"Give it a minute," Frank said.

We waited quietly, until there was nothing but the sound of birds coming in from above us. I could see a crimson light filtering in from where the basement doors had been. "I think it's OK," I said.

"Try not to unsettle anything," Frank said. "This house could come down any minute."

We crawled from under the table, made it out into the eerie glow of a saffron-colored sky. Trees and telephone poles were uprooted, scattered for as far as anyone could see. I looked and all the corn was gone from the miles of field. Only a skeleton remained of my house. Parts of other houses littered the fields. Cars, trucks, unrecognizable twists of metal, lay in piles. There was so much clutter it was difficult to focus, to make sense of what had been left behind. I looked, focused, and everywhere in the stripped field something moved. Something iridescent, white, wormed in the dirt.

"What the hell is that?" I said.

No one answered. I headed out to take a look and everyone followed. I got close and saw that there were miles of squirming trout, eel, shad. They worked with life, having been lifted from the river. I kneeled and picked one up. It finned out of my hand.

"It's fish," I said.

I untucked my shirt, held the tail out with one hand and walked into the field, collecting as many fish as I could carry. Danna and Stan and Frank followed, gathering their share. We walked deep into the field, taking a dozen each. We moved without talking. As many as we gathered, the field still worked with hundreds more.

The air had gone almost cold. As I looked, everything seemed caught in a pinkish hue. I bent, taking the best trout I could find. When I had all I could carry, I walked farther out, the dirt soaked and muddy on my boots. I thought to go as far as the river. But something caught my attention and I turned. A pig lilted high in the air. It was beautiful against the flushed sky. I took in its arching flight without saying anything. I stood motionless as the pig creased the sky. It seemed natural, as if it had always belonged. I stood, a pleasing sensation rising in my chest. Its wings tipped smartly in the breeze as it floated over the land and the river, effortlessly.

Acknowledgments

For my sight, my body, my care, I have numerous doctors, nurses, and pharmacists to admire and thank and, to protect their privacy, I will leave them nameless—you know who you are and what you've done—but I must express my boundless gratitude: many, many thanks.

I am filled with the deepest admiration for John Edgar Wideman, a teacher in life and art. Thank you for believing in me and supporting my work even when it wasn't going well. Your voice has lifted me when I thought I was out of the game.

There is no way to express the many ways in which a writer needs support, but I must thank those who've aided me in my every weakness. When it became clear to me that my health dictated I leave the science building and cross the campus to the English Department, Emory and Dorothy Estes and Larry Bromley made me at home and gave me important books. Intellectually and spiritually, they fed, clothed, and loved me. Clyde Moneyhun literally furnished me with a place to live, and he offered me more than the elements of fiction—his belief and his friendship. Harry Reeder not only taught me how to see and think more clearly, but he also generously gave me the computers that I needed in order to keep writing. There is no way to measure the value of these people in my life. I have been blessed. I also must thank David Wright, Audrey Petty, Jim Marino, Herman Fong, Margot Livesey, Michael Pettit, Jay Neugeboren, Noy Holland, Sam Michel, Maddy Blais, Lisa Shea, Chris Judge, Jennifer Hogue, Christine Caperton, Kathryn Stewart, Michele Tomiak, Rob Galvin, and the Bentley's crew (Al, Bruce, Diane and Dick, George, and, our lost friend, Brad). I am indebted to Carol Shields and Charles Baxter for noticing my work and selecting it for inclusion in *Scribner's Best of the Fiction Workshops 1998* and *Best New American Voices 2001*. A very special thanks to Buddy and Julie Miller for their talent and inspiration.

I am grateful for the friendship and support of Wendy and Walt Kohler. You've given us music and a family. Sue and Eugene Battistoni have provided sage advice and a safe haven, a welcomed place to live and write. Cindy Bielanski has been so supportive and faithful to our every need that there is no way to really thank her. My thanks—Wendy, Cindy, Sue, and Eugene—for seeing Debbie and me through the many crises. Each of you has turned a place into a home.

For his constant belief and support, his quiet kindness, his fellowship, I must thank John Kulka.

There is no way I can adequately thank those that have shepherded my work into print. I'm fortunate to have as a friend Okey Ndibe and my agent, Anna Ghosh, who believed in my work from the beginning. I'm genuinely honored to have André Bernard on my side. He is truly an editor in the largest sense of the word—a craftsman extraordinaire. I am thankful for Meredith Phillips (who has been patient and kind and all-knowing), David Hough, and everyone at Harcourt. Thanks to Lilian Kravitz for her beautiful, thoughtful photographs. My gratitude to everyone at Harcourt, whose excitement has been unbounded.

Acknowledgments

My gratitude and love to my brother, Sy, and his family, and to Debbie's family, for understanding that something moves me to write and for standing with me anyway.

I completed these stories in the ever-present absence of Debbie's mother and my mother and Mary—who left us partway through the adventure—though their ghosts are with me each morning I write.